LOVE ON THE EDGE OF REASON

A PINE HARBOUR NOVEL

ZOE YORK

WWW.ZOEYORK.COM

Tom Minelli doesn't know why Chloe Dawson has fled Pine Harbour, but she's pregnant with his baby and he wants her back. Not just back in town. He wants Chloe back in his life, and not as the casual hook-up friends they were before. But finding her proves harder than he expected—and when he does track her down, a snow storm rolls in right behind him, trapping them together in a cabin on the lake.

This one is for myself

CHAPTER ONE

Christmas Eve

IT WAS A WONDERFUL, magical night—for everyone except for Tom Minelli.

For reasons that had nothing to do with the event at hand, he left his best friend's wedding so angry he wasn't sure he should drive. He'd arrived the same way, but he'd buried it down deep until the groom—after kissing his bride—noticed something was wrong and dragged the truth out of Tom.

Now he stood on the frosty, snow-lined street in front of Matt and Tasha's house and glared at the fat, white flakes falling gently through the golden glow of the street-light. Somewhere, Chloe Dawson—town librarian and the bravest, smartest, sexiest woman he'd ever met—was alone tonight, and it was all his fault.

"Hey, are you heading out already?"

Tom turned around. His oldest brother, Zander, was standing on the front porch. He hadn't even heard the door open or close. He dragged in a ragged breath. "Yeah. No. I don't know. I just needed some fresh air."

"Matt said as much."

"Did he?" Tom felt his cheeks heat up, embarrassed that his older brother was involved now. He should have kept the news of Chloe's pregnancy to himself, but Matt had caught him off-guard and it slipped out before Tom realized what he was saying. Way to screw up the wedding celebration. "What else did he say?"

"Nothing."

"I doubt that."

Zander jumped down, his feet crunching on the snow. "He said he was worried about you, and you shouldn't be alone right now, but it's his wedding night, so he had to deputize someone to babysit you. What the hell is going on?"

"I need to go."

Zander didn't ask where. He just nodded. "I'll come with you."

Tom's chest ached. "Matt really didn't tell you?"

"I know nothing." Zander held his arms out wide. "See? I'm wholly unprepared for whatever Christmas Eve mission we're about to depart on. Will you stay put while I go back inside, tell my wife I need to go and kick someone's ass, and maybe grab my coat? It's freezing out here."

Tom gave him a tight nod, but inside his chest his heart thumped harder and faster at the reminder. It was bitterly cold tonight, the first really good freeze all week. The only ass that needed to be kicked was his own.

Where is she?

Matt had told him to trust Zander. His brother had resources and connections. But could Tom confess just how much he'd screwed up? It was hard to admit even to himself—that he'd been carrying this secret around for a week, that he didn't fix it sooner, that he waited too long to tell Chloe he was in, and most of all that his first reaction had been stupid and wrong and absolutely not cool.

His brother would rightfully think Tom had failed her. He had.

Zander stopped at the door, shooting another concerned look in Tom's direction.

"I'll wait for you to get your coat," Tom ground out. It was all he could say right now. Zander nodded, then quietly slipped back inside, leaving Tom alone with his dark thoughts. But when the door opened again, it wasn't his brother.

It was one of his sisters-in-law. The first sister-in-law, the one who had known him the longest.

"I'm fine," he said, and Olivia waved her hand, like she knew he was lying and didn't really care. *It doesn't matter*, her hand said.

Unlike Zander, she was already bundled up. Smart woman. It was cold and getting colder by the second. She marched right over to him. "What's going on?"

"Nothing."

"You led with *I'm fine*, which is a telltale sign that you are not."

He huffed in frustration. He hated that he was that transparent. "I don't want to detract from the evening. It was a really beautiful wedding."

Her face bloomed into a soft, happy smile. "It was, wasn't it? We really rock the holiday weddings in this group, if I do say so myself." Olivia and his other brother, Rafe, got married—for the second and last time—in a similarly intimate ceremony on New Year's Eve a few years ago.

But before he could pat himself on the back for distracting her from whatever she'd come out to say, the smile dropped and she gave him a serious look. "Is this about Chloe?"

He opened his mouth to deny it, but given the circumstances, lying wasn't in his long-term best interests. Or Chloe's.

But the truth wasn't his to share freely, either.

He pressed his lips together.

Olivia sighed. "Yeah, you guys have really stuffed that whole thing up," she said softly. "I saw her the other day, you know. She looked pretty miserable."

No, he didn't know. He didn't know anything, and the proverbial knife in his chest twisted a little harder. And the words that would have spilled out a week ago—*we're just friends, that's her choice, no comment*—all died in his throat.

None of that felt true. Hadn't for a while, but he'd been a fool and hadn't seen the warning signs. "Where did you see her?" He leaned in, thirsty for any scrap of information Olivia might know.

His sister-in-law rolled her lip between her teeth and looked to the side, evading his searching gaze.

"Olivia."

"If you dumped her—"

"We weren't dating!" He hated that it burst out like that. It was technically true, but technicalities didn't matter at this point.

"You were something."

"Yeah, we were. And we still are."

Doubt twisted across Olivia's face.

He knew that feeling, too. Because he'd found Chloe's apartment empty just before the wedding, when he'd gone to ask her to come with him as his date. But before he could explain any of that, Zander opened the front door, and behind him came Rafe.

Great, now it was a party.

He lowered his voice. "Do you know where she is? I want to fix it, I want to make everything right."

"I don't know," she whispered back, her eyes now as big as saucers. "But Tom—"

"What's going on?" Rafe stopped behind his wife and gave Tom a concerned look.

Olivia looked back and forth between her husband, and Tom, and then Zander. It was hard to read her expression, but not hard to read the way she shook her head after a minute and stepped back. "Come on, Rafe. Let's go back to the party. What is our daughter getting up to while we're both out here?"

Rafe laughed, but Tom cursed under his breath. Olivia wasn't giving up whatever she knew, because she thought she was protecting Chloe. That was supposed to be his job.

He had so much to fix.

Which left Zander.

I'm sorry, Chloe. But I can't just let you disappear. Not when I have so much to apologize for. So much to make right.

After Liv and Rafe were back inside, he looked at his oldest brother. "I need you to do something questionable, both ethically and legally. And don't ask a lot of questions, because time is of the essence."

Zander tugged on his gloves. "I'm your guy. Where are we going?"

———

CHLOE HAD THOUGHT of nearly everything. Everything, it turned out, except for matches.

She'd packed three kinds of hot chocolate mix, more socks than she'd worn in the last month, an entire bag of cozy sweaters, and a stack of books to read in front of the fire.

She just didn't have any way of *making* that festive blaze.

She'd been looking forward to this moment for days. Four days, to be precise. From the moment she'd realized she couldn't stay in Pine Harbour a second longer, except it was four days before Christmas and how exactly did one move at the last minute during holiday shutdowns?

It turned out, one did it right *before* a holiday shutdown.

She'd found a moving company that could box up her entire apartment—except for hot chocolate mix, socks, sweaters, and a stack of books—and stow it all in a shipping storage container. She'd also found a cottage that wasn't going to be occupied over Christmas, because the owners—the Vances, loyal library patrons when they were in Pine Harbour over the summer—were heading south instead.

Mrs. Vance had been a peach when Chloe had called her and asked for this favour, breaking all kinds of librarian code rules. Except she'd been an apologetic peach, because while she was happy to let Chloe use the cottage, it was empty.

Completely bare.

The kitchen had been swept clean—every shelf, every drawer—in preparation for a renovation that would start in the new year.

So yes, Chloe had the run of the cabin, but she'd been warned to bring everything herself.

And she'd forgotten *matches*.

Tears welled up as she moved back to the couch. Hot, frustrated, definitely hormonal tears. The kind of overwhelmed feeling she vaguely recalled from her teen years and had been happy to leave behind ages ago.

Hello, weirdness, my old friend.

Pregnancy hormones were some kind of crazy, that was for darn sure.

She pressed her hand to her belly. Her head swam, as it always did when she thought about what—who—was growing inside her. The size of a pea now, but it wouldn't be long before it was a lime. A grapefruit. A little person, cells duplicating over and over until there was a foot jammed into her cervix and all her organs had been completely moved to places they shouldn't be.

She was pregnant.

Pregnant.

Ms. Take-A-Pill-Every-Morning-At-Seven.

She'd never missed a pill in the past. Never. Before Tom, a period now known as BT. Because she didn't want a baby. But now she had a baby, or the start of one, she *loved* it.

She was still wrapping her head around *how* she'd gotten knocked up. In hindsight, of course, she knew. In the last few months—well into the Age of Tom—there had been a few times where it suddenly didn't matter quite as much that she didn't have her pills in hand at seven in the morning. She'd missed a couple by a few hours, because of an early morning booty call the first day, and sleeping in the next day, and she hadn't really cared.

Not enough to get a morning after pill. She'd gotten comfortable in her non-relationship relationship. And she'd never had a scare in the past.

When her period was late, she'd been genuinely confused.

And then she'd felt profoundly dumb, because what had she been thinking? *That it might be okay.* That's what she'd been hoping.

Deep down, she'd been okay with the surprise.

Except it hadn't been okay. Tom had reacted exactly as badly as she imagined her father had, back in the day, and she'd felt like a fool.

But she was a fool who still wanted her pregnancy. Maybe, deep down, stumbling through a re-do on her mother's path in life was the only way she'd ever have a child—fucked-up as that thought might be.

Chloe was nothing if not fucked-up, and frankly, she was fine with that. Because happy-ever-after endings were fantasy and foil. Fiction. She knew, deep down, that her own happiness was hers to control and create and contain.

So, she knew without a doubt that there were three things that would absolutely not happen:

1. She wouldn't marry Tom Minelli out of some misplaced sense of family values if he ever came around to suggest that. Fuck that noise.

2. She wouldn't raise her baby the way she'd been raised. This baby was—now that she'd gotten over her shock—wanted. When he or she or they arrived, Chloe would hold them in her arms and the first thing they would hear in this world was that they were *wanted*. No afterthoughts. No shuttling back and forth between parents bound by obligation.

3. She wouldn't put up with any judgement from the

tiny town of Pine Harbour, population six hundred, seventy-five percent of whom cast serious side-eye at single moms. It wasn't that she couldn't handle it. She was a bad-ass and didn't care what anyone thought of her. But she didn't want to raise her child somewhere *they* could get any flack for *her* choices in life.

Rolling her neck, she tossed up her options. She could go to bed early. This was never her first choice, but the master bedroom had a gas fireplace. It didn't have blankets, though, and the one she'd brought fit better on the sofa than the king-sized bed upstairs.

Next time she invaded a fancy cottage, she was going to be better prepared. Next time she wouldn't do it right before an overnight storm was due to arrive, and she couldn't safely get back across the narrow causeway to the mainland. The last thing she wanted to do was drive into the icy waters of Lake Huron.

For a split-second, she thought of Tom's flannel covered down-filled duvet, on his big bed in his little cabin, not that far from here. The last time she'd been at his house, she'd burrowed in the flannel, newly added to the bed in honour of the colder weather, because it felt so good. Light and warm and endlessly soft all at the same time.

No more burrowing. No more Tom.

She'd had her fun and now it was time to face the consequences. On her own.

She decided to hunker down on the couch with a cup of cocoa. She could imagine the flickering flames. But when she headed back into the main room, she pulled up short. The outside light was on.

It hadn't been on when she went into the kitchen, she was sure of that. It was possible the wind had somehow turned the light on. But if she saw evidence of anyone out there, when nobody was supposed to be here, she'd call 911 in a heartbeat.

She crept closer to the door, grateful for it being relatively dark inside the cottage. That helped her see past the well-light porch to the darkness beyond.

Nobody was there.

Holding her breath, she eased back from the door and waited.

Maybe it had been nothing. Maybe there was a motion sensor she hadn't noticed because she'd arrived in the daylight hours, and the blowing snow had triggered it. Or a bunny. Yes, she'd like that. A snow hare, hopping up onto the porch. Cute.

When the light flicked out, proving her motion sensor theory, she checked the lock one last time and retreated to the couch.

It was only after she curled up in her blanket and her thumping heart calmed down that she realized she'd been hoping the light meant she had a visitor. But he hadn't come to her all week. He wouldn't be coming now.

She read the same page in her book over and over again, trying her best to ignore the ache in her chest. This was a mess of her own making. She realized that. She'd known exactly what she wanted—and what she didn't—right up until everything changed. Now she couldn't fall into the same trap her mother had, hoping for something that would never come to fruition.

At the end of the day, she wanted happiness. For herself, her child, and her child's father, too. They all deserved that. There were many ways to be happy, many ways to shape a family. No reason to force a square peg into a round hole.

She just needed to protect her baby while she made that clear to Tom.

He would understand, eventually. He didn't have the capacity to be a full-time partner anyway, she reminded herself. He'd proven that the last time they saw each other.

CHAPTER TWO

A week before Christmas
When it all started to unravel

TOM WRAPPED up the monthly Search and Rescue team meeting ten minutes early. When people looked like they might linger, he dumped the coffee urn in the sink and started washing it with a loud clatter.

Take the hint, folks, he thought to himself. *Time to beat it, whether you like it or not.*

What none of them knew was that Tom had a date.

Not a date, exactly. No, that wasn't what Chloe was coming over for. But it was something.

She'd texted him just before the meeting started. It was a regular thing now, her texting him every few weeks. Often on a Sunday afternoon. *Doing anything in a few hours?*

The subtext was always, *want to do me?*

And he did. Endlessly, creatively, breathlessly. They'd been hooking up for months, and each time Tom was quite convinced it was the last. Sometimes she told him it was. A few times he was the one to speak the lie.

It never was the last time.

He knew not to push it with hoping for more, and yet, when she'd texted him today, he hadn't been able to help himself.

Chloe: Doing anything in a few hours?
Tom: I'm on duty this afternoon. Can't leave the park, but if you want to come visit me, we'd have the training centre all to ourselves.

There was a solid chance she'd pass.

She didn't. In an unexpected and delightfully uncharacteristic move, Chloe accepted his offer (request?) to spend time together somewhere other than the bedroom.

So now he was urging everyone to get the hell out. He had a woman to seduce. Or a countdown to a woman showing up in all her tattooed, pierced glory to seduce him.

He was her willing victim.

Chloe Dawson was the most gorgeous, intriguing woman he'd ever been with. She'd laid out crystal clear rules from their very first night together, and he had no problem following them. But there was a part of him that was hungry for more.

They both knew it. Most of the time, they both ignored it. But today felt like a tiny victory in that direction. If all went well, he'd ask her if she wanted to sleep over at his place on Christmas Eve, after Matt and Tasha's wedding.

"Hey," she said from the doorway.

He turned and his heart leapt, thumping eagerly against

his ribs. He always had the same reaction to her. It hadn't settled down over time, and it still took him by surprise. He simply adored everything about her. Her confidence, her intelligence. Her perfect mouth. Her bright eyes.

And her dirty, filthy mind.

In a single glance, he knew she had something special planned for today, and he was a goner. She was dressed for the increasingly cold December days, with a down jacket over jeans and tall leather boots, but as he watched, she unzipped and under the jacket she wasn't wearing much. A tank top that sliced low across the tops of her breasts and bared her shoulders.

Sex at his workplace was not smart at all.

But Tom never claimed to be smart around Chloe. He'd always been overwhelmed by her, amazed and impressed and rendered stupid.

He crossed the room, tugged her inside, and locked the door. Then he pressed her against the wall and took her mouth like it had been months since they'd last kissed and not a mere week.

She groaned, giving him her tongue. They'd gotten good at this together. He'd learned her body, her responses, and knew where she liked to be licked, where she needed a rough scrape of teeth or a soft, teasing probe.

Today she held back, gasping as he consumed her, until at the end when she chased his retreat and sank her teeth into his bottom lip.

His erection strained in reaction. Yes. He was up for literally anything—within the bounds of what Chloe had carefully established as on the table. No feelings. No commitment. Everything in secret and furtive and not at all what Tom really wanted, but beggars couldn't be choosers. And when it came to Chloe, Tom was one thousand percent a happy beggar.

"That was nice," she whispered, her breath hitching as she looked up at him.

"I've got more where that came from."

She smiled slowly, her eyes searching his face. "I know you do."

They could do it. Right here, against the wall. He could work her pants down her hips and turn her around. Tight, hard, fast. They'd done it that way before. Or there was the couch. She could ride him nice and slow, until he begged her to come.

Both would also be an option. He had stamina for hours with Chloe.

But she'd come here, to his workplace in the middle of the day—a nearly public date, a first—and he didn't want to miss the opportunity to gain a small advantage. "Do you want to do something fun?"

She laughed. "Don't we always?"

"A different kind of fun."

A look crossed her face. She wasn't sure. But after a moment of consideration, she slowly nodded. "Sure." She took a deep breath. "Outside? Somewhere we could talk?"

"Yeah. Definitely." He caught her hand in his and reached past her to unlock and open the door, taking the opportunity to steal one more a kiss before pulling her out into the cool afternoon air. He pointed at the climbing tower which the team used to practice rescue descents on. "Up there."

Chloe zipped her jacket up again and glanced at him sideways. "Wall climbing?"

"If you want. Or we could go up there and, if we're

quiet enough, I bet we'll see some deer come through the forest soon."

"Deer?" Her eyes lit up.

Bingo. She was tough on the outside, but under that brittle exterior was a soft, squishy heart that loved animals.

"Come on." He took her hand and led her to the stairs. "Up we go."

The climbing tower was four storeys tall, higher than any building and almost any tree in the area. It had an impressive view, which Chloe got sucked into as expected.

Tom grinned to himself as he stretched out the blanket he'd already stashed up there. When she turned around, she was suitably impressed. "Why haven't I been up here before?"

So many complicated reasons, most of them on her end, but he wasn't going to point that out. "No idea. We'll have to add it to our list of regular spots."

A quick reaction flickered across her face, then disappeared. "It's lovely up here."

"Even lovelier down here," he said, taking his radio off his hip and laying down. He held out his hand. "Come check out my fancy blanket."

She laughed and joined him, stretching out to mirror his body language. He pointed to the forest below. "Now, you'll need to be quiet."

"I'm a librarian. Quiet is my *thing*."

"I've never found your library to be that quiet."

"You always come at preschool hour, and I immediately kick you out. You haven't had the full experience."

He'd put that on the list of things he wanted, too. But first, deer spotting. "So we're going to be quiet…"

She laughed and poked him.

"And we'll watch for movement below. A rustle of trees, birds taking off unexpectedly. Lots of things that will let us know the deer are moving through. And then…" He pointed to the clearings where he usually saw deer stop. "There and there. Those are our best chances to see them."

"Deer," she breathed, her eyes wide.

"Yep."

"This is quite the secret spot you've got up here."

"I only tell my favourite people."

She snorted.

But he was telling the truth.

They lay there for half an hour. Every few minutes, Chloe would crack a joke, and he'd remind her she needed to hush.

"It's just so foreign to me to be this quiet if I'm not surrounded by stacks of books," she whispered back.

"Then I'll need to keep you busy." He covered her mouth with his hand, squeezing gently, then trailed his fingers down her throat and onto the fluttering pulse point at the base of her neck. "Can you be very quiet if I give you proper motivation?"

"No." He lifted his fingers, and she whimpered. "I'm just being honest."

He laughed and kissed her, then rolled back onto his stomach. "Watch. Listen. I'll give you something to do with your mouth if need be, but I want to see them, too."

Her cheeks turned pink as she propped her chin on her hands. "Okay."

She was rewarded less than ten minutes later when they saw a few trees rustle, then another, clearly leading in a path to one of the clearings below. Tom pointed it out and Chloe clamped her lips shut, her eyes wide.

When the deer sprinted into the clearing, she gasped

gently, then clapped her own hand over her mouth to keep that inside.

"So pretty," she finally whispered as they had a snack on one of the trees.

He was looking at her, not the visitors. "Gorgeous."

"Stop," she murmured.

He grinned. "Caught me looking." He crowded closer, kissing the back of her neck, then her shoulder. "It's because you *are* gorgeous. And sexy, and…" His fingers crept beneath her, first going to her collarbone, then lower. He tugged the zipper down on her jacket, and she rolled to the side, giving him space to play.

Her tits were marvellous. Firm and sensitive and always game for a bit of pinching—

"Ow," she breathed.

Maybe not that quickly. "Sorry. You okay?"

She leaned in, her eyes closed, and kissed him. Wet, slick, hot. "Mmm, just be gentle."

"You sore? Close to your period?"

She froze.

He pulled back. Chloe had never been one to hedge around stuff like that, and he'd always liked that about her. "Are you on your period? You know that's no big deal to me, right? We can—"

"I'm pregnant." She blurted it out, her face going white, and his entire world turned upside down.

"Wait, what?"

"I meant to tell you."

"You meant to—when? *After* we spent the afternoon screwing?"

"When I showed up, but then you were kissing me." She scrambled to her feet. "You started it. You wanted to…" She turned in a circle, her arms outstretched. When she faced him again, her expression was tight. Pale. Angry.

Shit.

Before he could get out the right sounds to make an apology, she was jabbing her finger in his face. "Look. You wanted something today. This little show with the blanket, and the deer? What was that, you trying to be Mr. Romantic? We both know that's not really you. Not by a long stretch."

He gaped at her even though that had always been her thing—he wasn't allowed to want more than fucking. *She* was the reason why he hadn't shown her this side of him before. But he couldn't say that now, because she was *pregnant.*

And she wasn't done yelling. Her words came faster now, tight and spilling over each other, like she'd practiced some of this and hadn't meant for it all to come out, but it was and she couldn't help it. "But I tell you that I'm pregnant, and you throw back a line at me about wanting to *screw?* Wow. You don't get to be mad at me because I gave in to what might have been the last sex I have for the next eighteen years. Which, by the way, didn't happen, so you don't get to shame me. Got it? I won't stand for it, Tom Minelli. You hear me?"

"I think everyone north of town hears you," he said, shock making him stupid. The words were out before he could cut them off.

She gasped, then turned and spun on her heel, heading for the stairs. "Do not follow me," she yelled as he ignored her.

Fuck, fuck, fuck. "Of course I'm following you. We need to talk."

"We don't."

"Chloe." She was down a full level from him, and he started taking the stairs two at a time. How was she moving this fast?

"I told you not to follow me. You are a terrible listener."

She'd just said more about him—about them—in thirty seconds than she'd said in the past year. His brain hadn't caught up. And she was still moving. "How can I not follow you? What the hell? Chloe, *stop*."

She jumped the last few steps, landed on the ground, and kept moving. Not stopping. Not listening.

Tom's heart pounded against his ribs. She was really storming out.

She was pregnant.

He'd pissed her off, but damn it, she'd blindsided him. She just needed to *slow down* and—

But she was already in her car.

He threw his hands in the air as she powered her Honda Civic to life. Great.

What the hell had just happened?

"Congratulations," he yelled at the retreating car. "I sure as hell hope it's my baby."

And then he felt like the complete ass that he probably was.

CHAPTER THREE

Christmas Day

AS SOON AS DAWN BROKE, and it was safe to drive across the causeway to the Vance cottage, Tom poured an entire pot of coffee into an extra-large Thermos and headed out.

Zander had talked him out of driving across the night before. They'd tracked her down using the last known ping off her cell phone, and then his brother had waited on the mainland while Tom had walked out to the island.

He'd just needed to see her for a minute, just to make sure she was okay.

It had been hard to stand in the shadows, to watch her like a creeper through the window. To know she'd spend the night alone, but the only way he could make this better was to return in the daylight with supplies in hand.

She'd retreated from the world. From him. All he had been able to allow himself the night before was making sure she was safe.

And once he'd seen to that, he'd faded back. He'd

almost convinced himself to stay away completely. *She doesn't want to see you.* But the storm warnings didn't look good, and Chloe wasn't from the peninsula. Still, he came back to his apartment and spent the night talking himself out of doing exactly what he was about to do. His bed had never felt so empty.

It was strange to miss Chloe in his bed when she'd never slept over. Not even once. But she'd been there many times, for a few hours. Warm and happy. Their secret little games, their shared pleasure.

And at the first brush with hard reality, that had all disintegrated. None of it had been real. But he'd spent the night missing her all the same.

He'd spent a week trying to figure out how to make up for lost time, how to make right what had to have been an awful moment for her—*hey, jerk, I'm having your baby, and oh look, you're being fucking stupid about it.*

He'd also spent a lot of the last week feeling sorry for himself, which is why it had taken him a week—and that was yet another mistake. He'd waited too long, and now he had that to regret on top of missing what could have been, what others had, what they could have had if he'd simply been brave enough to say it out loud.

I want more with you, Chloe.

He'd say it today.

But he needed to be alive for that, so he waited until he could see where he was going.

As his truck heated up and the windows defrosted, he stared out at the lake. It wasn't a long drive from his cabin to the island where the Vance cottage stood. She'd hidden in plain sight, practically under his nose.

He needed to know why.

But he needed to keep his cool if he had any chance of getting an answer to that question.

He put his truck in four-wheel-drive and powered through the drifts of snow on the single-lane causeway, holding his breath every time the wheels jerked beneath him. The track he'd walked in last night was now gone, and the freezing cold lake threatened on both sides. There was no way Chloe's little car would get back to the mainland.

It was beyond foolish to spend any length of time out on the lake during a winter storm. Even in a cottage as robust as the Vance home, which was full-season and larger than most houses in Pine Harbour proper, it wouldn't take much to be cut off from the mainland resources.

Tom would know. It was often his job to run rescues to fetch people from their islands when the rustic Christmas-at-the-cottage plan inevitably went sideways.

He and Chloe wouldn't need to be rescued, though—except maybe from the past.

He did a three-point turn in front of the house, backing in his truck to point straight at the causeway, then turned off the engine. It had rumbled loud and long enough to clearly announce his arrival. But even as his cab grew cold, he didn't move.

The adrenaline of going to see her yesterday, finding her apartment empty, and then tracking her down had carried him this far. But he didn't know what was going to happen when he knocked on that door.

Except he wasn't going to need to knock. She'd heard him arrive. Watched him sit in his truck like a coward, clearly, because now she was standing in the open doorway, hand on her hip.

He grabbed the Thermos of coffee and hopped out of the truck, stopping at the back to grab the box of gift-wrapped presents that were his excuse for coming to see her.

"What are you doing here?" she called out.

He could ask her the same question. If she wanted to leave, why didn't she go very far?

He stopped just shy of the threshold and stomped his feet lightly, brushing off the snow. "I came to make sure you were all right." His gaze dropped to her midsection, and her hand followed.

"I'm okay."

"You disappeared."

She took a deep breath. "Yeah."

"Can I come in?"

She hesitated a beat, then stepped out of the way, letting him in.

It was hard to step close to her and not lean all the way in and kiss her, but he'd messed this up, and that wasn't an option. But she wasn't a stranger to him, either. Why was she so hard to read? "Good morning. I should have led with that."

Her response was a soft whisper. "Good morning."

Damn it, why was this so awkward? *Because you were an ass when she told you she was pregnant.* He set down the box of gifts and unzipped his coat, inviting himself to stay awhile. "Merry Christmas."

"I'm not celebrating this year."

"Then Happy Regular December Twenty-Fifth to you. I brought hot coffee. Pre-made as double-double." Two cream, two sugar. Which was how she took her coffee, and not at all how he took his.

Of course, this gesture required her to know that he

knew how she took her coffee, which maybe she didn't. Maybe he'd been the only one watching carefully every time they were in adjacent booths at Mac's Diner. Maybe she really had been studiously ignoring him instead of it being a pretence like he'd hoped.

"You made coffee?"

"Yeah."

"For me?" She looked at him suspiciously.

"Ideally, for us to share."

————

IT WAS TEMPTING to snatch the Thermos and point him back out the door. Nope, she wasn't ready to talk. Wasn't ready to deal with the rioting feelings inside her that only got worse when Tom was close.

But on the other hand, he'd brought her coffee. Her kind of coffee, not his. And he hadn't asked her if she could have caffeine because of the bundle of cells inside her. She was pretty sure she'd toss him into the nearest snowbank if he did, because yesterday she'd thought it a grand plan to only bring hot chocolate with her.

This morning she'd regretted that choice—and then Tom had shown up with sweet, sweet coffee.

A sly move if ever there was one.

"Thank you," she said, and she meant it. For all the complicated mess that stood between them, she was grateful for his presence. Sharing would be a bit of a problem, though. "I have a mug, but you're going to have to use the Thermos lid."

He gave her a confused look. "Okay…"

"I'm not being petty," she told him, leading the way to the Vances' kitchen. The completely empty kitchen. She filled her mug that was sitting next to the kettle and gestured around. "They cleared this place out at Thanksgiving. It's being gutted in the spring for renovations, so... no mugs. Terrible hospitality, I realize. If you don't want to stay long, that's fine."

He looked alarmed. "The entire house is empty?"

She shrugged. "There's a couch and a bed. I brought hot chocolate and books. It's fine. I'm leaving tomorrow."

He threw his arm out wide, pointing at the window. "Do you have any idea how much snow has accumulated over night? I had a hell of a time getting across the causeway in my truck. I don't think your car is going anywhere until we can get it plowed."

Chloe frowned and took a sip of coffee, ignoring the new twist of worry in her gut. "The forecast said—"

"Forecasts mean nothing on the lake."

She resisted the urge to roll her eyes. He was always so safety conscious. "Then I'll wait until it stops snowing, and I'll get plowed out."

His jaw clenched.

"I know a thing or two about this town," she reminded him. "Everyone and their brother has a plow hitch. There's no need to be dramatic."

Instead of answering, he gestured to the fridge. "Is that thing empty, too?"

Not technically. She'd brought milk for her hot cocoa.

He gave her an incredulous look when she didn't reply. "What are you eating, then?"

"Crackers," she admitted. It was so cliched, but they felt good on her tummy. As did coffee, so she took another sip.

His face shifted from concerned to understanding. "Speaking of crackers...I think we should talk about it."

"It."

"I *want* to talk about it."

Again, she played dumb. "It?"

And understanding morphed immediately to visible frustration. "The fact that you're pregnant."

She nodded sagely, not at all feeling nearly that cool on the inside. "Oh. That. No, we're not going to talk about that. Not until after coffee."

He rocked his jaw back and forth, half-smiling, half-glowering. "Sure. We've probably got tons of time, anyway."

She shook her head. "You have a giant truck. You can leave after you've said whatever it is you came here to say."

"You just said you didn't want to talk yet."

That tripped her up.

"But when I go, I think I should take you with me. It's not safe for you to stay here without any food or a functional winterized vehicle."

"You aren't taking me anywhere."

"Then I guess we're staying here."

"*We* are not staying here. I'm staying here. You can—"

He put his Thermos lid down on the counter. "I'm staying. Either in here or in the cab of my truck. Your choice."

"That's a terrible choice," she exclaimed. She was mad at him, but she wasn't evil. "I'd feel bad if you froze to death."

"That's a relief."

"Go home, Tom."

His voice lowered, softened, and his gaze went extra-solemn. "I can't."

"Why not?"

"Because I need to make this right. I've messed up, and

there's a lot we need to talk about, and I'm worried about you."

There it was. All the things one should say when one has pissed off one's pregnant...girlfriend. Person? Buddy?

Because she wasn't his girlfriend. She wasn't his anything—admittedly, by her own foolhardy, terrible-in-hindsight choice.

Sharp, agonized longing stabbed in her chest. She wanted him to be this guy, for real and not out of some misguided sense of righteousness. But he was a thirty-three-year-old man who had never shown a whiff of interest in a wife and kid before this week. He'd loved the casual, no-strings sex she'd offered him because it was all he'd ever really wanted.

Chloe knew what everyone else thought of Tom. Mr. Responsibility, not a player. But she'd seen another side of him, one that came alive when offered the chance to sneak around. And as soon as she told him she was pregnant, he blew up and went radio silent. Even if she wanted more, deep down, he wasn't able to follow through on that kind of commitment. Beca

None of this was the right thing for him. He was going to sacrifice himself on the mantle of masculinity because he thought that's what she wanted.

It wasn't.

"There's nothing to make right here," she said tightly. "We do need to talk. I just haven't had a chance to gather my thoughts yet, and I don't want to say the wrong thing." Fingers shaking, she refilled her mug, and then stalked back into the living room in search of her crackers.

Tom followed.

She didn't offer him any saltines.

"So...crackers and hot chocolate and a stack of books.

That's what you have here?"

She gestured at the unlit logs she'd carefully stacked in the fireplace the night before. "It was all supposed to be in front of a roaring fire, but I forgot matches."

"I've got a lighter in the truck."

She wanted to decline the offer. The company. All of it. *Go away*, her hormones raged.

But she also wanted a fire. And he was right, they needed to talk.

"Chloe?"

"What?"

"Can I light the fire for you?"

She exhaled roughly. "Yes. Please. Thank you."

He nodded, his gaze unreadable. "I'll be right back."

She followed him to the door, and when he opened it, she groaned. A squall had blown up outside.

Tom raised his eyebrows at her. "What did you say? There's no need to be dramatic?"

"Where is this all coming from?"

Tom looked up at the sky, thick with clouds dropping even more snow on them. "The goddess of being snowed in with your favourite person?"

There was something in how he said it that made her squirm. Something familiar that pricked at her resolve. "I am not your favourite person."

He gave her a hard, lingering stare. "Yeah, you are." Then he zipped up his coat and dashed down the steps before she could reply.

She stayed at the door and watched him jog through the silent blanket of snow now falling heavily. She couldn't even see the lake on either side of the causeway.

The question of whether or not he should stay was moot. Now he would have to stay until it stopped. *Merry*

Christmas, you doofus, she told herself. This felt like an awful trap she'd set for herself, because what did she expect Tom to do? Just leave her be?

Yes. That would have been nice.

Ugh, except there had been that wee pulse of happiness when he'd shown up. It was a week late, but it was *something*.

When she heard the rumble of his truck, she'd jumped up, knowing it was him, and before she remembered she was mad at him, it had made her day. That was only natural, of course. He'd been a person who'd brought her a lot of happiness over the last year. Usually in the form of orgasms, but sometimes just laughs. Sometimes company.

Mostly orgasms.

Because she'd artificially held the line at orgasms, telling herself they didn't have much in common other than sex. She'd kicked herself out of his place pretty soon after, every single time.

She hadn't even bought him any Christmas presents. She glared at the box he'd brought in on arrival.

That just wasn't their deal. How dare he pretend otherwise?

She grabbed the box and moved it out of the way, pushing it against the staircase as reckless outrage surged inside her. She felt like she was on an emotional roller-coaster the likes of which she'd never experienced before. It wasn't fair to be outraged. Tom hadn't asked for this situation any more than she had. He was trying to make the best of it in the only way he knew how—it just wasn't the way that would work for her. *Tell him that. Breathe. Calm down.*

Easier said than done.

Especially when Tom returned from his truck, and he

didn't just have a lighter. He had a full gym bag over his shoulder and a canvas shopping bag in his hand.

"What's all that?"

He gave her a tight smile as he stepped in the cabin. "Supplies."

For what? But he turned away before she could ask him that question. And besides, she was pretty sure she knew the answer.

Tom shrugged out of his coat, hung it on a hook on the wall, then crouched in front of the fireplace.

She closed the door and lifted her voice. "What are you doing?"

He didn't look away from his task. "I'm lighting the fire for you."

So he was being literal about this. Fine. She'd meant in general. With the supplies. This tracking-her-down business. She watched the muscles play on his back, the soft cotton of his shirt bunching as he flexed effortlessly beneath it. "Are you rearranging the logs?"

He paused. "Nope. They were perfect the way they were."

She craned her neck. He was totally fixing her log set-up.

With a final adjustment, Tom lit the fire, then stood and turned around. "Can I make you something more substantial than crackers? I brought bacon and orange juice." Behind him, the kindling popped and sizzled as the flames grew.

Maybe it would go out. It wouldn't, but a girl could hope the park ranger would have an off day.

She glared at him. "Why are you being so nice?"

"Because I wasn't nice before and I have to make up for that. So how about some bacon?"

CHAPTER FOUR

TOM KNEW he was skating on thin ice with Chloe. Somehow, somewhere, they'd gone wrong, and it wasn't when she'd realized he wasn't prepared to hear she was pregnant. It was long before that.

He needed to figure out where that point was and bring her back to that fork in the road. He wanted to surge forward and find another path, but right now, that seemed like an impossible fantasy.

So he was cooking bacon. It wasn't much, but it was something.

He'd found a baking sheet in the warming tray under the oven, and when he'd packed up, he'd thrown his winter camping gear in the truck just in case she'd refused to let him stay inside—so he had a frying pan, too. *Score one for the outdoorsy pack rat.* He used that to keep the bacon warm while he made toast in the oven.

As he was buttering the last slice of that toast, Chloe came into the kitchen. She wiggled her now empty mug. "I've had coffee now, if you want to talk over breakfast."

He nodded slowly. "Sure. Yeah. Thanks."

She moved around him, grabbing his empty Thermos lid on her way to the sink. After she rinsed them out, she poured them both orange juice from the carton he'd had in his fridge at home. "So… I'm pregnant. And you're the father, by the way, but since you're here, I assume you've got that figured out already."

A stab of guilt cut him deeply. She didn't know what he'd yelled after her last week, but he did, and he regretted it to his core. "I've been thinking about nothing else for the last week."

"Huh."

"What?"

"I just didn't hear from you. Must have been some silent thinking."

He gave her an exasperated look. He couldn't help it. "Isn't thinking usually silent?" Then he realized how that sounded and sighed. "I could have thought faster. I admit that. But, like you, I wanted to be sure of what I was going to say. When I said the wrong thing, you took off on me. Fairly, of course. I own that. I didn't respond well."

She lifted her chin. "And now?"

"Now I'm sorry about how I reacted, and I'm grateful to be here to talk about this news, however you want to talk about it."

She grimaced and took a big sip of juice.

That expression sliced through his gut as the worst possibility seemed to loom true. He took a deep breath. "This isn't good news for you."

She shrugged, her gaze guarded. "It's…complicated."

"That's understandable." And it was. Goddamn it, it was. He swallowed any other response he might have because nothing mattered more than acknowledging how much her life had just changed.

Her eyes shifted back and forth as she searched his face. "You come from a big family."

"I also come from a complicated family. The two adjectives go hand in hand sometimes. I can understand messy feelings."

She took a deep breath and nodded. "I'm already attached to the idea of a baby. And I'm really surprised at that, I have to be honest. I'd never wanted kids." Her voice cracked, and she pressed her hand to her belly. "But I want this baby now."

Inside, he sagged in relief. He hadn't ruined her life. "Good. That's great."

"It's not *great*."

"No, of course not." Fuck, it was hard to keep up. "Can you give me a chance here to say the right thing? I support you, whatever you want to do."

She took a deep breath. "There isn't a right thing to say, though. This is an awkward accident with big consequences. Well, consequences I'm choosing, I acknowledge that. All I want is for you to be real with me. This is terrifying. I can only imagine what it's like to have it dumped on you. I'd much rather you admit that than go radio-silent while you figure out the 'right' thing to say."

He swore under his breath. "You're right. I hadn't thought about it like that."

"I know." She shook her head. "Like I said, it's messy. And if I'm being honest, I don't think either of us was truly real with the other, and I bear as much responsibility for that as you do. What we had was a lot of fun, but we were playing with fire."

His jaw flexed, a hard, painful twitch.

She didn't blink, and she didn't look away.

She wasn't wrong, but damn it, she was *wrong*.

The look on her face said it all, though. He needed to accept this was her perspective right now. She was looking back at their relationship and judging it harshly. He understood that. Their choices had led to her current situation, and she felt alone. Unsupported.

He took a deep breath and tried again. Why did this feel so clumsy? He was a grown-up. "If there are other options you want to explore…"

She shook her head. "I don't."

"Okay." His heart pounded in his chest. Her life would be forever altered if she had a child. He couldn't imagine being in her shoes right now. "Just know that I would hold your hand."

Silence stretched between them.

"I know," she finally said. Quietly. "Thank you."

He wanted to hold her hand now, too. They were going to have a baby. Holy fuck. Taking a deep breath, he nodded again, still trying to respect her boundaries and navigate the big feelings. "So what's your plan, exactly? You moved out of your apartment."

"I need some time to myself, away from Pine Harbour. I'll be back, in the area if not the town, but I'm leaving tomorrow."

He looked out the window. "I don't think either of us is going anywhere tomorrow."

"I'm leaving at the earliest opportunity, then. I can't be the knocked-up single woman in a town of six hundred busybodies. Please don't ask me to do that."

He raised his hands, ignoring the panic that had returned to his body. "I won't. Where's your stuff?"

"A sea container in Owen Sound. I paid for a month of storage. I'll figure out where I want it delivered when I find a new job."

"Wait, what happened to your job? Did you quit?" He couldn't believe it. Of all the insane overreactions...

Her face tightened, her eyes dangerously bright. "I didn't quit. The Pine Harbour library branch is being closed down. It's not public knowledge yet, but we were told last week." He opened his mouth to protest, because that wasn't fair. Or right. But she held up her hand and shook her head. "It's a sign. My time in this town has come to an end."

"But—"

"I won't have a job, Tom. What would you have me do?"

Stay. Fall in love with him. Make it work between them. It wouldn't be awful.

But Chloe wouldn't settle for *not awful*.

He didn't want her to settle, anyway. To just be his wife and the mother of his child, with no career of her own.

An awful helplessness threatened to take over.

Tom knew the danger there. Helplessness led to defeat, and he wasn't defeated here. This was a setback. He needed to regroup and take stock of their options.

"Right now, I want you to eat breakfast." He scooped up the plate of food and gestured to the living room. "Come on, let's eat in front of the fire."

She scowled as she followed him into the living room. "I'm not hungry."

That was a familiar refrain from her. Chloe was never hungry when she was stressed. At the end of a bad day of work, she wanted sex. She wanted to move her body and work out the frustration through physical release. He'd tried to feed her a few times at his place and it never went well.

He wasn't stupid enough to offer sex right now,

though. So he set the plate of bacon and toast on the coffee table and went back to the kitchen to get her more orange juice.

"You need to get away," he said when he returned. "Where are you going to go?"

She shrugged. "I don't know. That's tomorrow's problem."

"Day after tomorrow at the earliest." Tom hoped it never stopped snowing.

"Tomorrow," she repeated stubbornly.

That made him feel like he a countdown clock on figuring out a plan, but he couldn't let that thought dominate. It wasn't helpful. Right now, it was a long shot whether or not she'd eat his toast, let alone agree to stick around and try to work out a whole relationship with him.

He was used to Chloe being headstrong and opinionated. Not only used to it, he usually found it very attractive. He found it very attractive right now, even as she blithely talked about leaving him in her dust. She was a force of nature.

But it also made a part of him mad.

What about him? He had a job here, a life. *She* had a life here. Why couldn't she fight for the library? Why was she throwing all of that away?

He couldn't figure out how to ask her that without making it about himself, though. Replaying the last week in his mind didn't bring any clarity. Replaying the year that stretched before that in one gorgeous, sexy fever dream didn't help either. He missed that time already. Had missed it from the second she threw herself into her car and tore away from the training centre.

He was terrified he'd lost her in that moment, and nothing would ever be okay ever again.

He didn't like that feeling at all, so he let her finish breakfast in silence. She ate a few pieces of bacon, he got up to feed the fire a few times, and eventually she started nibbling on toast.

He gathered up the dishes and took them to the kitchen, where he washed them the best he could without a tea towel and left them to drip dry on the counter.

When he returned to the living room, Chloe was curled on the couch. She watched him cross the room.

He found it unnerving how she watched him. It was different from before. Now, she was looking for the truth of him, where before she'd been looking for a co-conspirator in an affair. The truth hadn't had much to do with anything when they were hooking up. Now it had everything to do with everything, and he was scrambling to keep up. Never before in his life had he felt so deficient.

"Do you want to know how I really feel?" she asked.

He squatted in front of her, his forearms braced on his thighs. "Of course. I want to be as real as possible with you."

"I'm scared," she admitted.

That made two of them.

"I've spent the last five years being gloriously, perfectly selfish, and that was a lot of fun. But that time is done, and now I need to figure out how to be a selfless, giving human being in eight and a half months, maybe less, and honestly, I'm not sure I can do it."

Did becoming a parent really mean they'd have to be selfless? Give up everything that had made them happy? That didn't seem right. "You aren't selfish. And we'll figure out the giving part together. We'll both do that parenting work."

She frowned. "How about you?" she challenged. "Are you scared?"

"Fuck yes. Terrified, because I don't know how to be a father. Or a good partner, clearly. So…yeah."

"That makes two of us, then."

There was a thing, the right thing to do here, and he couldn't see it. "What do you need right now?"

She sighed. "Space. Time. I've launched into something rather unplanned here and I'm not dealing well with my own recklessness."

He loved her recklessness, though. Now wasn't the time to say that. He couldn't pressure her. But he could stoke a fire—literally and figuratively.

"I'll be right back," he said, rising to a full stand.

"Where are you going?"

He tugged on his boots, then cast a wild-eyed look around for his hat and gloves. He didn't need his coat. He was going to heat up plenty just by stomping around, and hopefully, throwing an ax. "They have to have a stockpile of hardwood around the property somewhere. I'm going to chop some wood. We're going to be here for days, and we've already burned through half of the logs on the hearth." He pulled open the door and sucked in a breath of cold, clean air.

It didn't calm him down as much as he wanted it to.

"It's going to stop snowing any minute now," she called after him.

She was wrong about that. But she was right about other, more important things, and he had a lot of thinking to do.

He sorely hoped there was an ax. And a giant pile of wood that needed to be split.

———

CHLOE'S PULSE jumped as Tom stomped away from the cottage.

Days! No, they were not going to be there for *days*. For one thing, they didn't have enough food for Tom to last that long.

She would be fine. She had crackers for miles.

But secondly and more importantly, she wasn't sure she could handle days of Tom right now. Especially this new, earnest Tom. It was like he'd retreated into a chrysalis and emerged a fully formed grown-up with emotional IQ and a deep understanding of intimacy.

It had to be a trick.

No, not a trick. He didn't have any cruel intention. He never had. And he'd always been earnest in a way she'd adored. Right up until she told him she was pregnant, and then he—

He'd reacted in a perfectly human way.

Ah, crap. They were both being pretty human. Right now she was irrationally upset, and she didn't have the faintest clue why.

She stomped into the kitchen and glared at the clean breakfast dishes drying next to the sink, Tom's tiny bottle of biodegradable camping soap right there. The man had literally everything they needed in his truck. It was insane. He'd pulled a full kitchen out of his bag—everything from a six-spice dispenser to the sponge to clean up at the end of the meal. He probably *could* live here for days.

Weeks, even.

Weeks of awkwardness and confusion.

It was a nightmare.

They couldn't keep this up. She needed to get a handle

on her emotions, and he needed to accept that this wasn't a problem that she simply hadn't consulted him on.

She didn't need to. Not yet.

Eight months down the road would be a different story. They would need to figure out some kind of happy medium for co-parenting. But right now was the last time bit of time that would be entirely hers for the next eighteen years.

Eighteen. Years.

It was a long time. It was worth fighting through the assumed "right path" to make sure she actually did this the real right way, the way that would mean her child was wholly loved. But she had to fight smarter. No more scowling at the grumpy man on his way out to chop wood. For one thing, that gave him the moral advantage, since he was being productive. That wouldn't do.

Maybe she could figure out something to make for dinner.

In her exploring of the cottage, she'd realized the unheated mudroom off the back of the house hadn't been cleared out. That included a supply pantry of canned goods. It also had a nice view of Tom and his mad wood-chopping.

She put on her toque, tugged on her boots, and marched into the mudroom which was freezing cold, holy crap. Between surreptitious glances out the window, she took a quick summary of what was on the shelf. Spaghetti sauce but no spaghetti. Tinned tomatoes, kidney beans, corn…

She could make chilli.

Maybe.

She thought about calling her best friend Jenna for a precise recipe. Jenna and Chloe had bonded over cooking, after the other woman arrived in Pine Harbour to claim her injured soldier husband back, only to find out that nobody knew about her. Now Jenna and Sean were happily back together and had a baby.

But calling Jenna for help would require explaining why she was making chilli for Christmas dinner and if she'd talked to Tom and yes, he was going to share the chilli, and no, they weren't going to fall madly in love over the unconventional holiday dinner and live happily ever after.

No calling a friend for a recipe. Nope.

The internet would have to suffice, even though Chloe's experience in converting recipes into actual meals was spotty at best.

Cooking was not her strong suit.

From the other side of the cottage, she heard the front door bang open, and she startled. Wood clattered loudly against the hearth, then the door slammed shut.

Well, maybe it didn't slam.

It closed with purpose.

She watched Tom tromp back through the heavy snow to the stump he'd been chopping at.

And he started again.

She dashed her cans into the kitchen, then slid back into the glassed-in mudroom to watch.

He moved like a machine, grabbing a thick log from the covered shelter, stacking it on the stump. Without missing a beat, he picked up the axe and swung it, cleanly cleaving the log into two. He held the axe in one hand and grabbed one of those pieces with the other. Up. Chop. Repeat.

She watched the hypnotic routine until he shoved the axe aside and started stacking logs in his arms.

This time, when he stomped in the front door, she was busy at the counter opening cans of things.

She listened as he clattered logs into the wood cradle beside the fireplace. As he moved back to the door and sighed while he kicked off his boots. She could picture all of it so clearly, because Tom was nothing if not a creature of routine.

Ten bucks said that when he wandered into the kitchen to check on her, he'd be running his fingers through his hair, scratching his scalp. In the past, when she got to his place before him, she'd usually let herself in because he always left the door unlocked for her. And she'd watch with affection as he scratched his hair back to life after being squished under a hat all day.

And then—back in those simpler days when they were fuck buddies—she'd have grabbed his hand and dragged him to the shower to get all clean before they got dirty again together.

"Hey."

She glanced over her shoulder as he filled the doorway, leaning against the frame with one shoulder. His other arm swung up and he ruffled his hair.

Swallowing a smile, she nodded. "Hey. Thanks for chopping the wood."

"I needed to do some thinking. It helped."

"Then…you're welcome for the woodpile."

He laughed, and she was relieved he got it as the joke she intended it to be. "Listen. I think…" He crossed his arms over his chest and gave her a long, solemn look. "Maybe we're having the wrong conversation."

Her heart leapt into her throat. "What conversation should we be having?"

He walked closer. Gently, quietly. Like she was a deer

he didn't want to startle. "That's the thing. I don't know. I just know that we've got this big, life-changing thing that's happened to us—you more than me right now, I fully acknowledge that—and I want to do right by you, and me, and definitely the baby. Can we talk about that?"

"That's a big conversation."

"Yeah." He gave her a tight smile. "Good thing we're here for a while."

"Not days," she whispered.

He just shrugged.

There was so much about this situation that felt out of control. The emotions, the circumstances...but they could control their reactions. They could control how they started their lives as parents.

She took a deep breath and looked up at him. "I'm pregnant," she whispered.

He reached out and touched her cheek. Not a stroke, exactly. Just the gentlest of caresses. An acknowledgement, really. "I know. Wow."

Wow. Yeah, that was the word. She nodded. "And I'm losing my job."

"I'm sorry."

"I'm scared."

"Me, too. Less now that we're talking about it, though."

Another nod.

"We'll talk more. We'll talk all day, in little bits and pieces, until we put them all together. Okay?"

"Yeah."

He glanced past her to the counter. "What are you doing?"

"I thought I'd get some chilli simmering for dinner."

He swept his gaze over the cans she had out. "Sounds good."

She was pretty sure it didn't, not with what she'd found so far. "I, uh, need to look up a recipe."

"Can I open those while you do that?"

"Thanks." She handed him the can opener, ignoring how good his fingers felt against hers and the fresh smell of outside still lingering on his skin.

But when she fetched her phone from the living room, she couldn't get anything to load on the browser. She jabbed at the screen. The signal strength flickered from one bar to no signal, then back to no bar. Not enough to grab any kind of data service. "Can you search for a recipe?" she asked as she returned to the kitchen. "I don't have a great cell signal."

He dug his phone out of his back pocket and frowned. "Neither do I."

This happened sometimes in storms. It was one of the realities of living on the peninsula. She powered her phone down, but when she turned it back on, there was still no signal.

So much for Google.

"We can wing it, right?" She tipped her head to the side and looked at the cans he'd opened. "How hard could it be to make chilli?"

Tom cleared his throat. "Not hard at all." He was doing his best to maintain a straight face.

She jerked upright. "Wait, you know how, don't you?"

"Yeah, because I'm a grown-up." But his eyes were still gentle.

Waving at the pot which he'd somehow magicked onto the stovetop, she gestured for him to show her. "Be my guest, Gordon Ramsay."

Chloe paced back and forth as Tom turned on the stove. He dumped the tomatoes into the pot, added a bunch of spices, then started rinsing the canned beans. She was pretty sure she'd have remembered to do that.

Maybe.

She'd have to learn how to cook in order to feed their child. There was still time. The wee thing wouldn't be eating real food for…a while. She bet Tom would know. He was an uncle twice over. "When do kids start eating real food?"

"Six months, I think? Maybe closer to a year by the time they are actually *eating* a lot. Why?"

"Just wondering."

He glanced her way. "I think they make it clear that they want to put stuff in their mouths and you follow that lead. Also, there are books about these things."

"I know there are books," she said hotly. She was a librarian after all. She'd walked down that aisle yesterday morning.

It had freaked her out.

She was freaking out right now about it, too. She didn't know how to make chilli. Or anything.

Hot, angry tears pricked the back of her eyelids and she spun on her heel.

CHAPTER FIVE

CHLOE NEVER CRIED. Never, ever, ever. She swore, she yelled, she bit her lip until it bled. But she didn't cry, because crying made her feel like shit.

There was nothing worse than being so sad she couldn't keep her emotions inside, and then being alone to bear all of that on her own.

Except she wasn't alone.

Tom was right behind her, she could feel him, and she didn't know what to do with that, either.

"I'm going upstairs." Not looking in his direction, she grabbed the afghan off the couch, and the novel she'd been reading. "With my blanket and my books. And my…" She looked around for the saltines. "Crackers."

Silently, he grabbed them and held them out. Whatever she wanted. Whatever she needed.

Her arms overflowed as she stopped at the base of the stairs and looked in his direction, although not right at him. "I need some space. I needed all of this space, but then you showed up."

"I understand," he said quietly. "I'll stay out of your hair."

And he did.

She curled up in the quiet master bedroom and tried to distract herself with the book. It took flipping through fifteen unread pages to calm down. Then she fell asleep, and didn't wake up until the weak, blizzard-filtered light had shifted to the other side of the house. Long shadows stretched across the bed, and for a second, she didn't know why she was upstairs.

Then she smelled the chilli wafting up from the kitchen and remembered losing it on Tom and stomping upstairs.

She rubbed her gritty eyes and looked at the ceiling, trying to process what the hell was happening inside her body.

Downstairs, dishes clattered in the kitchen. The sound ricocheted through the empty house, easily carrying up to where she lay.

She was struggling to process what was happening here in this cottage, too. Maybe the first step in her own journey to real honesty between them was admitting what she didn't know, what made her anxious.

And what she did know. What she'd experienced growing up.

She stopped in the washroom to pee and wash her face, then she went to find the chef. The father of her future child.

Her unwanted but not unappreciated roommate for the duration of the blizzard.

She found him stirring their dinner.

"That smells really good," she said as she eased her way into the kitchen.

"Hey." He glanced over at her. "You're up."

"I guess I slept for a while."

"The whole afternoon. Full disclosure, I came up to check on you. I'm not sure where that falls on the spectrum of giving you some space, but…"

She made a face. "I deserve that."

"I was prepared for you to throw something at me. Not a book. Maybe crackers."

That made her laugh. "Those are almost as valuable as books!"

"Do you want some with your chilli? We might want to ration our bread a bit."

What had she gotten them into that they needed to carefully measure out food to last through a blizzard? "Are we going to be okay here?"

He waved his hand. "Oh yeah. I've got hard rations in the truck if we get desperate."

"Do I want to know what those are?"

"Vacuum packed things that approximate food popular in the fifties."

"Gross."

"Better than going hungry."

Her pregnant stomach wasn't sure about that, and she made a promise to herself to make the crackers last as long as possible.

"Can I ask how you're feeling now?"

She blew a raspberry, and he laughed. Then she sighed. "This is a crazy rollercoaster of emotions. I don't say that as an excuse, just a statement of fact."

"I don't know what to say to make it better."

"You don't need to say anything right now." She held up her hand. "I do want to talk. Tonight. But let's eat first."

He grinned. "I won't stand between the pregnant lady

and sustenance. Coffee and food always come first, I promise."

———

TOM SERVED up chilli into their mugs, then gave her the spoon from his camping pack, and he took the fork.

She watched him pull the utensils apart with interest. "You don't have one of those sporks? I mean, I'm not complaining. This way we both get something to eat with, so that's great."

He shook his head. "Never did understand those. They're a crap spoon, and a crap fork. What are you saving, an ounce or two in weight? Carry both and eat properly."

"Huh."

"I have strong opinions about most things sold at outfitters to rubes from the city."

"I've never stepped foot in an outfitters," she said, the corners of her mouth turning up in a smile.

We'll have to change that, he wanted to say, but now was not the time. He was painfully aware of how precarious their relationship was. Suggesting outings was way down the map, and he hadn't even started drawing the damn thing yet. While he'd been chopping wood, all he could think about was that somewhere along the way, they took a wrong turn. It wasn't enough to just look at last week and how much he screwed up what should have been a good-but-surprising-news moment. They needed a whole new plan, but first he needed to put a hard pause on what he wanted so he could figure out what she needed, wanted, and was going through. Until he figured out what set her off and what kind of reassurance she needed from him, there would be no flirtation about future dates.

Hell, there hadn't been any dating in the past. That had to be reckoned with as well.

"Uh, okay, I'm going to get my crackers," she said. "My contribution to dinner."

He carried their food to the coffee table and set it down. While she'd slept, he'd cut and decorated the mantle with evergreen boughs from outside, and he quickly adjusted those before she came back.

When she did, she stopped and breathed in the scent before sitting down. "Merry Christmas," she said quietly as she stared into the flickering flames.

He smiled. "I thought we weren't celebrating today."

"I won't force my humbug attitude on you." She touched his hand. "You slaved over…everything, after all. Thank you."

It was a peace offering, and given her wariness, it was more than he expected.

Today hadn't gone as he'd hoped. She hadn't fallen into his arms and allowed him to make grand promises. But she'd shared some hard truths about how she felt, and pushed him to be honest in the same way with her.

It wasn't what he'd come for, but it was progress in the right direction.

While she'd slept, he'd been able—after much cursing and refreshing—to pull up a forecast for the next thirty-six hours. The storm was only going to get worse. He couldn't have asked for better news, not that he'd frame it that way to the woman who wanted to run away as fast as she could. But he was grateful tomorrow would be another opportunity for him to show her he wasn't going to flake.

"I've never been a big Christmas person," he admitted. "My mother is…"

Chloe cleared her throat. "Particular?"

That was an understatement. "Well, you know my mother. She's intensely Italian for someone who has no Italian blood. Growing up, it was all about mass on Christmas Eve, and big meals around that. Christmas morning we had presents, but the biggest effort was over and done with. And by the time I was a teenager, we'd basically merged Christmas Day with the Fosters. What do fourteen-year-old boys get each other?"

"Smokes? Booze? Porn?"

He laughed. "Yeah, pretty much. And video games. So it's a day I'm happy to upgrade to chilli and a fire, let's put it that way."

"Same here, to be honest." She stretched her legs out. "My favourite holidays were spent in the Caribbean. That was an annual tradition for a while, but I haven't been able to do that since I moved up here. Junior librarian on the totem pole doesn't get the sweet week off between Christmas and New Years—until this year, ironically."

"When did you start travelling for Christmas?"

"College. When you're willing to fly last-minute and you aren't picky about what kind of resort serves you rum, you can get some sweet deals. And I got pretty good at figuring out which textbooks I could sell back mid-semester to find the money."

He frowned. So that meant she hadn't spent a holiday with family in almost a decade. He knew she wasn't close to her family—hadn't gone back to visit them in Toronto in the year they'd been hooking up—but this was a new layer of distance.

She dug into the chilli, ending the conversation about

Christmas traditions or lack thereof, and he joined her. It was simple food, and not really heavy, but he'd managed to make it taste good and she finished her whole mug.

"Delicious," she said as she pushed it away. "I'll clean up, Gordon."

"I'll add some wood to the fire and think of some turn-of-the-last-century entertainment options for our evening."

She stuck her tongue out at him. "I brought a dozen books. Do you want to read one of them?" She pointed to the stack she'd set on the mantle, then picked up their dishes and cleared them to the kitchen.

While he waited for her to come back, he perused the collection, finally choosing an erotic thriller. But he didn't crack the cover, even after she returned and started reading herself. Curling up on the couch and reading sounded lovely—for a different night. Tonight he didn't want to hide with pages in between them. Minutes ticking by with so much left unsaid.

Book in hand, he paced around the room, trying to figure out how to put that in a way that didn't come off as pressure. Then he saw, high on an otherwise empty book-shelf, a deck of cards. He snagged it and spun around, holding them out.

Chloe scrunched up her face.

He shrugged and put them down. Fine.

She sighed. "I guess I retreated into a book without discussing anything, didn't I?"

"Little bit."

"I honestly wasn't avoiding talking. I was a pretty solitary kid growing up." She gestured to the stack of books. "I come by my profession legitimately. I spent a lot of time in the library when I was little. And then when I was not-so-little, too."

The way she said it, he got the impression she was sharing this information with a purpose. He sat down. He was eager for any glimpse behind the Chloe curtain. "What was the first book you remember reading?"

"I don't know. I don't remember not reading, honestly. But I think I remember the first book I signed out from the library."

"Oh yeah?"

"Gordon Korman's *No Coins, Please*. Did you ever read him?"

"Bruno and Boots?"

"Yep, exactly. So I'd already read the MacDonald Hall books, or a couple of them, anyway. I wanted to read *Live at Nickaninny*, and my mother wouldn't buy it for me. She thought it was too old for me. So I went to the library, and asked about his books, and the librarian encouraged me to read *No Coins, Please*."

"Aw, that was nice of her. She got you a new book and stuck to your mom's rules."

Chloe snorted. "Hardly. *Live at Nickaninny* was signed out by someone else. As soon as they returned it, she set it aside from me." She leaned over and poked Tom in the chest. "Never underestimate the subversive nature of a librarian, Mr. Law and Order."

He caught her finger for a second and smiled. "Noted." He let her go, and she flopped back.

Looking up at the ceiling, she took a deep breath. "Did I ever tell you my parents are divorced?"

"I think so."

"They weren't married long. A year."

"That's pretty short."

"They got married because my mother got pregnant —with me."

Ah, for fuck's sake. His chest ached for little Chloe, and big Chloe, too. "You grew up knowing that?"

"Yeah."

He nodded slowly. "So that's how you see it going for us?"

She kept her level gaze on his face, but she didn't answer the question directly. "How do *you* see it going for us? Based on actual evidence in our...relationship. Not some rose-coloured glasses hope for what might be."

"If I'm bound by past actions, then I guess I don't know what to think." He took a deep breath. "Is this why you're leaving? Why you need to get away? Because you think people will think we're just together because of the pregnancy?"

"Yeah."

"It doesn't need to be like that. Nobody knows, and it's nobody's business—"

She groaned. "Enough people know about us. And those that don't, will soon enough. And yeah, that's a big factor—the biggest—in why I'm getting the hell out of Dodge." She rolled up to sit, wrapping her arms around her legs. Her next words spilled out fast and furious, but not angry. Resigned, and he hated that for her. "Don't pretend you don't know how this goes down. You're the stud, and I'm the slut. I was good for a fuck, until I got knocked up, and now you're doing 'the right thing.' You said as much yourself, and I don't want that."

They were hard words. Course words. Brittle. Meant to hurt, meant to protect herself. He could see the wall she was building again, but it didn't matter. He could build ladders even taller.

He took a deep breath. "I didn't mean it like that. I wouldn't. What we have between us is private and nobody's business, but if anyone were to ask me, or if I were to hear anyone talk about you, I'd be clear that your company was always the best part of my day. That's the actual evidence you asked for. For a year, you were the best thing that happened to me, day in, day out. I felt lucky to have *any* part of you."

She didn't say anything. No more harsh words.

So he built the ladder a bit taller. "Tell me more."

"About what?"

"About any of it."

Her eyelids fluttered shut, and she sighed. "I don't know where to start. Jenna knows about the baby. I needed to tell someone. And Olivia knows I'm moving, so I'm sure it won't take long for her to figure out the rest."

He gentled his voice as much as he could. "And the world is still standing. Look at that."

"Don't make light of my fears." Her face turned white, and his heart did a free fall. Not gentle enough.

Maybe he could never be gentle enough, but he was going to try. He held her gaze. *Trust me*. It was too soon to ask that of her. He had a lot to show her first. "I'm not. I'm sorry."

Her shoulders lifted and fell in a helpless shrug. "We can't re-write history. We were what we were, and that's not something I want to bring a kid into."

We were what we were? She had no idea what she meant to him. His mouth ran dry, and he rubbed his hand over his face. But this wasn't the time to correct her. "Maybe we can use this time to figure out what we're going to be."

Her lips twisted in a sad grimace, but she didn't say no.

He leaned into the couch, relaxing next to her. Showing her he had all the time in the world for her to sort out her feelings. He could give her space again, too, if that's what she wanted. "Should I go chop more wood?"

She laughed quietly. "It's dark out."

"I'll be fine. I'm a pretty good orienteer and the stump is like fifteen feet from the door."

She sighed. "You know what you can do?" She turned and looked at him. "You made dinner, and that was lovely. I napped the day away. The least I can do is play some cards. You can deal, mister."

"Uh…" He hadn't been expecting that. "Yes. Absolutely. What do you want to play?"

"How about Slap? Or War. Something simple."

They sat across from each other at the coffee table, and after he shuffled, he admitted he didn't know how to play Slap. Chloe held out her hand for the deck of cards. As soon as she was holding them, she squared her shoulders, cleared her throat, and launched into a precise set of instructions on how to play the card game.

So precise it would make a military instructor cheer.

He'd never fully appreciated her skills as a teacher before, but that was probably a big part of her role at the library.

Again, not the moment to be asking about *that*.

Tom was realizing he'd missed a lot of moments over the last year. To ask about her job, her family, her thoughts on major holidays.

And then when two major things happened in her life, he was not there for her, not the way he should have been.

So when they finished their third round, her winning the last round to take the best two of three, and she stood up to say good night, he didn't argue. He wasn't in a place to argue. He'd come here uninvited to convince a woman to give him a shot at something bigger than he probably understood—and the more he thought about it, the more he realized he'd never really gotten to know her.

Not beyond how much he enjoyed their time together, which had been primarily physical.

Christmas night was a weird time to realize you'd been a bit of a dog toward the woman carrying your child.

"Good night," he said as gently as he could. "Sleep tight."

"I will." She glanced at the couch. "Uh…"

"I'll be fine."

"I only brought the one blanket…"

"I don't need a blanket."

She smiled. "Good, because I wasn't offering to share it."

"Good, because I wasn't asking." He grinned back.

"Great."

He stepped towards her, herding her to the stairs. "Great."

She took one step, then another. Slowly.

An old feeling tugged hard in his gut—a pulse of awareness that she was reluctant to leave, that he didn't want her to go upstairs alone. He'd spent a year chasing magic at the end of that rainbow with her. Now look where they were.

But it didn't stop him from turning his body, opening his arms up for a hug. If she wanted, he'd wrap her in his arms. It would kill him to let her go, but it would feel so good, it would be worth it.

"Night," she whispered.

"Chloe…"

She reached for him. Not a hug, just her hand. She wrapped her fingers around his forearm and squeezed.

That was enough for his entire body to react as if she'd used a defibrillator to hard reset his heartbeat.

Could she feel the jolt? Her eyes flicked up to his face and she held his gaze long enough he wondered if she'd been rocked in the same way.

"See you in the morning, Tom." And then she was gone. Climbing the stairs, carrying that feeling away with her.

He was left standing in the quiet living room with literally nothing. No blanket. No woman, no clue, no plan.

He'd see her in the morning. He'd really see her. He'd watch and listen and pay fucking attention, because something needed to change in a big way.

Turning away from the stairs, he took a step, his toe colliding with a box. The entire room was empty, and he was normally light on his feet. How the fuck had he missed something big enough to trip on?

Cursing under his breath quietly, he stepped back and looked down. Sticking out from beside the newel post was the box of presents he'd brought in, the gifts that had gone untouched and fallen by the wayside in the tension.

The bottom of his stomach dropped out, and he was tempted to kick the box across the room. Instead, he threw himself on the couch and stretched out, ignoring the chill of the air on his skin. He'd slept in trenches and outside. He had a sleeping bag in the car, but he wasn't going to get it.

Maybe this was the penance he needed to pay. Maybe he should go upstairs and stretch out on the hardwood floor outside the master bedroom. Show Chloe that he would suffer for her.

That doesn't make any sense.

Did any kind of grovelling gesture ever make sense, really?

Tom rolled over, trying to get comfortable on the couch as he listened to the silent house, on a silent night. What a strange Christmas this had been. A truly spectacular disaster of a holiday, but he didn't miss any of the other options for today—a friend's house, a sibling's home. He didn't want to be anywhere else.

Except for upstairs.

He should have asked her which book she recommended from the stack she'd brought. That's what he wanted to right now. He wanted to listen to her voice as she talked about something she knew inside and out. He wanted to fall asleep being told what was what by Chloe Dawson.

Instead, he fell asleep feeling like a lonely fool.

CHAPTER SIX

CHLOE WOKE up to the smell of bacon, and she hurried downstairs, her nauseous tummy wanting some of that *right now.*

"Morning," she said breathlessly. "You're cooking again."

Tom looked up from buttering toast and gave her a quick nod before resuming his task. "Hey. How'd you sleep?"

She'd had better nights. She'd tossed and turned and thought about him a million times, and at least once, she woke up to hear him lightly snoring from the couch, and it had hurt her to be so close and yet so far.

In every book she'd ever read with a couple stranded in a snowstorm, one bed and one blanket, they figured out a way to share both. Why couldn't she do that? She thought about going downstairs and curling up with him on the couch, covering them in her afghan, and sinking into the warm comfort of his body.

But her bruised heart wouldn't let her.

And now in the light of day, she felt off-kilter in a

whole different way. How had she sleep? No way could she tell him the truth there. "Okay," she said, proving herself a total liar. "You?"

"Same." Another quick glance up. "Okay."

Maybe he was lying, too.

Of course he's lying, you ninny. He didn't have a blanket and you made him sleep on a couch made for a normal-sized man, and he's built like a lumberjack. "You could, uh, take the bed tonight, if you—"

His head jerked up again, this time his gaze holding on her. Sharp. Piercing. "No. The bed is yours."

Oh, it was going to be an awkward morning. She swallowed and reached for a cracker to nibble on. "I'll make coffee, then?"

That got a smile. "Sounds good."

Chloe grabbed the milk from the fridge and was shocked to find three more packs of bacon waiting there.

"Did you bring…" She counted on her fingers. "Five pounds of bacon with you yesterday?"

"I guess. I grabbed what I had in the freezer. It's easy to cook anywhere, nutritionally dense."

"You make it sound like you have bacon emergencies regularly."

That made him laugh.

She closed the fridge and leaned against it, watching him cook. "You always order sausage at the diner."

He shot her a quick look over his shoulder. "Do I?"

"You do. I didn't even know you liked bacon."

"But you knew I liked sausage," he said quietly, and how he said it—as if he liked that she knew something so mundane about him—made her stomach flip-flop in a new, non-pregnancy related way.

"I know things about you," she said. She wasn't sure

why she was feeding that feeling, but the flip-flops got stronger, and they were better than feeling queasy. "I know you don't put sugar in your coffee."

"You can put sugar in my coffee if you want."

She smiled, remembering yesterday's Thermos of double-double sweetness. Today they were having instant coffee, from a canister he'd already set out. "I won't do that to you."

As if right on cue, the kettle started to boil.

She prepared their cups with instant coffee grounds and hot water, then added milk to both. After putting sugar in her own coffee, she brought his Thermos lid to him, setting it on the counter beside his hip.

"Thank you," he said, turning, and she stepped back, bumping into the counter.

He was suddenly right in front of her.

"The thanks should be all mine," she whispered. "You're stuck here with me, feeding me and making sure I've got all the things I hadn't thought about. This isn't the greatest way to spend a holiday break."

He braced his arms on either side of her body and leaned in. His eyes bored right into her, hot and promising and very, very dangerous. "Don't think for a second I want to be anywhere else. Okay?"

She nodded, a tiny little wiggle up and down. She got it. She didn't know if she could trust it, but she believed him.

Every muscle in his face tensed as he searched her expression, then he roughly stepped back. "Good."

A lump formed in her throat as the space in front of her suddenly went cold.

He took a long, ragged breath. "You know what we should do?"

She couldn't think straight. Kiss? Fight? Kiss and fight at the same time? "What?"

"Go for a walk."

Spinning around, she looked out the window. "It's storming out there. It's so bad you can't drive across the two-hundred-foot-long causeway in your monster truck. We're not going for a walk."

He closed the gap between them, and there was that delicious warmth again. Right up against her back. He lowered his voice, his breath warm against her ear. "We'll just walk around the house. We'll go slow, but it'll be good to move and get some fresh air."

"That would take an hour in this weather."

"So it takes an hour." He said it like that wouldn't be any kind of hardship at all.

That was hard to argue with. She straightened up and looked at the oven. "Your bacon is burning."

He got the tray out of the oven, and it wasn't burnt, just extra-crispy. It was perfect, actually, and Chloe ate more than she thought she would.

After breakfast, they got bundled up and headed outside. The wind immediately got under her coat, cooling her down, but with Tom in the lead, making a little trail for her to follow, it wasn't that hard to make it around the house.

And he was right—when they collapsed on the porch again, she was warmed up and it had felt good to move her legs.

"Now it feels good to not move," she panted. "That had to have been like five hundred knee-ups, don't you think?"

He nudged his leg against hers. "Your knees had to lift higher than mine did."

"Good point. Is it too soon for me to invoke the whole exercising-for-two excuse?"

He chuckled. "Nope. That's a get out of jail free card you get to use for nine months. Milk it."

"I will." She shivered, and he thumped his hand against the porch.

"All right, inside we go. We can't have you freezing for two."

Back inside, she kicked off her boots, then shucked off the too-big slush pants Tom had pulled from the magical, all-giving truck cab for her. She carried all her wet stuff to the hearth where Tom was adding another log to the fire.

He pointed to the coffee table. "Cards again?"

"You want to redeem yourself?"

"Hell yes."

And he did. He won two games in a row, and then when she insisted they could do best out of five, he won the third game, too.

"If we'd bet on that, I'd call you a card shark," she muttered. "Where was that Slap skill last night?"

He laughed long and hard. "Slap skill. Chloe, I grew up in the middle of four kids, and am best friends with four brothers. You don't want to know about my training in this regard."

She poked him with her big toe. "Sure I do."

"So many kidney punches. It was brutal." He grinned. "Probably a morality tale for leaving children to fend for themselves in a pack."

She wouldn't know.

His face sobered. "Your childhood was nothing like that."

She shook her head. "Nope."

"Tell me about being a single child."

So much of her childhood had been defined by the battles back and forth between her parents. The divorce proceedings went on and on. Custody disagreements, child support fights.

"Resentment," she finally said. "That was the theme. But I think that's more about my parents being who they are, rather than me not having any siblings." She touched her fingers to her belly. "I want something different for this baby. No drama. No conflict. Just a perfect acceptance of them, and us as co-parents without any societal stricture forcing our hands to be anything else. I just want us all to be happy, Tom."

His face darkened. He didn't say anything, but he didn't need to.

She sighed. "You don't agree with that idea?"

"For others, absolutely. People shouldn't stay together for the kids, and they shouldn't fight each other if they decide not to be married. But yesterday, you said we weren't a couple in love. Something like, that's not what we were."

"It's not." She believed that so strongly.

"Because it wasn't a possibility for *you*."

"For good reason."

"I get that now." He didn't mean it to sound loaded, she could tell, but it was. She hadn't told him about her parents. Hadn't had any reason to until she found herself at risk of repeating their mistake. "I swear to you, I do, Chloe. I see you. But I don't know—I've been thinking about where we went wrong. At what point could I have said something and sent us down a different path? Because clearly we went too far down the friends-with-benefits track. And I can't see it."

"Can't see what?"

"The point where you would have been open to hearing how I really feel about you."

"What are you saying?"

"On some level, I always knew that you couldn't risk your heart with me, so I never asked you to. But you want to know the truth?"

No. Yes. "I don't know," she whispered, her heart hammering and her vision going blurry.

Tom rocked back on his heels, then pushed up to stand. He paced back and forth as he let loose a stream of words she never expected him to say in any form. "I fell in love with you the first minute that I saw you. Not lust. Love. I saw you, wanted you, craved you. The only thing on offer was sex, so I took it. I grabbed it with both hands." He stopped pacing and looked at her helplessly, his hands swinging at his sides. "But I've been hopelessly, pathetically in love with you for a year. Every time you crawled into my bed, every time you made me feel so unbelievably good I wanted to shout about it from the rooftop, I had to bite my fucking tongue. I almost told you a million times that I loved you, and now it feels like you're punishing us both because I didn't."

"I'm not punishing you. I'm sure as hell not punishing myself. I'm making the safest, clearest decision I can for myself and my baby. So you say that you love me. What am I supposed to do with that information? Throw myself at you regardless of how I feel?"

"No." He sagged. "I shouldn't have said that last bit."

"Probably not. Because every time you chose not to tell me how you really felt, there was a reason for that."

"I was working within the terms you set out."

"The terms we *both* liked." He truly didn't see himself the way she did. She stood up, too. Her voice cracked.

"You *didn't* want our relationship to be different. Not then. Maybe now in hindsight you're filled with regret, but over the last year? You wanted it exactly as it was, with this extra layer of feeling good about yourself painted on top. Maybe that was exactly what you needed—you could pretend to love me without having to do any of the hard work of actually being in love with someone."

"So let me do the hard work now. Let me prove to you that I'm here, that I'm all-in."

It was so tempting. She could see, maybe for the first time, why her parents got married.

But it hurt, too, because she would never know if he was actually choosing her for who she was, or her for being his baby's mama.

So she shook her head. It was the only thing she could do, because hot tears rushed to her eyes and closed up her throat.

"Ah, Chloe, no…" He stalked back, stopping right in front of her, and pulled her into the front of his warm, flannel shirt. "I said the wrong thing. You're not punishing me. I see you. I see what you want, for yourself and the baby, and I want to give you that. Whatever you need. I can love you and let you be free."

"I just lived the wrong life for any of this. We are not supposed to repeat our parents' mistakes, you know? And yet, here I am. Doing exactly the same thing my mother did. Desperately hoping I might be loveable when I'm really just fuckable."

He swore under his breath and pressed his lips to her hair. "I don't think that. That's never in a million years how I'd describe you. Think of you. Anything. At all."

"But it's how you treated me," she whispered. "And I treated you the same right back. I know that. I know what

I did, what I chose. And it was *fine*. I liked being friends with benefits. I really did. But I won't have that kind of relationship with a child in the mix." The thought actually hurt. Physically caused her pain, and the tears flowed harder as the agony of it all racked through her body. "I hate crying," she said as she desperately wiped her eyes. "God, what a mess."

He wrapped his arms around her tighter. "I'm sorry."

She tried to catch her breath and shake it off. "It's hormones."

"It's also losing your job and having a shitty boyfriend. You've got a lot going on."

"You're not my boyfriend," she muttered.

"I want to be."

That made her head swim. "I think we both deserve a cleaner start to parenting than that."

He breathed in, his whole chest moving against her. "Maybe."

She stepped back. The hug had been good, but too much could be dangerous. Taking another deep breath, she tried to make light of what had just happened. "One of those horrifying parenting books said that pregnancy hormones can make you cry."

"Did you throw it across the library?"

"I would never throw a book," she said disapprovingly. "But I did consider taking it out of circulation."

He chuckled gently. "Is that how a librarian takes a hit out on a book?"

"Yeah." She sniffled. "Listen, about earlier…and now… the hugging…."

He stepped back and crossed his arms over his chest. "Got it."

"It's just—"

"No, I understand." He shoved his fingers through his hair. "Listen, I'm going to chop some wood. Then I'll get dinner started."

She frowned. "We could cook together."

He nodded, a short, hard clip of his head. "We could."

"Do you not want to?"

He gave her an incredulous look. "Do I not— Chloe, there is nothing I don't want to do with you. I want to cook with you. Play cards with you. Read a book with you, go to sleep with you. Keep you warm, chop you wood, hold you tight until you believe how much you mean to me. There is nothing I don't want to do with you. You're the one throwing up boundaries. I'm just trying to respect your limits."

What was she supposed to say to that? What could she say over the too-fast, too-hard beating of her heart?

"Let's cook together," she finally whispered. "Please. And then after we eat, let's go for another walk."

CHAPTER SEVEN

TOM CHOPPED TWICE as much wood today as he did yesterday. He soaked through his undershirt, and when he dumped the fourth armload of logs on the hearth, he stripped down next to the fire, right in front of Chloe.

She'd seen his bare back before.

Behind him, she flipped a page in her book. Loudly. He grabbed a clean shirt from his bag, tugged it over his head, then turned around, letting the heat of the fire dry his back before he pulled the shirt down over his torso.

She didn't look up once the whole time.

"Good book?"

That got her to look at him. She smiled. "Great."

"Which one is that?" He sat at the other end of the couch, and she pulled her feet back, giving him room.

"The thriller you picked up and put back down last night."

"You stole my book."

"Apparently. It's a page-turner. You missed out."

"I got to play cards with you. I missed nothing." He leaned over and snatched the book from her hands, careful to keep his finger on the page she was on. "Let me see… *'Careful,' I warn her. 'I don't want to be careful.' She pushes up, sitting squarely on my lap as she grinds away. 'I want you to fill me up before we go out. I want to feel your*—, you were reading this while I was outside chopping wood?"

She grinned.

Tom flipped the book over and read the back. "I had no idea it was that explicit. Who is this guy?"

"An asshole." She shrugged. "Sometimes I like reading about characters I can't stand."

He gave the book back. "I want to read it when you finish. I'm going to raid the pantry again."

She set the book aside and stood up. "I'll come with you."

He followed her to the mudroom off the back of the kitchen. The temperature had dropped again, and it was cold enough to take his breath away. Quickly, he scanned the shelves. "Soup is fast."

"S-s-sure," Chloe chattered. She grabbed a can of peaches and cream corn. "I like corn, too."

"Deal. We can add that to…chicken noodle?" There were two cans of that. Simple but classic.

"Yum."

Sold.

He stepped back, doing the world's fastest visual inventory of what else they had. There was a cardboard box on the top shelf. "Take the soup fixings," he said, hanging them to her. Then he grabbed for the box, ducking out of the way as a light rain of dust showered past him. "What's this?"

Chloe shrugged. "I couldn't reach that."

It was heavy. He set it on a lower shelf and opened the top flap. Chloe laughed when she saw that inside were a set of dishes, wrapped in paper. "Hey, matching mugs. We can upgrade you from the Thermos lid."

Tom shook his head. He grabbed a couple of bowls, but left the rest in the box. "Nothing wrong with my lid mug. It's kind of our thing now." She giggled, which made him happy, and he gestured to the kitchen. "In we go."

Back in the kitchen, he dunked the cans in a sink of hot water to thaw them, then joined Chloe on the couch again.

He tapped his finger against her book. "Are they still having sex?"

"Nah, they've moved on to fighting about how to take down the bad guy now."

"Sounds about right."

She put the book down and looked at him.

He shrugged. "What? It does. Fucking and fighting. It's human nature."

"On the page, maybe. I'd rather real life was more of lying on a couch and reading all day. There's something underrated about just being warm and safe and entertained."

That sounded pretty good. He grabbed one of the other books and joined her again, stretching out, one of his legs up on the seat of the sofa. She let her leg fall softly against his calf, and he opened the book.

She had a point.

As he got into the story—this one more of a humorous mystery—he found himself pulled out of the conflicted angst of their current situation. Yeah, that was still there in the background, but right here, right now, he was chuckling at shit on the page, and enjoying the warm press of her leg against his.

This moment, removed from everything else, was pretty damn perfect.

At one point, Chloe drifted asleep, and he watched her have a nap. When she woke up, he went back to reading his book like he hadn't been staring at her like the creeper she would think he was.

The day was ticking by. Their fight earlier was still on his mind. She hadn't brought it up again, but maybe it was for him to broach.

When her tummy gurgled from the other end of the couch, he put his book down. Standing up, he held out his hand. "Cook together?"

She slid her fingers over his, squeezing for a second before pulling herself up. "Soup, ho."

The first thing she did in the kitchen was grab a couple of crackers, which she carefully washed down with a glass of water.

"You feeling okay?"

She wrinkled her nose. "It's always there, a weird quiver like I could get sick, but I won't. The crackers help a lot."

He'd buy her all the crackers in Pine Harbour when the storm ended. "Let's get some soup going then." He started with the corn, adding spices and seasoning to that in the pot before adding the two cans of chicken soup. "And…done."

She laughed. "So fancy."

"Only the finest tinned cuisine at Chez Vance." He nodded toward the mudroom. "I guess they're not renovating that space?"

"I guess not."

"How did you exactly end up here, anyway?"

"Uh…" She gave him a sheepish look. "I brazenly told them I wanted to use it? Mrs. Vance is a library regular all summer long. I was going to try to find a hotel room somewhere, but Olivia said something when I bumped into her about the town being surrounded by idyllic escapes that never get used in the winter. And I…wasn't ready to leave just yet."

She looked at him, and he realized that was about him. She hadn't been ready to leave him fully in the dust, maybe. Or she'd wanted to give him another chance to talk, after she'd had some space. Either way, he was grateful.

"I immediately thought about this place—I'd been out here a couple of times, to drop off and pick up books when Mrs. Vance broke her leg the summer before last."

"Ah ha."

"I promised to be a model houseguest. She said I was welcome to stay, but I'd have to bring everything I needed because they would be the opposite of model hosts."

"It's a pretty nice place to hide out."

"Except you found me in less than a day." She crossed her arms. "How exactly did you do *that*, by the way?"

He stirred the soup. "An accomplice who shall remain nameless had someone find out where your cell phone was."

"I turned it off."

"Did you do that after you got here? It pinged off the cell tower at the head of the road Christmas Eve morning. Then it was just a matter of looking for the house with the lights on. This was the only one."

"I would really not be good on the run."

"Are you saying librarians are more suited to being subversive street fighters than fugitives fleeing from the man?"

"Precisely."

"Good to recognize your limits—and your strengths."

He wanted to tell her to stay and fight, not to run again, but there were other things to say first. "Listen," he said after they'd settled back in front of the fire with their matching bowls of soup. "I've been thinking about what you said about your parents, and I'm sorry. I understand better now why you don't want to get stuck in something that isn't right."

She tilted her head. Listening, giving him space to say more, which was good, because he had a lot more to that train of thought.

"I know there isn't any *one* thing I can say to you to prove that we won't hate each other in a year. I've heard that, finally. I don't even know if there are a dozen things I can say or do. It's not going to happen in a single conversation. It's going to have to be everything, over time." Her lips parted, and he sped up, wanting to get it all out before she protested. "We can figure that out together, because I apparently spent a year showing you—accidentally—that I didn't want a relationship, when it's very much the opposite. I regret that, and I accept it could take another year to show you that I do want one now."

"Wow."

He exhaled. "Was that...was any of that close to the right thing?"

"Was it real?"

"Very."

"Then it was the right thing to say."

He smiled in relief. "Good things happen when you lie on a couch and read all afternoon."

"Maybe we should switch books. I could use some clarity like that."

He bumped shoulders with her. "Deal. I want to read the rest of that scene where she wants to be filled up."

Chloe smiled and blushed.

"Eat your soup," he said gruffly. "And I'm going to stop talking now before I ruin a good thing."

That made her laugh, and *that* made him happy.

After they finished eating, they washed up together. As Chloe set the second bowl on the counter to dry, she looked sideways at him. "I have a confession to make."

"What?"

"I almost didn't let you into the cottage when you showed up. I didn't want you here."

That wasn't exactly a secret, but it was good to talk about. Name and put on the table. "I'd have left. Eventually. I don't want to make you uncomfortable."

"Good. But I'm glad I let you in. Maybe that's the real confession."

He wanted to kiss her so much it hurt. He clenched his hands at his sides instead. "I'm glad you did, too."

She swayed towards him, then nodded and stepped back. "Time for a walk? I want to go for another lap of high-knees around the house, because that was *so much fun, Tom*."

"*The funnest, Chloe*. I know it. But it's gotten colder out there," he warned her.

"I'll have to work harder to stay warm, then. Brace yourself for snowballs."

———

CHLOE HAD an ace up her sleeve: Tom had no idea she was a master snowball builder. He may have childhood experience of besting his brothers and best friends, but she'd spent three years volunteering at an elementary school when she was in university. That was more recent.

Advantage, Chloe.

Of course, he had arms honed from chopping wood like a Norse god. Advantage, Tom.

But he was also hampered by a misplaced sense of chivalry and he wouldn't use that strength against her.

Advantage, Chloe, again, and she intended to use it.

They did the same tromp around the house they did earlier. The path was still there. It had filled up again, both from fresh snowfall and some blowing around, too, but the beaten down stuff underneath was easy for their feet to find. Casually enough that Tom wouldn't notice, she scooped up a bit of snow with her fingers and tested the clumping strength of the powder.

Perfect.

As he rounded the third corner and ducked out of sight, she grabbed her first ball-sized weapon and packed it tight, then held it loose as she followed him around the bend.

Dusk had fully settled on them, a gorgeous dark blue sky that popped above the bright white of the snow shimmering in the light streaming out of the cottage windows.

"Hey, it's stopped snowing," she said. Both as a factual observation, and a way to get Tom to twist around.

"That's great," he said, stopping. He started to turn. "Maybe—"

Thwack. She nailed him square in the chest. "Gotcha."

With a roar, he leaned over and armed himself, but she was already packing snowball number two. This time he was harder to hit, because he was moving back and forth. Excellent defence.

She turned and sprinted back the way they'd come, making a smaller snowball as she ran.

"A moving target is a nice challenge," he called from behind her right before a ball smacked her in the elbow.

"Quarter point," she hollered back. "You only get full points for torso shots." She stopped and whipped her next shot at him.

"Missed," he taunted as they squared off.

She scooped up another. "I like to lull you into a false sense of security."

"False sense of nothing, woman." He wound up and took aim. She twisted away, but it still got her on the butt.

"Ow," she yelled out. "My bum!"

"Your poor behind?" He had no sympathy. Nor should he, she was totally playing that up. "Turn around, Chloe. Take the final shot like a real warrior."

She smiled to herself and turned back.

He was right there, and the snowball she'd let fly with her left hand—surprise!—hit him right in the face. "Snowball warriors are ambidextrous," she said, cackling as he tackled her into the snow.

As far as tackles went, it was pretty gentle. He cradled her in his arms on the way down and quickly rolled off her.

Maybe too quickly. Her pulse was beating erratically, but she wasn't confused in the least about why. It would have been nice to have him on top of her, pinning her into the soft, fluffy bank.

"That was fun." He groaned as he pulled her up again. "And now we're both soaked. Let's get back inside. Cruel, cruel woman."

Shivering, she pushed through the cottage door and hurried over to the fire. Snow had crawled up her coat sleeves, freezing her wrists where her gloves met her jacket. It had also slid down the back of her neck, and now cold, wet drops were crawling along her spine.

"That was f-f-fun," she said, her teeth chattering as she pushed off her slush pants. They kept the snow off her clothes, but they weren't warm.

Snow pants needed to get packed next time. Not that there would be a next time.

Tom dropped to his knees in front of her and put his hands to her wet socks. "Lift."

"Tom…"

"Let me help you." He didn't look up at her, didn't give her any room for argument, so she lifted her leg and he peeled off the first sock. He repeated the gentle care on the other leg, then stood. His face was tight and concerned. "I think you could use a hot shower. I'll go put the kettle on. Let's get you warmed up inside and out."

He turned, but she reached out and caught his elbow. "Wait."

Twisting back, he did his best to hide the look of wanting on his face, but his best wasn't good enough.

The burning need inside her matched it. "I've had enough hot cocoa," she whispered. "I need something else now."

He whispered her name. *Chloe.*

It wouldn't be a good idea to confuse their situation with sex. But being intimate with Tom had always felt good. It had made them both happy.

She wanted that now. To be happy, to feel good, to hold Tom close and bring him into her body. She wanted him to warm her up, not cocoa. Not an empty shower to match the empty space in her chest.

Stepping closer, she slid her cold, stiff fingers under the hem of his shirt. He didn't flinch, just took her chilly help.

When he was bare-chested in front of her, she dropped her hands to his belt. He groaned under his breath. She didn't miss how his cock flexed against his fly.

Whatever else they didn't have—total honesty, secrets laid bare, a basic understanding of what made the other tick—they had this. She affected him no matter what.

It felt *good*.

But more importantly, it felt right.

CHAPTER EIGHT

TOM COULDN'T BREATHE. All he could feel was her fingers below his waist. All he could hear was her name on his lips, a low, groaning whisper.

Chloe, Chloe, Chloe. He'd hurt her. Set her up and left her alone when she needed a friend more than anything else.

And now she was offering—

No, she was asking.

She wanted him to—

His brain was working overtime to process what his body knew intuitively. They'd done this many times before, but never like this. Never with their true feelings on full display. His true feelings. And oh, how he loved this woman. Wanted her. Needed to show her everything.

She swayed her hips as she walked backwards, tugging him by his belt, until her heels hit the bottom step.

Then he took over, swinging her up into his arms.

"I can walk," she laughed.

He wasn't laughing. "I can carry you," he ground out.

Upstairs was just as empty as down. Two vacant

rooms, nothing but long shadows. But one room, one blessed, amazing room, had a big bed, and that was his target.

That was where he would strip her down. Make her feel good.

"Shower, Tom," she whispered, brushing her lips against the bare skin on his neck.

Swearing, he turned, bumping her back into the wall.

She laughed again.

He growled and pushed against her, holding her in place as he covered her mouth with his and swallowed that laugh. Every amused peal was fuel for him, helped reinforce that yes, this was what she wanted. This wasn't wrong.

He wasn't hurting her, wasn't taking advantage.

But then she shivered in his arms, and he swore. "Sorry," he ground out. "Sorry, fuck me, sorry, hang on. Where the hell is the bathroom up here?"

"Across the hall." She twisted and pointed, then wiggled her legs. "P-put me down already."

He did as asked, and she led the way across the hall. There was one towel hanging on the back of the bathroom door. Bright purple. He recognized it from one of his few visits to Chloe's apartment. "You had to bring your own towel, too?"

"Ye-es. And I only brought one, s-so we'll have to share."

He could dry off with his t-shirt. He reached into the tub and turned on the shower, cranking the hot water tap all the way around. His dick needed to cool it, because Chloe needed to warm up. Her teeth were chattering now, the cold sinking in to her core.

She peeled out of her long-sleeved t-shirt and yoga

pants, and oh, how he'd missed her sweet, soft body. He loved her wide hips, the way her thighs jiggled as she bounced in place, and the slight sway of her perfect ice-cream-cone shaped breasts. Here and there, all over her body, ink decorated her curves. He'd missed her tattoos, too.

He'd make time tonight to tell her every single way he adored her. How all of this was so important to him.

"In you go," he said. It sounded brusque, and that wasn't his intent.

She gave him an amused look even as her jaw bounced uncontrollably. "I'm f-f-fine."

"Sure. Get warm, please?" He needed her to not be cold. He needed her to be okay, to be cared for—by him.

She obliged, getting in first and then holding the curtain out of the way so he could join her. Steam quickly built up around them as she stood under the spray, rolling her neck back and forth under the water.

"Better?"

"Mmm." She turned and let the water slide down her front.

He closed the gap between them, easing her back against him, and wrapped his arms around her middle. Gentle, careful. She was so precious to him, but she was playful, too, and he had all the time in the world for loving teasing. "I'd call that snowball fight a draw, wouldn't you?"

She gasped. "Not at all. I won fair and square."

"You won. I don't know it was fair. You started with a sneak attack."

"Legitimate strategy for victory," she murmured.

When she reached for the shampoo, he held out his hand. "Can I?"

"Please."

He worked the suds into her hair, probably using too much, but it felt good. And then he got to do it all over again with conditioner. "Stay under the hot water for a minute, okay? I'll go find you something warm to put on."

She shook her head. "There's a gas fireplace in the bedroom. We're good."

He got out, shook off the excess water like the mongrel he was, and dashed across to the bedroom. The gas fireplace immediately started heating up the room when he turned it on with the flip of a switch.

When he got back to the bathroom, she was out of the shower and drying off her hair. He took the towel from her hands and finished the job for her, then used it to hold her next to him as he kissed her mouth. Softly, hotly, and with a promise that he hoped was equally erotic and adoring.

"To bed," he murmured.

Her eyes lit up. "Yes."

They kissed again in the doorway, and across the hall. But as soon as Tom pushed the bedroom door shut behind them, closing in the warmth from the fire and making the room their private cocoon for the night, Chloe pulled away.

She kept her eyes on him, smiling, as she crawled onto the bed ahead of him.

This was familiar. This pull of desire, this wanton offer in invitation. *Come and get it.*

He chased her, falling on her, and then kissed her. Soft at first. He whispered her name, and she nipped at his lips. If she wanted it harder, hungrier, he'd oblige. He pressed her thighs apart and kissed his way down her belly, stopping right at the dip between her abdomen and her mound. He pressed his face there, reverently, and breathed her in. The start of this had been botched well and truly, but he was going to spend the rest of her pregnancy making that up to her.

He kissed the bottom nip of her belly and whispered, "Hello in there."

She giggled.

Looking up, he caught the small smile on her lips as it faded into a heated look. "I've missed you between my legs," she said huskily.

"What have you missed, exactly?" He licked his lips, eager to please. Whatever Chloe wanted, Chloe could have.

"Your mouth. Your...tongue. Lick me, Tom. Gently to start."

He brushed his lips over her curls, then lower, down the seam of her sex. "How gentle?"

"Soft little licks," she whispered. When he glanced up again, her eyes had drifted shut. She was so beautiful like this, overcome with desire. The sexiest, most uninhibited woman he'd ever met. "Hold me open and taste me."

He caressed her lips, feeling them plump and swell under his attention, and then, when her hips rolled in a silent plea, he pressed her legs further apart still and found the wet, pink centre of her.

Little licks.

Soft, gentle touches.

He worked her up slowly, patiently, until her desire ran clear and eagerly from her body. Then he slid a finger, two fingers, into her core and gave her something to fuck against as she found her pleasure on his face.

When she came, it was slow, but not gentle. She wrapped her thighs around his shoulders and clamped down, jerking against him in a long, sustained climax that felt pretty damn good on the giving end.

She finally collapsed back on the bed, her bare limbs sprawling wide, and she reached for him even as her eyes stayed closed. "So good," she murmured. "Your turn."

He was tempted.

But she was tired and something was holding him back.

"Tomorrow," he said quietly, curling around her. "Can I sleep up here with you?"

"Mmm." She nodded and rolled onto her side, giving him her bare backside to rub against.

He might not get much sleep tonight.

But it would be worth every moment of frustration to have a chance to hold her again. For a first time, in fact, because she'd never slept over at his place.

What would the Vances say if they knew their cottage was home to this particular first? Hopefully they would never know that particular detail.

It was their little secret. Tom and Chloe, finally having a sleepover.

———

CHLOE HAD a few thoughts happen all at the same time when she woke up. It was still night, because it was dark out. She had no idea where her afghan had gone, and her toes were really cold. But the rest of her was warm, and the key bits—the dirty bits—were pretty turned on.

The last point was probably because there was a big, manly hand cupping one breast, and a matching one possessively curled over the opposite hip. And a super manly, extra big erection was poking her from behind.

She smiled and wiggled back against it. *Tom*.

He roused immediately, as if summoned to service her. "Morning," he mumbled.

"I'm not sure about that," she whispered. "It's still dark."

With a nudge, she pushed him onto his back, then she scrambled around, looking for her afghan, which had slipped down to his feet.

It was doing neither of them any good down there.

She threw it over her shoulders like a cape, then settled between his thighs. He rubbed his eyes as he looked down his body at her, a big, dopey smile on his face. "Hey."

"I'm Blow Job Girl, here to save the night," she said, pointing at her cape.

His erection stiffened in salute.

She wrapped her fingers around his heavy, solid cock, enjoying the feel of him in her hand. She liked the sounds he made even more, when she dipped her head and licked him, then swallowed the tip in her mouth. Her gag reflex made itself known immediately, so she eased off, using her hand more and her mouth as the bonus at the top.

"So good, Chloe. Fucking yes, suck me."

She smiled to herself as she licked around the thick crown of his erection. He didn't care what she did with her mouth. He was just happy she was going down on him in one way or another. A definite point in Tom's favour. He was vocally appreciative of her skill and creativity in the bedroom.

"Gonna come for me?" she asked, twisting her wrist. She piled on some dirty talk, her favourite little trick that drove him wild. Talking about a blow job was almost as effective as actually giving him one. "Come on, Tom. Come in my mouth. My wet, hot little mouth."

His next words were too strained to make out, but it didn't matter. She'd jerked him to an orgasm in no-time flat, and now she was very proud of herself.

She dashed to the bathroom, where she grabbed her towel and got the corner of it wet so she could clean him up. When she returned, he was still spread-eagle on the bed, panting.

"You're proud of yourself for that, I bet," he said, his voice gruff.

"Very."

"As you should be." He took the towel from her and cleaned up his belly, then he hauled her back onto the bed beside him. "Your turn now."

"I'm pretty good from last night."

He tumbled her forward, onto her belly, and slid his fingers up the back of her leg, towards the juncture of her legs. "Pretty good? We can top that."

And he did, his words in her ear and his fingers playing back and forth along her slit until she lifted her hips and urged him inside.

When she came, he held her tight until the aftershocks faded, then covered her up again. His fingers brushed her shoulder, then his lips followed, as he focused his attention on the tattoo that peeked out there. "I haven't told you enough how beautiful this ink is."

She shrugged off the compliment. Her tattoos were mostly for herself. "I like it."

"I know." He traced the same path with his fingertips, moving the blanket as he explored, but keeping her covered up, too. "Will you get one about the baby?"

She stretched and yawned. "They discourage tattooing pregnant ladies."

He pinched her lightly. "After."

"Maybe. Probably. I've gotten one for every major life event so far."

"I didn't know that."

"You didn't ask." She wouldn't apologize for pointing that out. He hadn't. He'd admired, licked, touched, and teased, but he'd never asked. She wiggled her shoulder at him. "The flying books are for my graduation from my Masters program."

"When you became the stern and sexy librarian I adore so much?"

"Exactly."

"And the spinning globe is…Christmases in the Caribbean?"

She smiled. She liked that one, too. A mark of her independence, of finding a peace with the holiday season which had always been fraught with tension growing up.

He kissed his way down her spine, raising a slow, aching line of arousal. Would another round of sex before breakfast be out of place? She didn't think so.

She rolled away from him, catching him off guard. She used that advantage to push him over, tumbling and twisting until he was on his stomach and she was perched on his back. "Let's talk about your ink, mister."

She already knew the broad strokes of the story. It was the same tattoo other soldiers from Tom's only deployment overseas had. *Brothers in Arms* in Latin. But he hadn't told her why they all had it. They'd never had that kind of relationship before. But now? Now she wanted to know more.

He flexed his back, making the words come alive. "What about it?"

"When did you get it? Right when you came back from Afghanistan?"

"A few months later. It came up one night at the pub. We were all there, all of us who'd deployed together from the unit, which was rare. And we were talking about the guys who died." He rolled one shoulder in a shrug.

Chloe had spent enough time around the men of Pine Harbour to know this was him brushing it off as no big deal, but that was incomprehensible to her. She slid off his back and curled up on her side on the bed, looking at Tom's profile. "It's your only tattoo."

"Yeah."

"You went along with the group."

He turned his head to look at her fully. "Yeah." He gave her a faint smile. "It wasn't a mistake, though. I'm glad I have it. I'm glad we all had that experience."

"How many of you?"

"Five. It took all fucking day to get them done, and we all just sat there, shooting the shit, watching each other suffer one more time. It was a good day. Bittersweet, but good."

"You ever think about getting another one?"

He shook his head. "But I would get a tattoo with you. About our kid, about each other. About anything."

"Not each other."

His smile grew, more on one side than the other. "Not taking that chance?"

"Nope."

"Fair enough."

"But maybe the baby's initials, worked into some-thing…" She took a deep breath, her heart suddenly pounding again. "We have to name the baby."

"At some point before he or she arrives, yep."

"We have to agree on a name."

He laughed out loud. "Now you're just inviting trouble."

"Seriously, Tom. What would you want to name a baby?" She scrambled to her knees.

He rolled onto his side and lazily swept his hand over her naked thigh. "Whatever you want."

"That is not how real life works. I suggest Finnegan and you veto it. That's how real life works."

"Finnegan Dawson Minelli is a mouthful," he said wryly. "But veto is a harsh word. I'd rather convince you there are alternatives that don't remind people of puppets from childhood."

She gasped. "It's a good name."

"Great name. How about Hank?"

"No. Veto. Hard veto."

"Hank Williams, come on."

She shook her head.

"Johnny."

"As in Cash?"

"Of course."

"Are all your suggestions going to be vintage country music singers?"

"Yes."

"You're not taking this seriously."

He slid his fingers up over her hip and onto her soft belly. "We have time for serious later. I'm having fun right now. And so are you."

"Am I?"

He circled her navel, then stroked lower. "Are you?"

She shivered, determined to keep him focused on the conversation. "What about Hazel?"

"I like it." His voice was silky. Focused, but maybe not on baby names.

"Then we better have a girl."

"I like Mabel better."

"That was a sneaky veto on Hazel, wasn't it?"

"You learn fast." He stopped trying to distract her with sex and stretched his arms wide on the bed. That was distracting, too, though.

She loved his body. The rough honestness of it, the parts that were strong because of endless work, the parts that were pale for the same reason, like his shoulders that rarely saw the sun because he was always wearing one uniform or another. But she'd demanded a conversation about baby names, and now she was going to get one, apparently.

He gave her an all-business look. "So, Hazel or Finnegan. Those are your top choices?"

"You say that like they're preposterous. Yours are Hank and Johnny, so you don't have much of a judgement leg to stand on."

He gave her a look of soft, mock reproach. "And Mabel."

"I'm not sure if that one was suggested in good faith."

"It was."

"Oh, then I like it. Mabel Dawson Minelli."

He blinked up at her. "Damn, that's good."

It really was. She tumbled to the side again and laughed. "Wow. The baby that Christmas named."

He followed, nestling his face into her hair. "I will tell her about this someday. The PG-13 version."

"How her name was almost Hank Williams Minelli?"

"Hank Dawson Minelli."

"You keep doing that. Adding my name in there."

"I like it that way."

"Good. Me too." She yawned again. "We should get up and make breakfast."

He nodded. "We could. Or you could get back down here and we could go back to sleep, since it's still dark outside."

A much better plan. She curled up against him and closed her eyes.

CHAPTER NINE

IT WAS LATE in the morning when they woke up again.

Late, and bright. Blue-sky bright.

Tom's stomach sank as he realized this meant the storm was well and truly over, and it wouldn't be long before Chloe would be hoping for a plow so she could hit the road.

So she could leave him behind, and get on with her search for a safe place to be single and pregnant.

He hated that his town wasn't that for her.

But if she weren't single…

God, that was such a tempting and dangerous thought. It was way too soon. He'd promised her he would take it slow and show her he was committed to her. But it would be so much easier if they lived in the same place. The same town, at a minimum, even if not the same house.

They showered together again, then he put another packet of bacon in the oven before checking his phone.

When he still didn't have a great signal, he did a secret dance of joy.

"How's your cell signal?" he asked as Chloe came into the kitchen, newly dressed.

She shook her head. "Not good. I managed to refresh a forecast, but it said storming, and…" She pointed at the sunny sky out the window. "Clearly not accurate. Maybe it was an old forecast, maybe it's just not right. Either way, I think we're stuck here another day. Do we have enough bacon?"

He grinned the biggest shit-eating grin he'd ever grinned in his life. "Oh yeah. We're good for another two days."

She pressed up onto her toes and kissed him right on the mouth. "Excellent."

And it was. They played cards, finished their books, traded their books, recreated a scene in the dirty book where Tom went down on Chloe in front of the fireplace because wasn't that conveniently written—and neither of them checked their phones again the entire day.

Dinner was bacon sandwiches, which led to a debate about what percentage of their diet could be bacon and bread before it bordered on an imminent heart-health concern, and that led to making out in a chair in the kitchen because they just couldn't keep their hands off each other.

By the time they headed outside for their post-dinner walk, Tom was quite convinced this was the best day ever.

That ended ten steps into their walk, when headlights appeared at the far end of the causeway. The rumble of an engine promised it was a truck, and from the wall of snow being thrown up all of a sudden, pretty clearly one with a plow.

Tom swore.

"What?" Chloe shouted.

"Nothing," he muttered. "Let's get back to the porch." He wasn't sure he trusted any of his friends or brothers not to run Chloe over.

The wall of snow curved as the truck cleared the causeway and plowed past his truck, Chloe's car, and around the corner of the house, pushing as much snow as possible out of the way.

When it backed up, the passenger window was rolled all the way down.

It wasn't one of his brothers, or his friends.

It was his sister-in-law, Olivia, and Chloe's friend Jenna, who was driving her husband's truck. "We're the rescue squad," Liv said as she hopped down. "Sorry it took us so long, but we couldn't sneak away without attracting attention because of the storm. Kind of hard to steal a plow when they're all in use."

Sneak away? Rescue?

Tom bobbled his head back and forth between Chloe and Olivia twice before he realized she wasn't talking to him.

She was looking right at Chloe and trying to do some Woman ESP thing with her. With his Chloe. In front of him.

"We're fine," he said. "Thanks, though."

Liv nodded, but her gaze was still locked on Chloe. "Are you?"

He looked at the mother of his future child, whose mouth was hanging open. She snapped it shut. "Yep. Yeah. We are. All good."

"Okay…" Olivia looked back at Jenna, who'd joined them.

Now he was outnumbered three to one. He could take them, but he wasn't sure he understood exactly what was going on. They were worried about Chloe, clearly. But she'd said they were fine.

"So are you heading out soon?" Jenna asked. "Do you need any help packing up here?"

Chloe blinked. "Uh…"

For a second, Tom thought she might have had a change of heart. *I'm staying with Tom,* she could say. She didn't.

"Yeah, in the morning I guess. Do you guys want to come in for hot chocolate?"

"Sure."

"Yes."

Both of them swept past him as Chloe opened the door.

Now it was Tom's turn to gape, speechless. "I guess I'll go chop some wood," he finally muttered, not that anyone was listening.

———

"TELL US EVERYTHING," Jenna said as Chloe put on the kettle. "Why does Tom look like he wants to murder us? He doesn't want to murder you, does he?"

"We interrupted their love nest," Olivia said. "No murders." She looked at Chloe. "Right?"

Chloe went to the fridge and got out the milk. Then she went out into the mudroom, closed her eyes, counted to ten, realized it was too cold to hide there for long, and grabbed a couple of extra mugs.

When she returned, Jenna was frowning. "Are you okay?"

"Of course she's not *okay.*" Olivia had an answer for everything. They could really have this conversation without Chloe. "Tom loves her, but he's hurt her—clearly

—and he hasn't had enough time to convince her that this time, he'll do right by her."

Chloe dropped the box of hot chocolate she'd picked up. "Wow, that's creepily accurate, actually. How did you do that?"

"Practice." Olivia sat down. Jenna followed suit.

Okay, so they were staying a while.

That was on her. She'd invited them inside, but she hadn't known what to do. Telling people to go away was clearly not her strong suit.

"Besides, you were upset the last time I saw you," Olivia continued. "And now you look…better. Are things on the mend?"

"It's complicated." In more ways than one, but the library closure was still a secret, and Chloe felt honour bound not to tell the residents of Pine Harbour—and that included her friends.

Her heart twisted.

"So…" Jenna looked back and forth. "This is a good thing? I thought you wanted to get out of town because Tom wasn't ready to—" She cut herself off, glancing quickly at Liv.

Secrets were so complicated.

Chloe sagged back against the counter. "That wasn't a fully formed plan, let's be honest. And now? I don't know what's going on with Tom. I don't know what's going on with me. I don't know where I want to go or when I might leave. I really just want to…" She trailed off.

She really just wanted to have another snowball fight with Tom.

Anything beyond that was still terrifying for her. Sure, last night they'd talked about baby names, but that had been a sex-fuelled hormonal connection thing. That wasn't real.

She might call the growing fetus Hank Williams, though. That had a certain ring to it.

She looked at her friends. Really looked at them. "Who else knows about me?"

Olivia shrugged. "About the fight? Or about the baby? Not many on the first point, and I think just the two of us on the second."

Chloe gaped at her friend. "How did you know I was pregnant?"

"You were a hot mess and mainlining saltines when I saw you. I've been there, done that. And then Jenna didn't need a reason why we had to come and rescue you, so I figured if you'd confided in the midwife and not me…"

Chloe laughed weakly. "I will never, ever cross you again."

Liv smiled. "Hey. Your secret's safe. I promise. I don't know if Tom told Zander, but I think he'd be the only other person. I didn't tell Rafe."

Jenna nodded. "I haven't told Sean. Some secrets, husbands don't need to know about. Zander probably doesn't follow that same rule, so maybe Faith knows?"

Four people. And Tom had been right. The world was still standing.

Chloe took a deep breath and held it until she started to see spots at the edges of her vision. "I don't know what to do," she finally burst out. "At all. I was freaking out, and then—" The kettle boiled, and she cut herself off to make four cups of cocoa. She set two of them in front of her friends.

Both of them were looking at the other two mugs

sitting side-by-side on the counter. Her mug. Tom's Thermos lid.

She shrugged. "It doesn't mean anything."

Olivia gave her a dorky smile. "I think it does."

"He's outside chopping wood. He'll be cold when he comes in." His big, strong hands would be red and rough, and they'd wrap around the mug and warm up so when he touched her, they wouldn't be ice cold.

She was selfish, that was all. She didn't want freezing hands on her skin.

Except if Tom wanted to…

She closed her eyes.

Jenna coughed.

Olivia sighed.

Chloe opened her eyes and both of her friends were grinning. "Shut up," she said. "Shut up, drink your hot chocolate, and get out. I'm not ready to be rescued yet."

———

"BYE, TOM!"

He set the axe down and turned around in time to see Olivia and Jenna pile into the truck they'd driven in not that long ago.

He lifted his hand to wave goodbye, and a snowball pelted him on the shoulder.

Without looking back, he leaned down, made his own ammunition, and then spun on one foot.

Chloe was nowhere to be found.

It was dark, and he was far enough from the house that there were long shadows around the trees and between the windows. She could have come out the front, where her friends left, but probably…

He pivoted and stalked toward the mudroom on the back of the cottage.

Another snowball sailed in his direction and he batted it out of the way. "So this is how you want to go," he yelled out. "In battle?"

"Always," she called back, and then he saw her, just a blur, sprinting around the side of the house.

He gave chase, and when he rounded the corner she was waiting for him.

Her eyes bright, her stance wide. Her smile huge.

"Hey," he said. He was grinning, too.

"You're going down." She stepped back and wound up.

He lobbed an easy one right at her chest. She twisted to avoid it and he pelted the other snowball he had ready right at her ass.

She tumbled sideways into the snow, and he pounced, ready to declare victory. But Chloe played dirty, and she was waiting with a pile of fluffy cold stuff to shove in his face and then, as he howled in protest, down the back of his coat.

"Take that," she crowed, climbing on top of him. "What do you say?"

"I love you."

Her smile dropped and she gave him a wide-eyed stare. "What?"

"I love you." He struggled to sit up in the snow, with her perched on top of him like a pleased kitten. He gave up. Flopping back, he sank a bit further into the snowbank as he looked up at the sky and hollered. "I love this woman, and I'm tired of keeping that secret inside! I. Love. Her."

The words bounced and echoed, and they felt good as they rained back down on him.

Chloe was looking at him, her eyes big and mouth a tight little O of surprise.

"Do you hear me?"

"I think everyone north of town hears you," she whispered. He'd yelled that at her when she'd told him she was pregnant. She'd misread his emotion then, but there was no missing what he was saying now. And she was all ears.

"I know I stumbled when you told me about the pregnancy, but nothing is more important to me than you and the baby. Let me move with you. Wherever you want to go. I can take a leave of absence from work."

"What?"

"I have to follow you. Wherever you go, like a creeper. Except a creeper who will respect your boundaries and live arms-length away, whatever you want. But damn it, Chloe, if we're going to do this, I need to be near you to do it."

"What would you tell people?"

"I don't know. I don't care. People can get fucked is what people can do. They don't matter. You matter. Our baby matters, and snowball fights matter, and I love you. That's it. That's as real as it gets."

"That's pretty real."

"Also, I'm freezing my nuts off right now."

She scrambled off him and held out her hand. "Come on."

He jumped to his feet, suddenly feeling ten feet tall. She hadn't run away screaming. Maybe there was some hope for this new plan. "I'll follow you anywhere."

"Right now, I just want you to follow me inside and get dried off." She laughed and shook her head. He was pretty sure she muttered something else under her breath, but she didn't let go of his hand.

Inside, she dragged him over to the fireplace, and then left him there. She disappeared, then returned a moment later with a cup of hot chocolate. "Here," she said, shoving it into his hands. "This is still warm."

"Thanks." He watched in confusion as she stripped out of her own winter gear. "Do you want some cocoa?"

"I have a cup, too. Be right back." She was scurrying. And she wasn't looking at him.

Slowly, he laid his wet stuff by the fire and found a new, dry shirt for himself. "Do you want to wear one of my shirts?" he asked, turning around.

Chloe had stripped all the way down, and was wearing just a tank top and a pair of panties. "Sure." She smiled and reached for the flannel shirt in his hand. "This one looks cozy."

His brain scrambled to keep up.

He leaned down to grab another shirt from his bag and his gaze caught on the cardboard box he'd stubbed his toe on two nights ago. "Hey." He reached out, caught her wrist as it popped out the arm of his shirt. "Wait."

She searched his face. "What is it?"

He sat on the couch and pulled her on top of him, her legs spread so she was straddling his lap. "You haven't opened your presents yet."

She looked sideways at the offending box. "I didn't get you anything."

He shook his head. "That's not true." He rubbed his fingertips over her belly, still soft, their wonderful accident still small inside her. "Yes you did."

"Tom…"

"Shhh. I want you to open your presents."

"It doesn't feel right. I know you got them for me before—"

He cut her off, kissing her lips until she softened against him. "I didn't buy any of them until after you told me you were pregnant," he whispered.

"You didn't?"

"We didn't have that kind of relationship."

Her mouth dropped open, and he kissed her again, enjoying the sweetness of her surprise. "That's what I thought when you gave them to me," she said softly. "I was like, *you big jerk, I didn't get you anything, we don't have that kind of relationship*."

"And I knew that it was pushing things. I just—well, I'm glad I brought them. And I'm glad we talked things out before I gave them to you." He wrapped his hand around her side, his thumb stroking the edge of her belly. "But when I say you got me something special, I mean it. And the things I could get you pale in comparison. So please, open your damn presents. They were... I mean, I had a few days to try and put together a way to show you that I was onboard, and...well, it didn't go exactly as planned. But they're a part of showing you how I really feel. They're real, I promise."

She climbed off his lap and went to the box. There were five presents in there. He knew them by heart.

"Bring the whole box over," he said. It wasn't heavy.

She gave him a curious look as she set it on the coffee table. "Is there any order I should open them?"

"No, I'm not that organized."

She gave him a crooked smile and pulled out one of the small packages first. She ripped into the paper, and sighed. "Aww, this is cute."

It was a yellow sleeper with bunnies on it. "I picked

yellow because I don't care if our baby is a boy or girl. I just want them to be healthy."

She beamed at him. "Nice."

"And I did some research. Apparently, the zipper is better than snaps for middle of the night diaper changes."

Her eyes went wide again. "Really?"

"Yeah."

"Shit. Okay, good to know." She bit her lip.

"Keep going." His heart pounded in his chest. Maybe this hadn't been a good idea. But he wanted to see it through.

The next one was the heavy present. A bottle of non-alcoholic sparkling wine which she wiggled at him. "We can drink this when I finish, yes?"

"Yes." Yes, yes, a million times yes.

"Good." She stared down into the box. "There's a big one that seems kind of jammed in there, and then two smaller ones. Which next?"

"Pull that big one out." He was proud of this one. He licked his lips as she ripped the paper off, and laughed when she gave the present inside a confused look. "You need to, ah, open the package, I think."

She did as much, and the body pillow started to inflate in her hands. The squeal she let out was downright sinful. "What is happening?"

"It's a body pillow. Pull it all the way out of the package."

She did, then she danced around with it. "It's my new boyfriend."

"I thought I might be your new boyfriend."

"You're my it's-complicated." She gave him a soft smile. "These are all amazing."

He gestured to the box. "Keep going. There are two more."

The next one was a massage bar, vanilla and lavender, which he ordered online from an all-organic prenatal something something. It cost him twenty bucks plus expedited shipping, and it was worth every penny for the moment she held it out and asked if he'd use it on her tonight.

Hell yes. And every night for the rest of her pregnancy.

She took a deep breath before she picked up the final present. Holding it in her hands, she came around the coffee table and sat next to Tom.

"Thank you," she breathed, leaning in to kiss him. "I just…this is all perfect. I'm sorry I was too angry before to see that you were trying."

"I was bumbling, mostly. This was my big plan, and it wasn't enough. But I'm glad you're opening them now."

She went to stand up, and he stopped her. "Open this one here. I want to show you something about it."

Nodding, she carefully ripped the paper open.

Inside was a hand knit blanket. Yellow and blue striped. It was a bit fuzzy in parts, but clean. Meticulously clean. That's what came with having a control freak for a mother. He turned over the top corner and showed her his initials on the inside.

"This was yours?"

He nodded. "My baby blanket. We can put it in the nursery, or let the kid drool on it. Whatever you want."

"It's in amazing condition," she said, stroking it carefully.

"I wasn't allowed to wreck it." He shrugged. "Our kid can do whatever he wants to it. Or she. Mabel Hank."

Blanket gripped firmly in her hand, Chloe climbed into

his lap. She looked at him, really looked at him, and he held her gaze.

See me, he offered. *Look at whatever you want.*

"I don't know what to do next," she finally said. "I'm grateful you came after me, though. And I'm grateful for all of these presents."

"You could come home with me." He ignored the pounding in his chest. It might be pushing her too hard. He had a fine line to walk here. "When the storm passes. We can take it day by day. I'll help you move wherever you want to go, but you don't have to go far if you don't want to."

Did she want to move away? She couldn't deny how relieved she'd been when Tom had found her, hiding in his own backyard. She hadn't run far in the end. "I'm terrified of what people will say," she said, her voice cracking. "Which sounds silly when I say it out loud."

There was a part of her that desperately wanted to be accepted in Pine Harbour, and she hated that. Hated it so much it hurt all over again. She forced a smile on her face, even as Tom shook his head.

"It doesn't sound silly to me. I think I've spent a lot of my life trying to be *good* or some shit like that, too. Don't we all fall into that trap?"

"But you are good," she murmured. "With the search and rescue team, and all the community work you do."

His mouth tightened up, his brows pulling together in a frown. She wanted to ask him about that, but *what's wrong with your face right now* wasn't the right way to frame it. But as she wrestled with the words in her head, he smiled, the cloud passing. "So what do you say? Should I call movers and put my stuff in storage, too, and we can be nomads together?"

She burst out laughing. "No." That was silly. And a good kind of silly, because it helped her see what she needed to do next. "I'm not going anywhere. I'll get my apartment back, and we can figure out what the next step is with the whole telling the world I'm having your baby and we're happy about that, so mind your own beeswax, everyone. Deal?"

He nodded. "Deal."

CHAPTER TEN

THE NEXT MORNING the sky had cleared a bit. They bundled up, went outside, and stood in the back of Tom's truck, trying to find a line-of-sight cell signal so Chloe could call her landlord. What Tom was expecting to be a very matter-of-fact conversation about how she'd changed her mind didn't go exactly as planned.

"What do you mean, you've rented out my apartment?" Chloe's mouth fell open, and Tom had to force himself to look concerned instead of victorious.

This was, officially, bad news. But if she couldn't move back into her apartment, there was another obvious option right down the road. His place. Except Tom knew Chloe wasn't ready for that—which meant they needed more time.

"No, of course, I understand that I gave notice, it's just —Yes. No. Oh. Okay, well, that's something. No. I realize that—Yeah. Thank you." She ended the call and gave Tom a very frustrated look.

"I'm sorry," he said, holding out his arms.

She folded against him. "I don't have to pay him the

next two months of rent, at least. He found someone who wants it for the first of January. A new midwife is moving to town, apparently. Someone who works with Jenna." She gasped. "*Jenna would never*. Would she?"

Tom was at a loss for words. "No?"

Chloe spun in his arms, forcing him to brace himself to keep them both upright in the snow-covered truck bed. She yanked off her mitt, dialled her friend's number, then jammed her mitt back on her hand all in one quick sequence.

Jenna answered on the first ring. Tom was holding Chloe close enough he could hear both sides of the conversation. "Hello?"

"Did you tell someone named Kerry that there was an apartment available in Pine Harbour?"

"Uh… No? Are you okay?"

"My landlord rented out my apartment already! To—"

"Oh. Kerry."

"Yes. *Oh, Kerry.*"

"That was, uh, okay, I know how this happened." Jenna laughed. "You're going to think this is funny."

Chloe sighed. "Hit me."

"We've had a big increase in the number of patients on the peninsula, so Kerry and I are going to open a satellite office. This morning—like, an hour ago—we met with the landlord of a storefront on Main Street. I wasn't there for the whole thing, because I've got a client in labour so I'm on my way now to check on her."

"And the landlord who owns half the storefronts on Main Street is also my landlord. Oh. Crap."

"Sorry."

"No, it's okay. That is funny, I guess." Chloe took a deep breath. "I'll get over it."

"I can talk to her if you want."

Chloe shook her head, and Tom's heart leapt for joy. "I'm good. I'll…figure something out."

They would figure it out together.

"So you're opening a satellite office in town, eh?"

Jenna laughed lightly. "Sure are. If you can get over Kerry accidentally stealing your apartment, she might make a great midwife for you. Just saying."

A midwife for Chloe. Tom hadn't thought that far ahead, but yeah. There would be appointments galore. He kissed the top of her head, a snowflake landing just in front of his lips. He kissed that, too.

Chloe ended her second call and turned, lifting her face to his as she shoved her phone into her pocket. "So. This is a complication."

Another snowflake landed on her nose. It was hard for him to feel like this was anything other than perfect. "Two days ago, you had no intention of returning to that apartment. Now you're committed to not doing that, which leaves you with all the other options in the world."

"Like moving." She wrinkled her nose as the snowflake melted.

"Or…" He paused, waiting for a sign she was ready to hear his invitation.

Two more snowflakes drifted between them. "It's starting to snow again," she whispered.

"We'll go back inside in a minute," he said. Being outside made him brave. His heart hammered in his chest. "But if you want, when we leave here…we don't have to go far. We could go to my place."

"Okay." She smiled at him.

That had been too easy. He rewound the conversation. "Not to hang out."

"Are you going to put me to work?"

He burst out laughing. "Shit, I'm bungling this. No. Chloe, I'm asking you to move in with me. Which can be a big deal if you want it to be—it will be for me, secretly— but we can keep it low-key if you'd rather."

"Low-key," she repeated slowly.

Ah, fuck. He'd had a good run there of saying the right thing, but now he was back to bungling everything. "No? No. That's not a nice thing to say. Of course I want it to be a big deal. I want a lot of things—"

She grabbed the front of his jacket and hauled him down to her level, kissing him.

Kissing was better than stomping off in a huff—by a long shot. He smiled against her mouth and sank into the warmth of the embrace. Her cold nose rubbed against his, and snow flakes dropped on both of them, fatter now, wetter, but it didn't matter. Kissing her was all that mattered. He'd asked her to move in with him and she'd grabbed him by the jacket and mauled him.

It was as good an answer as he ever could have hoped for.

But it wasn't an exceptionally clear one. "Is that a yes?" he finally asked when they broke apart, grinning at each other.

"I guess," she whispered, her cheeks pink and her eyes bright. "But—" She laughed. "Of course there's a but. I'm so scared, Tom!"

"I know."

"One thing at a time, okay?"

He jumped off the back of the truck and held out his hands to help her down. "Deal," he said when she was in his arms again. "Low-key but excited. How does that sound?"

"Perfect." She glanced at the sky. "And we've got lots of time to sort out the details. It looks like that break in the weather is over already. What do you want to do next?"

The thing to do next was get naked, and stay that way for thirty-six hours—or as naked as was reasonable when the temperature outside was stubbornly stuck at minus twenty.

Chloe had adorable double-thick wool socks and a thick sweater she wrapped around herself when she made coffee.

He liked looking at her tug them on just as much as he enjoyed peeling them off her when she hurried back to bed.

And when she tumbled under the afghan, legs spread on either side of him, her softness made way for his hardness.

He loved being inside her. Loved the sounds she made and the greedy way her body clung to him. Like maybe she could love him too, at least like this.

This was a start. It was a connection unlike any other. Real, honest, open. Vulnerable.

He made himself go slow. To show her how much she affected him. He didn't hold back anything—not his reactions, or his requests, or all the ways he found her incredible. He poured it all out there so she could see him.

Really see him. The thought terrified him, truthfully, but it was too late for fear.

The next step was getting her off this island and back to town. When they finally packed up, he really hoped it would only be to go as far as his cabin on the edge of the lake. He would follow her wherever she wanted to go, though. And if she needed space, she would get it.

"We're running out of groceries," Chloe finally said the next morning.

"Time to return to real life?"

"I think so." She paused, an uncomfortable look crossing her face.

Tom kicked himself. Her real life included job uncertainty at the worst possible time. "Do you want to talk about work?"

She sighed. "No. Not right now."

It wasn't in his nature to let stuff go. When someone on his team or in his life had a problem, he wanted to lean in and help fix it. Talk it out.

Except Chloe had been central to his life for more than a year, and her personal life being off-limits had always been a firm boundary of hers for more complicated reasons than he ever could imagine.

He couldn't change all the ground rules of their relationship in a single weekend.

For that matter, he couldn't change any of them without getting her buy in. If she didn't want to talk, that was going to be how it was. It was enough that she was willing to move in with him—in a low-key, no strings kind of way.

One thing at a time. "Do you want to go to the diner for breakfast?"

Her entire expression changed, lighting up at the promise of a truly robust meal—her first in a few days.

First Tom would take care of the basics. Food, shelter, security. Until Chloe trusted him on that level, they wouldn't get a chance to build anything on top of it. He could be what she needed in the most elemental of ways, and through that, show her he could be depended on to stick around and be a partner in her life, too.

But he couldn't just feed her, over and over again. He'd have to build on that and find other ways that made her face lit up in the same way.

———

WHEN THEY ARRIVED at Mac's, there were three vehicles in the parking lot that Chloe recognized, which meant that inside were two of Tom's siblings and one of his friends.

So it would be a baptism by fire. Chloe cringed inside at the baby-related metaphor, but it was appropriate on more than one level.

"Ready?" Tom asked her after she'd slowly scanned the parking lot.

She scrunched up her nose. "No." Leaning forward, she grabbed her bag and pulled out a small makeup pouch. She slicked some hot pink gloss over her mouth and took a mascara wand to her eyelashes. Time to armour up. It had been days since she'd last cared about what her face looked like, and she regretted not taking some time before they left the island. But a little bit of flash was all she needed. "*Now* I'm ready."

"But now I can't kiss you," Tom protested.

Silly man. Chloe arched her eyebrow high.

His lips twitched as he leaned in, and she lightly pressed her mouth against his. "Worth it," he said when he pulled back.

Shaking her head, she pointed at the rearview mirror. "No transfer. You're all good."

He caught her wrist and kissed the inside of her arm, then her palm, and finally the tips of her fingers. "Yes. I am."

Well, damn. A fresh wave of warmth slid through her.

"Okay, now I'm *really* ready. And starving. So let's do this."

He grinned as he pushed his door open. Then he hustled around to her side and helped her down, which she didn't need but quite liked anyway.

The warm feeling carried her all the way inside, but as soon as they stepped into the diner, nerves took over. Chloe hated nerves. She hated that tremor of anxiety that whispered she wasn't good enough, hadn't done the right thing.

She'd watched her mother wrestle with that kind of doubt growing up. It had been exhausting, so Chloe had done the hard work as a grown-up to learn about self-talk and being true to herself.

And then Tom stalked into her life, literally a full-grown Boy Scout, and she'd fallen for him—months ago, maybe even as soon as they met.

She'd denied herself the truth of that, limiting their relationship to a secret affair, but the universe had had other plans.

Baby plans.

Tom's hand was firm and warm in her back, but he wasn't pushing her forward. "Do you want a table of our own?" he asked quietly as he waved at his brothers. Rafe and Olivia were squished into a long booth with their daughter, Sophia, who was dipping toast wildly into egg yolk, and Zander's family was on the other side.

In the next booth behind them, Jenna was sitting with her husband, Sean, a sleeping baby in a bucket car seat next to him. Friendly faces.

They were all friendly faces, at least for Tom, but Jenna was probably the friendliest of all for Chloe.

"No," she said. "Let's join them."

Jenna had read her mind and was already on her feet, moving around to sit on the same side of the booth as her husband. Chloe slid in first, sitting across from Sean, who gave her a wink and a gentle smile.

Chloe hadn't known him before he went overseas with the military. She'd known of him, of course. The elite athlete, the youngest of all the Foster brothers. Driven to succeed, he ran ultra-marathons and was a career military officer.

Was.

Past tense.

That had all changed on his tour of duty in northern Iraq, where he met Jenna. The first time Chloe had met the midwife, it was when she'd arrived in Pine Harbour, furious that Sean was hiding his injuries from her.

Chloe had been Team Jenna from day one. But so was Sean, in his own way, and now she saw a lot in his smile, in the gentleness of his eyes. *I know what it's like to have a rough shift in your life. It's going to be fine.*

His rough shift had been orders of magnitude rougher than hers—a pregnancy wasn't anything like an actual life-altering explosion. It was more of a metaphysical explosion, where Old Chloe ceased to exist in a single moment, and then slowly fragmented back together. She felt like herself, but permanently altered already. And the baby was still months away from arrival.

"How's the coffee this morning?" she asked as Tom settled in next to her.

"Strong." Sean paused as the waitress arrived and poured them cups. "Which is nice, because Jenna had a middle of the night delivery and I couldn't get back to sleep."

From the next booth over, Faith pivoted around. "Was that your first back from maternity leave? How'd it go?"

As Jenna launched into a birth story, Chloe sank into her coffee. She wasn't ready to think about stuff like that. She wouldn't be ready in nine months, either.

Tom wrapped his arm around her and she leaned into his warmth.

"Love you," he murmured.

The words were as sweet, lovely, and perfect as they had been at the cottage. She leaned in even further.

Their embrace didn't go completely unnoticed. But Jenna's story was more interesting, apparently, so Chloe was grateful for that distraction. The reactions were brief glances and wide grins, and she couldn't ask for better than that.

Once their food arrived, they tucked in. It was the biggest meal Chloe had had in days, and when it was over, she felt pleasantly stuffed and quite ready for a nap.

Tom read her mind. "Ready to head back to my place?"

She nodded. "Yep."

"Catch you guys later," he said, standing up and holding out his hand to help her do the same.

She felt the curious gazes follow them to the door, but all that mattered was she'd survived what was a completely benign event without bursting into flames.

Eating breakfast together as a couple with everyone wasn't that different from eating together with everyone and pretending she didn't have a massive crush on Tom—the first year of their acquaintance—and definitely less complicated than doing the same and pretending she wasn't hooking up with him in secret.

Just how much she was scared of relationships was

probably something she should have examined earlier in her life, but what was done was done.

And now…here they were.

Heading back to Tom's cabin on the lake, to crawl into his big cozy bed, and be together.

As he navigated his truck back to the highway, he reached across the cab and squeezed her hand. "So that went well, right?"

She smiled. "Yep."

"We should celebrate. My initial research suggested that ice cream is excellent for pregnant ladies. We could hit the grocery store next. Stock up for both celebrations and craving emergencies."

"Research?" This wasn't the first time he'd mentioned it. And the thought of Tom knowing more about pregnancy than she did—at least academically—freaked Chloe out. On the other hand, stocking up on ice cream was a smart, proactive step, and appreciated.

He made a cute, rueful face. "Desperate Google searches for how to win back your pregnant girlfriend are surprisingly robust on the results front."

"They suggested ice cream?"

"That's one of the steps in a ten-step system."

Chloe didn't think ice cream would have worked on her a few days ago. "And how about snowstorms?"

"Surprisingly not mentioned that often, which is weird, because they are quite effective as a give-me-time-to-say-the-right-thing device."

"You could add that to the internet canon."

"I wouldn't know how."

"I'm a librarian. I could show you." And she would. "Do you want to create a Wikipedia page?"

He laughed out loud.

Her smile got bigger. "Yes, let's get some ice cream."

At the store, they took turns pushing the cart and choosing food, so when they got to the checkout, it overflowed in a way it never did when she shopped on her own.

It helped that Tom knew how to cook, apparently. A pang of regret sliced through Chloe on the time they hadn't spent together in his kitchen, but that didn't matter now. They would make up for that lost time now.

First up was an ice cream celebration.

Then they took a nap, and when they woke up, Tom gave her sous chef duties on making a baked tomato sauce he claimed was dead easy.

And it actually was. A can of tomatoes, which she had a lot of fun squishing between her fingers in a big casserole dish, a disturbing amount of butter—guaranteed to make it delicious, probably—and an onion which Tom chopped in ten seconds flat.

"That's it?"

"That's it," he promised. "In forty-five minutes, the oven will turn that into the best thing you've ever put in your mouth."

"But I've put you in my mouth," she murmured, and it took him a second.

Just a second.

Then his eyes lit up and he growled, leaning in for a possessive kiss that scorched every cell in her body.

"The best *tomato sauce* you've ever put in your mouth," he corrected, his voice rough, after they broke apart.

Chloe sucked in a happy, excited breath. "I'm going to hold you to that."

While the sauce baked, Tom made a green salad and

put on the water for the spaghetti, and Chloe curled up on one of his kitchen chairs.

Tom wanted her to move in here.

She still had the key to her apartment, and could play off having given notice as the flighty and irresponsible millennial librarian everyone in town thought she was.

But if she was going to lose her job and have a baby, staying with Tom would be smart. She could save money until she went on maternity leave. And he loved her. That had to count for something.

Spending time together would be more than nice. It would be an excellent test for parenting. It would give them time to explore a real relationship, which they would need to understand really clearly if she had to move.

If Tom would follow her.

So much depended on her job situation, which needed to be sorted out.

She'd reacted hormonally to the news of the Pine Harbour branch being closed. She'd rationalized to herself that if it was being shuttered, it wouldn't matter if she buggered off for parts unknown.

But now it mattered for other reasons.

Tom had promised he'd follow her anywhere. That might be necessary—and it could be an opportunity, too. To focus on building their relationship away from the curious gazes.

On the other hand, those gazes were attached to a lot of support.

Babies were a lot of work.

She made a noise, somewhere between a groan and a whimper, and Tom whipped his head around. "What's wrong?"

"Nothing. Just thinking." She shook her head. "Nothing. Really."

"Still feel kind of surreal?"

She laughed. "I think that's a given for the next eight months. Keep making me delicious dinners, though, and I think somehow I'll find a way to survive."

"You don't know that it's delicious yet."

"You promised," she said solemnly. "And I trust you with my mouth."

That earned her another growl, another kiss, and before they were done with *that*, the oven dinged.

Tom hadn't lied. It was the most delicious tomato sauce she'd ever had. "I don't get it," she said after carefully scraping up the last drop on her plate. "How do those three ingredients turn into pure magic?"

"I don't think too much about the how. I worry that messes with the alchemy."

"Because it is magic, isn't it?"

He nodded sagely. "It really is."

She let out a happy sigh, then stood up. "I'll wash up."

"No need." He stood as well. "Everything in this house is dishwasher friendly."

Chloe had been a low-budget renter her entire adult life. She was so oriented to hand washing dishes it didn't even occur to her to look for a dishwasher, but if she had, she would have missed it—it wasn't in the kitchen proper, but around the corner in a small anteroom that had been added to the cabin as an after thought.

"It's a bit ugly," Tom said as if issuing a warning.

A bit was an understatement. This anteroom made the uninsulated pantry at the Vance's cottage look like the Ritz Carleton. Exposed drywall, a random piece of plywood screwed in the middle of the wall—"That was a plastic window that had to go," Tom explained—and then the pièce de résistance: a giant cast iron sink with a built-in counter that looked like something out of a horror movie. Like a serial killer might use it to wash up after dismembering a body.

But next to that was a modern dishwasher, incongruous in its surroundings, but much appreciated nonetheless.

"Function over form is never a bad thing," Chloe said diplomatically. "Do you use the sink?"

"Nah. It kind of scares me, to be honest."

She giggled. "Oh God, same."

He set the dishes he was carrying on the counter with a rough clatter, then glanced over his shoulder as he leaned down to open the dishwasher door. "We can get rid of it if you don't like it."

Her mouth dropped open, and the offer stretched between them.

That wasn't something you offered your girlfriend when she crashed at your place because she'd impetuously given up her apartment.

That was more like an offer to the mother of your child as she settled in to your home.

Chloe was much more comfortable in category A. "I, uh…"

She didn't know what to do here. *What's the deal?* But she wasn't up for that conversation, either. Not yet.

"Low on the priority list," Tom finally said. "Hey, can you grab the casserole dish?"

"Sure." She scooted into the kitchen, happy for the breathing room, and steadied herself against the counter.

What was her problem?

Two dysfunctional parents and a lifetime of being

resented, that was her problem. She knew it. She just didn't know how to deal with it.

After they finished tidying up together, they took a shower together and brushed their teeth side by side before collapsing in his bed. It felt so good to curl up in Tom's arms and close her eyes.

When he was wrapped around her, the clamouring thoughts went away. The worry about being rejected—a bone-deep fear logic couldn't touch—faded to a small whisper.

"Love you," he said again, his voice a soft caress she desperately wanted to deserve, and she sank into his warm body, soaking up the feel of him.

"Today was a good day," she murmured. It had been. Doubts aside, it had been perfect.

"Tomorrow's going to be a good day, too."

CHAPTER ELEVEN

THE NEXT DAY was not a good day.

It was an awful, wibbly-wobbly day that felt like a week, and a terrible week at that, because Chloe woke up to morning sickness that put all her previous queasiness to shame.

"Do you want crackers?" Tom asked, clearly trying to be helpful. Chloe shoved him out of the way and threw up all over his bathroom.

No, she didn't want crackers.

What was happening inside her body? This was not okay. In a panic, she called Jenna. "What can I do?"

"Lots of little meals," Jenna said. "And rest."

If she couldn't handle the thought of crackers, how was anything more substantial going to happen? "Food terrifies me right now."

"Tea, then. Water. Small sips, take it slow. If it gets really difficult to keep liquid down, go to the hospital and we can get you hooked up on an IV."

"An IV?" Panic heaved hard inside of her, joining everything else.

"Worst case scenario only," Jenna added quickly. "I can bring vitamins around right now, and some ginger tea that might settle your stomach."

As soon as she hung up the phone, Chloe turned to Tom. "I want Jenna to be our midwife."

But it turned out it wasn't that easy. Jenna was going to be on holidays around their due date, so while she could do their first few appointments, it would be another midwife who would follow them closely and attend Chloe's delivery—Kerry. The apartment thief.

"She's great," Jenna said as she nudged the cup of ginger tea across the table. "Come in to the Walkerton office on Monday and meet her. We won't have our Pine Harbour offices open for a couple of months, unfortunately."

Monday was New Year's Eve, but instead of celebrating with a party, Chloe would be meeting a midwife, and urgently, because of her brutal morning sickness. Well, didn't that just make the whole thing even more real.

Tom drove her the hour south to Walkerton, where the midwives had their offices. That was life on the peninsula. Everything except the local grocery store was an hour away, a long drive down the single highway connecting them to the rest of the province.

Chloe wasn't sure if it was nerves or morning sickness that was twisting up her insides as they got closer. Both, perhaps.

But when they arrived and checked in at the front desk in the cozy office suite, decorated in shades of plum and soft, touchable fabrics, a new feeling took hold. Quivering of another sort—excitement.

She didn't know what to expect, but she suddenly felt like she was in the right place. There was an overflowing bookshelf of pregnancy resource materials at one end of the couch, and if there was anything that could make Chloe feel at home, it was a lending library.

While they waited, she filled out the intake forms. Jenna popped out to say hi in between appointments, and then a new face was standing in front of them. A woman about the same age as Chloe, with dark curls that bounced around her face, and an easy warm smile.

"I'm Kerry. And you must be Chloe."

She stood. "Hi. This is Tom. The dad."

"Hi Tom. Come on back, both of you." Kerry led them to an examination room and gestured for them to sit.

Chloe decided in that moment not to mention that Kerry had stolen her apartment. That didn't matter anymore. She'd spent a couple of days curled up in Tom's bed, and frankly didn't have the energy to think about moving anywhere ever again.

Kerry gave them a brief overview of the midwifery model of care, then they figured out a rough due date based on Chloe's last period. Mid August. Chloe had already figured it out from the times her and Tom had had sex, and the date was pretty close.

"That makes you seven weeks pregnant now. A little early for such intense morning sickness, so let's keep an eye on that." Kerry rifled through a folder on her desk, then handed over an information sheet with Hyperemesis Gravidarum spelled out ominously at the top. "This is the worst case scenario, mind you. I'll give you a call at the end of the week and see how you're doing. Or you can call me at any time if something changes." She explained the procedure for paging her, day or night, and how a back-up midwife might respond if Kerry was sleeping before or after a delivery. "If all goes well, our next appointment will be in four weeks. Until then, just follow your body's cues for eating and drinking and sleeping."

———

EVEN THOUGH IT was New Year's Eve, and Tom had the day off work from his day job at the provincial park, the Search and Rescue team was doing a practice that night. It was an annual tradition that they joked helped ward off a real rescue call on one of the longest nights of the year.

"I need to go to the training centre for a few hours," he said to Chloe on the drive home.

"Okay," she said brightly.

"Do you want me to make some dinner before I leave?" He felt weird about abandoning her, but tomorrow he'd be at work all day. On Wednesday, he worked during the day and had his weekly army reserve parade at night.

This wasn't new. They'd been hanging out for a year. She knew he had a lot on the go.

But that was before she was pregnant, and sick, and living in his house where he could see how sweetly vulnerable she was.

He wanted to stay home and take care of her forever, but that wasn't practical or realistic. Also, it probably wouldn't go over well with Ms. Independent, who was making a face at the thought of food.

She shook her head. "I'm kind of scared to eat anything substantial. I think I'll have crackers in bed and watch a feel-good movie."

He grinned. "That sounds amazing."

"I know, right?" She laughed, a long, trailing lilt of lovely noise that stirred the sweetest of feelings inside him.

————

HOURS LATER, he was still grinning as he walked into the search and rescue team meeting.

"Someone's happy," Sean commented dryly.

He really was. He finally had the girl and they were going to have a baby. Speaking of which—the two of them were relatively alone, with the few other team members already there in the kitchenette noisily making coffee. Tom dropped his voice nonetheless. "Hey, did Jenna tell you…?"

Sean raised his eyebrows and shrugged. "I know nothing, if I'm supposed to know nothing, but if there were something know, I may have guessed. Secrets are safe with me, though."

Tom didn't think it was possible for his grin to get any bigger. "We went to the first midwife appointment today."

Sean held out his hand. "Congrats, man. That's awesome."

They shook on it, then Tom raked his hand through his hair. "It is. Chloe's been sick for a couple of days, and I wish I could make it better for her, you know?"

"Yeah."

"Did Jenna get sick?"

"A bit. She had this tea that helped."

"She brought that over the other day."

Sean laughed. "Right. She said Chloe had the flu. Which isn't funny," he hastened to add.

Tom waved it off. "No, I get it. I don't know how long we're going to keep it quiet, but for a bit, you know?"

"Mum's the word. Listen, can I give you a word of unsolicited partner advice?"

Tom thought about all the times he'd offered his own

thoughts on his friends' love lives. Chickens coming home to roost, but he didn't mind. "Consider it solicited. What do you got?"

"Follow her lead. Don't try to baby her too much, but be ready when she needs it. We've only done it once so far, and Jenna was a rockstar, but the whole transition to motherhood thing is a rollercoaster. No, more of a… Honestly, it's like they're in training for a marathon. And you're the support team, not the coach. Got it?"

Tom took a deep breath. "Yeah. I can do that. Thanks."

"Once everyone knows, you'll be bombarded by advice from the others."

"Ha." Tom shrugged. "Fair turnabout. I've had a lot of thoughts on how you guys should fix things with your women for years."

Sean chuckled, then pointed his cane at the kitchen. "You can buy me a coffee to make up for that, now that you know how damn hard it is to negotiate the minefields."

It was the least he could do. He went and poured them both mugs, tossing a toonie into the tin.

Sean took his mug and lifted it in a cheers. "Happy new year, man."

It was going to be, that was for damn sure. Everything was slotting exactly into place. Maybe not in the order he'd imagined, but that didn't matter.

All that mattered was that in the end, they were together and happy.

———

WHEN HE GOT HOME, well before midnight, Chloe was

asleep in his bed, the end of a movie quietly playing on his TV. No crackers in sight.

He refilled her water glass, then washed up and joined her in bed.

No champagne for them this year. Hopefully next year they'd have a glass while a baby slept peacefully on his chest.

He fell asleep with that thought in his mind—and woke up to the sound of heaving.

A quick glance at the clock told him it was early, but time to get up. He put on a pot of coffee, and set a new box of crackers on the counter.

"This is bullshit," Chloe said weakly as she joined him in the kitchen.

"I'm sorry." He held his arms out wide and she came in for a hug. "Dare I ask if you want something for breakfast?"

She shook her head.

They spent New Year's Day lounging around and reading together.

The next morning—the first day back at work after the holidays—was a repeat of the same scene.

"Bullshit," Tom said when Chloe shuffled into his arms.

"Right?"

He smiled against her hair. "Are you calling in sick?" The winter was light at the parks. He was already rear-ranging his own day in his head. Maybe he could come home and make her a light lunch…

But she was shaking her head. "Nope. This is my new normal. I'll soldier through. Besides, there's a meeting about the library closure today. I don't want to miss that."

He set his hands on her shoulders. "One thing at a time. How about we get dressed for work?"

She wrinkled her nose. "That's another thing. My body has decided it hates waistbands already. I may need to do some shopping."

"Do you have anything in storage that would work? We could dash down the peninsula at the end of the day?"

"The thought of driving an hour to paw through boxes in the dark does not appeal." She shook her head. "I'll just order a few comfy things online."

"What if the boxes were here instead?"

She frowned and cocked her head to the side.

He waited.

Then she laughed. "Okay, one thing at a time. Let's get dressed for work."

———

CHLOE TOOK a deep breath as she followed her coworkers into the small conference room at the back of the Pine Harbour library. She couldn't remember them ever using this room themselves. It was booked regularly by community groups, and used occasionally by some local high school students taking classes remotely. It was rarely empty, but today it had been signed out by the director of their regional library service.

This was a meeting she would have missed if she'd continued on her ridiculous plan to flee the peninsula. A niggle of guilt spiked inside her, mixed with relief that Tom had found her and stayed with her while she worked through her fears—or at least the top layer of them. There was more to unpack there, she knew that. For example:

how much anxiety she had around this library being closed unfairly.

"Thank you all for coming in today." The director smiled at their small group. Two full-time librarians, two assistants, and a deputy director who worked part-time hours in three libraries up and down the peninsula. "We know the news right before Christmas was not what you wanted to hear. It wasn't what we wanted to communicate, either. The funding cuts have hit us hard, and we're scrambling to adjust while still meeting community needs across the county."

What about Pine Harbour's community needs, Chloe wanted to protest. But she knew there would be a time for questions, for their voices to be heard, and this wasn't it. Not yet.

"Blunt talk time: we don't have enough money to operate all the branches we have across the county. Before the start of the next fiscal year, some will need to be permanently closed. Others will be able to continue operate at reduced hours."

Screw not asking questions yet. Chloe shoved her hand in the air. The director paused and nodded at her. "Yes?"

"What is the difference between those two groups of libraries? Why aren't we on the slate that is simply having hours reduced?"

"Age of the building, village population, proximity to schools, and utility costs were our primary factors. We haven't fully finished our analysis—the leaked documents before Christmas didn't reflect that preliminary stage —but…"

Chloe's head started buzzing. Preliminary stage. Incomplete analysis.

All she heard was that there was a chance to save her

library. She flipped to a new page in her notebook and wrote down the factors the director outlined.

Utility costs
Age of building
Proximity to schools
Village population

She couldn't do anything about the village population —Pine Harbour was small, no denying that—but what if the library could move to another building? Moving came with its own set of costs, of course, but maybe they could crowdsource those funds. She also wondered—and maybe hoped—the school proximity data didn't take into consideration the distance ed high schoolers, or the home schooling population.

It was time to gather some numbers of her own. She wasn't going to challenge the director in this meeting. She would follow up with a polite email tomorrow. Get it in writing, and reply in kind.

For once in her life, she was going to buckle down and have some serious impulse control.

"Chloe, do you have something to say?"

She looked up to find the deputy director giving her A Look. Like, *fix your face* kind of look. Apparently her impulse control didn't extend to her expression as she processed what she was hearing.

"I have questions," she said carefully. "But I'm not sure if this is the time for them."

The director gave a slight nod of her head. "Consider this an open forum."

Chloe felt like she was tiptoeing onto a tightrope strung between two skyscrapers as she glanced around the room. Other than Jenna and Olivia, she hadn't found a lot of support in Pine Harbour for being brash and loud. But none of her co-workers wanted the branch to close, right?

"Is there anything we can do—or rather, is there anything that can be done, by anyone—to change the status of this branch on that preliminary list? Anything that could move it to the reduced hours list? Is it the building that's the problem, or are we not properly capturing library usage?"

When she stopped, silence reverberated off the walls.

Had she fallen into a trap?

"Our goal is avoid job loss as much as possible," the director said slowly. "If that's your concern."

The other full-time librarian shook her head. "That's not *my* concern. I'm close to retirement, and would be happy to move to a larger town for the next few years. But this town uses this library. I agree with Chloe. What can we do to protect it for them?"

This time, the silence wasn't as scary. It was thinking space, full of deep breaths and flipping through pages. Finally, the director leaned back in her chair. "I'm not making any promises."

"But?" Chloe leaned in. So much for playing it cool. She was eager, more eager than she'd ever have guessed, and she wanted to grab something concrete right now.

"We need to reduce operating costs by forty percent. That's not possible in standalone libraries like this one. And by the summer, the budget just will not exist for this branch to remain open."

It sounded ominous. It was ominous. But what Chloe heard was that the library would need to move to a shared space.

She knew who she had to talk to next.

On her lunch break, she grabbed her bag with her hidden box of crackers, tugged on her parka, hat, and mittens, and told the others she was going for a walk. It was a brisk five minute stroll to Olivia's house.

"I need to talk to you about a hypothetical situation," she said when her friend opened the door. "And you can't ask any questions because I'm not supposed to tell anyone just yet."

Liv held the door wide open. "Come in to my office."

Before she had Sophia, Olivia had worked as a waitress at Mac's, and then did location scouting for a movie company. That led to her current job as the local assistant to movie star Hope Creswell, who had come to Pine Harbour to film that movie and fell in love with a local man, Ryan Howard, and his three children. And the biggest thing that Olivia did for Hope was leverage her star power into helping local charities and businesses—which meant Liv had all the connections. At some point in the near future, Chloe would need the right connection to organically present an opportunity to the library. Olivia was the person who could make that happen.

Her office was a desk in her living room. Toys scattered the floor around it, but there was no toddler in sight.

"Soph's having a nap," Olivia said. "Do you want tea?"

Chloe consulted her stomach, which tentatively thought tea sounded fine. "Yes, please."

"I'll put the kettle on. What's this mysterious, hypothetical situation?"

"The library might need a new home."

Olivia looked surprised. Chloe knew the feeling. "I'm guessing I can't ask why?"

"I'd rather you didn't. I shouldn't even be here, but I don't know enough about the political dynamics to know where to start looking for alternative locations, and I don't trust the higher ups to get it right."

"What's the timeline?"

Chloe hesitated. "Hard to say. Soon, though." She took a deep breath. "It's a budget issue, I can say that much. Confidentially. Our current location is too expensive. Overhead costs, infrastructure repair…a lot of language I barely understand, to be honest. But the bottom line is that libraries in shared spaces are less expensive than ones in dedicated locations."

Olivia nodded slowly. "When does the budget year end?"

Chloe felt the blood drain from her face. She was not good at keeping secrets, or being subtle.

"Oh." Olivia sighed. The kettle on the stove started to whistle, and she turned it off, then added tea bags to a pot and poured the water over them. Chloe could see the wheels churning in her brain. "So what you need is a space to become available, one that might not cost anything. And soon."

"Yes," Chloe said quietly. "It might buy us some time."

"I'm on it." She poured the tea into two cups and passed one over. "Does Tom know?"

"I'll tell him tonight."

Olivia smiled.

"What?"

"I like that you're together now. Have you officially moved in to his place?"

Chloe made a scrunchy face to cover a smile she couldn't stop from spreading across her face. "Well, I'm staying there."

Olivia laughed. "Like a couch surfer?"

"Like a commitment-phobic woman with trust issues."

"It's obvious he wants you to move in with him."

"I know. But I'm not sure we know each other as well as he thinks we do." They were getting there, though. "So we need to get to know each other better. As partners, in life and parenting. One thing at a time, and, uh, maybe we don't need to worry about what's official or not."

"I hear a lot of words that sound like you're hedging your bets."

"I do that like a pro, yep."

"But you're racing into the fight to save your library." Olivia's eyes went wide. "Is this why you were crying before Christmas? Have you known about this for a while?"

Chloe made another face. "Stop being freaking psychic."

"That's shitty news to break before the holidays."

"It wasn't great, no. I really thought…" She trailed off, then shook her head. "Anyway, I'm glad Tom found me and convinced me there's good reasons for me to stick around."

Olivia chewed her bottom lip. "Hmm."

"What?"

"Nothing. It's just that…I'm surprised you care." She held up her hand. "I know that sounds harsh. But you've always been a little bit…take it or leave it about this town. Which I get! I really do. The old guard can be a bit much, and you love to beat to your own drum. But if, hypothetically, the library were closing, wouldn't that be a good excuse to get out of Dodge?"

That was harsh.

It was also true. If she didn't have a job here, she wouldn't have to live here.

Chloe frowned. "Even if I was—am—on the fence

about this town, that doesn't mean that the people here don't need a library. I can fight for them and think about leaving at the same time." She took a long sip of her tea. "Hypothetically."

From the bedroom, a little voice called out.

Naptime was over, and not a moment too soon.

"I have to get back to work. Don't tell anyone about this conversation, okay?"

Olivia gave her a concerned look. "I'll get you a list of places that could maybe accommodate a new service space. On the down low."

"You're the best."

"So are you," her friend said. "I hope you realize that."

CHAPTER TWELVE

TOM BEAT CHLOE home from work. Normally he'd have stuck around the office a bit late. In the past, he didn't have Chloe to get home to, though.

He liked this new normal.

He liked making her dinner—soup tonight, to go with her crackers—and he liked the way her face softened when she walked in the door and saw him waiting for her.

"Hey," he said gently.

She exhaled as she smiled. "Hey."

"Long day?"

"Yeah." She kicked off her boots and hung up her parka, then joined him on the couch. "What smells so good?"

"Chicken soup."

"For the soul?"

"For whatever you want it to be for. How do you feel?"

"Knock on wood, I've been okay all day, and now I'm starving."

"Then let me feed you while you tell me about the meeting."

She followed him into the kitchen. He grabbed two big bowls out of the cupboard, and a ladle, then pointed to the table.

Rolling her eyes, she followed his unspoken instruction. *Sit your pretty ass down.* "So," she said. "The list of libraries to close is, in the words of the director, preliminary. Which means there may be a chance to keep it open, but not in the current location. It's too old, too expensive to maintain. Maybe they can make some short term cash by selling it? We're under a huge budget crunch across the county, and it'll be the small libraries that get the axe first."

He swore under his breath.

"I went to Olivia's at lunch and shared some of the details with her. I think there might be a chance we could move the library to a lower-cost location and keep it open at reduced hours."

"That's great."

She exhaled roughly. "I don't want to get your hopes up. Or anyone else's, either. We need to keep this quiet."

"Do you have any idea when it'll be made public knowledge?"

She shook her head. "That didn't come up. It sounds like the library service was caught flat footed by the budget shortfall for next year and now they're hustling hard to make it work. Even if we can't save the branch, one way or another, the library won't be closing until the summer," she added. "I did some maternity leave research during a lull at the end of the day, and I think I can apply for coverage at that point, even if the baby hasn't arrived yet. So that buys me a year until I need to go back to work...somewhere."

Tom would take a year. "We'll figure it out."

She watched him, her eyes big and uncertain as he set the bowls on the table between them.

"I may have enough seniority that I get a position at another branch in the county. The director made the right noises about avoiding job losses." She worried her bottom lip.

Tom knew what it was like to have to balance a budget around government funding. And he knew how empty those noises could feel.

Instead of sitting down, he skirted around the table and crouched in front of her. Wrapping his hands around hers, he stilled her fluttering fingers. "Whatever happens, we'll handle it together. Do you think people are going to notice that you're shacking up with me?"

"Olivia asked about that at lunch."

"We could make it official. Get your stuff from storage and bring it here, hang a Tom and Chloe sign over the front door."

Chloe gave his cabin some significant side eye. He got the point. There wasn't a ton of room. But he'd been in her apartment. She didn't have a lot of stuff. "Where would it all go?"

"There's always the barn," he pointed out.

She looked at him blankly. "What barn?"

"My barn." He frowned. "Have you never been back there?"

"No."

Their lives had really been quite separate. He shook his head. "Let's go for a walk after dinner."

The soup disappeared quickly, then they got dressed in their winter gear, which reminded him of their snowball fights at the cottage—and that made him happy and a little bit horny. *Not the time, Minelli.* He grabbed a flashlight off the hook by the door.

"What are you thinking about?" Chloe asked as he opened the door. "You're grinning like a dork."

"Snowball fights and warm showers," he murmured.

She stopped right beside him, close enough for him to feel her sweet warmth. She glanced up and gave him a grin of her own. "Nice."

Maybe it *was* the time for happy and horny. Maybe, if she was feeling okay at the end of the day, he could make her feel extra good tonight.

But first, an overdue tour of the back of his property.

One reason she hadn't seen the barn was because it wasn't visible from the house. It was actually an old maple syrup processing shack, hidden deep in the woods at the back of his property, but the people who'd owned his cabin before him had used it for gardening equipment, and expanded one side of it to be a shed for a small tractor. It was this side that Tom led Chloe to, to the big double doors that slid open smoothly. He found the light switch that lit up the barn, revealing his makeshift gym and the long wall of shelves at the back, half filled with army gear and camping supplies.

"Wow," she said, glancing around. Her gaze stopped on the squat rack he'd built himself and the barbell resting in front of it. "Do you do workouts in here?"

"Not much in the winter." He pointed to the puffs of air left by their breath. "Too cold. But it seemed like the best use of the space, and Sean and I had a lot of fun building the metal frames for this thing. It was a good project."

Mentioning Sean reminded him of how hellbent Jenna had been on convincing her husband she loved him, brain injury and all. Chloe had had her back the whole way. Tom hoped he could be as persistent and loving as Jenna had been. Chloe had good reason to be skittish, but he was going to prove to her their love was worth any and all risks.

"Do you think there's enough room in here for your stuff in storage? Anything that can't be out in the cold, we'll make room for in the cabin."

She looked around. Her face was hard to read, but eventually she nodded. "Yeah. Okay. They say the storage unit is climate controlled, but it's basically the same thing as this. I don't have much that can't be left here—until we sort out something more permanent, of course."

"Of course." He held out his gloved hand, and she folded into his embrace. "It's a good first step."

————

ON FRIDAY AFTERNOON, Chloe was setting up a January Means Murder display of mysteries at the front of the library when Tom's mother came in.

Anne Minelli was a regular patron, so this was…fine. Professionally speaking. Personally, the Minelli matriarch scared Chloe to the depths of her soul, and she wasn't sure the woman wouldn't be able to smell her pregnancy, or detect that the next day, Chloe was moving all of her sex toys into Tom's house.

So she kept her head down, waited for her colleague to help Anne, and then scampered off to the back room and waited until she was gone.

"I hid from your mother today," she confessed to Tom when she got back to his place.

He laughed.

"It's not funny."

"Was she hunting you down?"

"I don't think she even saw me."

"Then it's funny."

"We need to tell her I'm living here. And that I'm pregnant, I guess." It was a lot of change to process at once—for Chloe as much as Anne.

"We will."

"That's scary."

He nodded. "It is."

"You aren't helping."

"How can I help here?"

"I don't know."

He laughed again, harder this time, and held out his arms. "Come here."

That helped. She snuggled in. "We need to tell her before she hears it through the grapevine."

"You're right." His voice was low and warm, steady and comforting. She didn't look up at his face. Instead, she burrowed in tighter. "Chloe, she's going to be happy. We're grown-ass people. We can have a baby."

"I know." But her voice sounded small. Was she a grown-up? She'd hid from the future grandmother of her child.

She needed to get over her fear.

Tomorrow. She would get over it tomorrow.

"It's okay to be nervous," Tom said in her ear. Then he hugged her tight. "I'm nervous, too."

That helped. She crawled up his body, hungry to kiss him. "Let's be nervous together," she whispered against his mouth. "We can tell your parents I'm moving in first, because they're here, and then we can call my mom."

"Deal." He caught her lower lip between his teeth,

tugging before soothing the sting with the soft push of his tongue.

Her stomach roiled, but she ignored it. She needed Tom right now. Needed his warmth, his solidity, his eagerness for her.

"Do you want to wait until the end of the first trimester to tell our parents about the pregnancy?"

"A thousand percent yes." She kissed him again. "Avoidance is my favourite way to deal with a problem."

"It's not a problem."

"It feels like a problem."

"Ah. Then yeah, I guess it is a problem." His eyes twinkled, though, telegraphing that he wasn't concerned.

She took a deep breath. "Thank you. For everything, but especially for this. Being with me every step of the way."

"It's exciting."

It was something.

———

THE NEXT MORNING, before they headed to Owen Sound to collect Chloe's belongings from her storage unit, Tom ran into town to get something light for breakfast while Chloe drank her ginger tea and slowly let her daily morning sickness pass.

The bakery was a part of his mother's cafe, so the errand wasn't entirely about breakfast.

"Morning, Ma," he said as he slid around the counter to join her behind the register.

She gave him her cheek, and he kissed it.

"What's wrong?" she asked.

"Nothing." Truly, nothing. "Everything is great. In fact,

it's extra great, because Chloe—"

"The librarian?"

He didn't know why she did that. The interrupting thing. It was kind of annoying, but there was a lot about his mother that tried his nerves. Luckily, Tom was an expert at brushing it away. "Yes," he said patiently. "Also, my girlfriend."

"Since when?"

That was a more complicated answer. He went for the most generous explanation. "Quite a long time, although we kept things casual. Which I know you don't approve of, so let's move past that, because she's agreed to move in with me."

"Tommaso!"

Now it was his turn to roll his eyes at the way his very Anglo mother threw an Italian accent—learned from her husband—on his full name. "Don't full name me, Ma."

"Don't give me reason to," she retorted. "Whatever happened to proposals and engagement periods?"

"I love her," he said firmly. "Let's focus on that. And she's agreed to move in to my place, so that's happening today. I wanted to give you a heads up before the rest of town hears about it."

"I heard a rumour about what happened at Christmas."

His mouth twitched. He'd blown off his family with a simple lie about having to work, and there had been zero pushback. Apparently that had been the silence of disapproval. "Rumours can't be trusted."

"Did you and the librarian stage a home invasion of the Vance property?"

"No."

"I don't believe you."

He laughed. "Okay. I gotta go. Can I grab some muffins?"

His mother reached out and grabbed his arm. "Just tell me she's not a criminal."

"Good Lord, Ma. No, she's not a criminal."

"Because she has those tattoos."

Jesus Christ. Sometimes he really wondered what decade—or century—his mother was stuck in. "So do I."

She frowned. "And I didn't like that you got it."

"The entire town is aware of that fact. Muffins?"

"Be my guest." She paused. "Your librarian likes the cranberry ones."

His librarian had a nice ring to it. He gave his mother a one-armed sideways hug before scooping up a half-dozen muffins and heading back home.

He found Chloe curled up on the couch, asleep under a blanket. Her face was drawn and pale, and his heart squeezed tight.

While he waited for her to wake up, he made coffee. The hiss of the maker must have roused her, because she wandered into the kitchen when he poured a cup. He slid it across to her and filled another while she peeked in the bakery bag.

"How did it go?"

"She was her usual caustic self," he admitted. "But she made sure I grabbed your favourite muffin."

"Lemon poppyseed?"

He laughed. "She told me cranberry."

"Those are good, too." Chloe's brows pulled together as she thought about it a second. "And maybe I order those more often?"

"She tried, let's leave it at that. Which was better than her first response."

"Oh no."

"Oh, yes. She wanted to know why we weren't engaged, and what was wrong with marriage."

"So the baby news in a month or two will be something fun."

He cleared his throat. "One thing at a time. Our new motto."

"Right." She wrinkled her nose. "But you know I'm not interested in anything traditional, right?"

He knew that. Loving Chloe came with a lot of boundaries. No talk of forever, nothing formal. No strings that would be hard to detangle should things go south.

It rubbed against everything he'd thought was maybe in his future one day, but it didn't feel wrong. He would take the reality of loving her over the idealistic but ephemeral fantasy.

"No expectations," he said. "I'm just sharing what she said in the spirit of honest disclosure."

She laughed out loud at that.

But once they were in his truck and heading south down the peninsula, she brought it up again.

"Do you want to get married?" There was an edge to how she asked it.

Deep in his chest, something desperate ripped loose from his heart. "I just want you, and our baby. That's all that matters."

She nodded. "Good."

Good. Except it wasn't the whole truth, so if he was being honest—and he should be, in the spirit of full disclosure—he should share more. "It might be nice," he added. "But I don't need it."

This time she was still, but eventually he got another nod. "Okay."

CHAPTER THIRTEEN

IT WAS way too early for her to have a belly, but most of Chloe's pants really didn't fit. And the stuff she'd dug through from storage—most of which was now shoved into Tom's barn because there wasn't room for it all in the house—wasn't much better. Why didn't she own more yoga pants? Why had she donated all of her hip hugger jeans? Feeling desperate at the slow delivery window offered by the online maternity clothing stores, she texted Olivia.

Chloe: I have another favour to ask.
Olivia: Shoot. And I've got some info for you, BTW. I was going to stop by after lunch. Which you should come to next week.

Lunch was at Dani Foster's house. Dani, Tom's little sister. Olivia's sister-in-law. And hostess-with-the-mostest. Chloe wasn't ready for that. Also, she knew that Dani's weekly Sunday lunch wasn't Tom's thing most of the time. So she ignored that and got right to the point.

**Chloe: Do you have any maternity pants I could borrow? I
want to barf every time I do up a button.**
**Olivia: Absolutely. I'll bring you some. We need to talk
about the first thing, anyway.**

She showed up thirty minutes later with an overflowing garbage bag. "Rafe was so happy I was getting
this out of the closet."

"My tummy thanks you." Chloe lifted Tom's t-shirt,
blessedly long enough to hide the fact that her current
pants weren't done up.

Olivia laughed and threw a pair of jeans at her. "Try
these on. You may never go back. I didn't for like three
years."

"I'm trying them *all* on, are you kidding me?" Chloe
shimmied into the first pair and let out a happy sigh. The
waistband was a long, hugging piece of spandex that
smoothed over her sensitive midsection instead of digging
in at exactly the wrong spot. "Tell me about the secret
other task while I do a fashion parade."

Olivia glanced around the cabin. "Is Tom out?"

Chloe appreciated the diligent dedication to
subterfuge, not that it was necessary. "Yep, Sunday afternoon training with the search and rescue team. But he
knows about the closure."

"All right." Olivia whipped out her notebook, all business. "I have a shortlist of options. None of these places
know that I've scouted them, because I'm a professional.
But I also have another idea, a bit more out of the box."

"Let's start with the shortlist."

"The new emergency services building at the highway
has an under-utilized training wing. In the long term, it's
designated for emergency response coordination, but I

think they might be open to a short-term lease. And since they're both county services, there may be some accounting savings to be found."

"How would the fire and EMS departments feel about people coming and going all day?"

"Hard to know without asking them. I'm not actually a mindreader, although I enjoy you giving me credit for that."

Chloe laughed. "Touché."

"Next option is the old municipal building, where the art gallery is now. The second floor is empty, but I think it comes with the same higher operating costs, especially in the winter, and I don't know how great the elevator is for accessibility."

Chloe knew the space, and was pretty sure that was a non-starter for her bosses. "Could be trading up into the same set of problems, yeah."

"And finally, but this may not be available in time, a little birdie told me that the Optimist hockey group is moving out of their offices in the arena in the summer."

"Oh!" Chloe stopped trying on clothes. Olivia had her full attention now. Like the new fire and EMS station, the arena was owned by the county. That gave them two viable options that would basically be a neutral cost. The rent for the library would reduce the expenses for another county department. "That's genius."

Olivia beamed. "And just to round out the idea pool, the out of the box option is staying where you are, but giving up some of the space—leasing it out to cover the operating costs. If the library board is going to consider selling the building, why not think about retaining the primary investment?"

"Very good questions for someone other than me."

"We need a town hall so I can ask those questions of the right person."

Chloe puffed her cheeks out as she thought through the options Olivia presented. Basically, there were three options. That was good. "Yeah, we need something. Okay, I'll figure out how to keep the balls in the air a bit longer, and put these ideas into the director's ear."

Olivia gestured between them. "Let's celebrate with comfy clothes."

"You are truly a lifesaver on many levels. I cannot wear regular pants a second longer."

"Still feeling crappy?"

"I'm literally on a tea, soup, and cracker diet these days. It's rough. But my next midwife appointment is in two weeks, and hopefully by then, I'll be feeling better."

"Good news for Valentine's Day?"

"Fingers crossed." It would be nice to actually be romantic with Tom on cupid's day, instead of crawling into bed early while he rubbed her back.

Olivia stuck around until Chloe had oohed and aahed over the entire bag of clothes, then headed back to her family.

The options she'd presented were so well thought out Chloe didn't want to wait until the next day to put them in front of her boss, so she went to her computer and logged in to her work email remotely. There was no time like the present to get a discussion going. She opened a new email window and began typing.

———

SOMETHING HAD SHIFTED when Tom got home. Chloe was in the kitchen, humming.

"You sound happy," he said, dropping a kiss on the back of her neck. "And you're…cooking?"

"I'm prepping. Let's not get crazy. I felt like something fresh."

"Salad for dinner sounds great." He went to the fridge and grabbed leftover chicken to add for some protein. "Cheese?"

"I'm good, but add some if you want it."

She bustled around, grabbing plates from his cupboards and filling water glasses, and it was nice.

It was even nicer when they sat down and there was a moment when she glanced across at him and he realized she was about to tell him about her day. Without him asking, without any hesitation.

Right up there with wanting to figure out how to be transparent about what he wanted was his craving for her to share right back. Maybe she was starting to trust that he was on her side. Team Chloe, all the way.

"Olivia came by while you were out. I think we have a decent plan to save the library. Or the start of a plan, anyway."

"Yeah?"

Chloe nodded slowly, her mouth set firmly. A warrior expression. A woman on a mission. "I regret that I didn't fight for this before Christmas. We lost a few weeks."

"You were reeling. Two unsettling pieces of news, back to back."

She chuckled. "Unsettling is a polite way to describe it."

"Terrifying?"

"Life changing," she said softly. "But not terrifying. Not for long."

Another little share.

It was the sweetest thing he'd ever heard. Just as good —fucking great—was the way she held his gaze as she poked at her salad.

He grinned, and his own happiness was reflected on her face. "Great salad," he rumbled.

"You haven't even tried it yet."

He didn't need to. But then he did, and it tasted amazing. Maybe it was heightened by the unexpected optimism zinging off her.

The next thing she said surprised him, too. "I was thinking that it might be time to tell our parents about the baby."

"Are you ready?"

"No." She laughed. "But at some point, I need to rip off that bandage."

"I want to say it doesn't matter how they react, but…"

She held his gaze. "It doesn't matter. It might hurt in the moment, but we'll get past it. I'll get past it."

He squeezed her hand. "I'm right beside you. And I'm really excited."

"I know." She said it softly, sweetly, then took a deep breath. "Hey, want to go for a walk in the snow after dinner?"

"You *are* feeling better."

"Enough for a tromp around the house."

They went further than that. They went all the way out to the barn, because Chloe remembered that one of her boxes also had books in it, and she didn't want those exposed to the moisture. On the walk back, she took the flashlight so he could carry the books.

Halfway back to the house, she stopped abruptly. "Look," she whispered. "A bunny!"

He saw it. Just past the glare of the light was a snowshoe hare. *A bunny.* The sheer delight in Chloe's voice did funny things to his heart.

All three of them stood stock-still for a moment, then the hare silently bounded off into the woods.

Chloe let out a happy sigh, and they plodded back to the house.

Once inside, he set the box on the table so Chloe could dig through it once she was out of her winter layers.

"Ah, there is the book I was looking for," she said, holding a middle-grade fantasy novel aloft.

"You have the most eclectic reading tastes of anyone I know."

She wiggled her entire body happily. "Thank you, I take that as a compliment. But this isn't for a re-read. One of our pint-sized patrons wants to read it."

He twisted his neck to look for the telltale label on the spine. "It's a library book?"

"Nope." She danced—still in a good mood, clearly—to her bag and stashed it in there. "But the library copy went missing, and who knows when we'll be able to acquire another one."

So she was going to give some kid her own copy.

Pine Harbour was going to miss the fuck out if the library closed. Tom frowned. "How often do you give people your own books?"

She shrugged. "Not often. And I have a lot of books. It's fine."

"It's more than fine," he said. "It's really nice."

"Book friends share," she said simply. "Speaking of which…can I read the thriller on your bedside table?"

He gestured to the bedroom. "Be my guest."

They read together for an hour, tucked under the covers, all cozy and warm. After a while, Chloe shoved the blankets off, and there was something in the way she did it, a new curve to her abs under the sweet layer of softness that caught his eye.

"Look at you," he murmured, crawling down her body.

She set her book down. Confusion was writ large on her face. "What is it?"

He beamed up at her. "Your belly."

"It's the crackers," she sighed.

But it wasn't. There was a firm roundness that had not been there before. The swell was different. He knew every inch of her body. Loved the soft parts, the shadowy dips. This was new and exciting.

"Can I touch you?"

"Of course," she breathed.

He started at her hip, and she squirmed.

"Hold still," he growled, and she grinned, he could see it in his peripheral vision. But she settled for him as he traced his fingers to the edge of her panties.

One of his most favourite things about Chloe was her matter-of-fact choice of underwear. Plain cotton, always, often in a cute cropped short style that revealed the bottom curve of her ass. Usually black, sometimes white. Tonight they were pale pink, ruthlessly innocent looking.

He followed the top ribbon of elastic over the dip between her hip and her belly, and then he felt it. Low, right above her pubic bone, the firm swell that had caught his eye.

"It's too soon," she protested.

He was no expert, but her body was changing and he could see it and feel it. "I love it anyway," he said, kissing her hip. Then he glanced up. "How are you feeling?"

He'd meant it to sound innocent. He wouldn't rush her. But it came out husky and full of honest need.

She smiled softly. "The same. But if you want to…"

He wanted to. "Gently?"

She nodded and he stood.

"Let me make love to you." The words were rough, but he was endlessly gentle. There was no other way to be right now, not when he'd just felt the start of her belly, where she would grow his baby.

With a soft sigh, she wrapped her arms around his neck and kissed him, an endless caress of her lips and tongue and warm, sweet breath. He ghosted his hands over her back, down to her hips, her ass, and then up again on her sides, to where she shivered as he neared her breasts.

"Tom," she whispered.

It hadn't been that long.

She'd been sick, and they'd both gone back to work. There was a lot in the mix.

But damn it, he'd missed this. Her.

She buried her face in his neck, her lips brushing against his skin. "Want to hear something funny?"

"Always."

She stretched out, a flushed, wanton woman. "I thought it would be weeks before I wanted to do this again, if at all, and I was kind of sad about that. I was hoping maybe by Valentine's Day, we'd get back to this. It's like you read my mind."

He grinned. "I like that. But you can hit the brakes any time."

"I'm good." Her eyes were bright. "This is nice."

He covered her with his body. Kissed her, caressed her.

Stripped her bare and tasted her all over before stretching out and tugging her up to straddle him.

"Get on top," he said, and he could hear the reverence in his voice. Could she hear it, too? He felt closer to her tonight than ever before in their relationship. Like their partnership was clicking into place in a whole new way. "I want to see you."

He wanted her to set the pace, too. To guide their pleasure tonight.

She made a noise deep in her throat as she tugged down his briefs and his cock swung out and up, ready for anything. Then it was his turn to make sounds, because the pace she'd decided to set was slow, torturous. Amazing.

Raking her fingernails over his hip, she lightened her touch just before reaching his groin.

"Touch me," he panted.

She obliged in the most literal of ways, grazing her fingertips against his balls, making his nuts tighten up and pulse.

"Chloe…"

She smiled. "Missed this."

His cock flexed, nodding in agreement. Fuck yeah.

Taking him in hand, she rocked her hips forward, rubbing her sex against his hard length. The warm, wet contact short-circuited his brain and drove his hips hard off the bed. She tightened her grip, giving him a tight sheath to buck into, and on the third pulse, she lifted up and fit him against her entrance.

"Already?"

"Want you," she whispered as she sank onto him.

Tight.

Hot.

He reached for her, cupping and squeezing her hips, her bottom, and then higher, filling his hands with her breasts. She shuddered at the lightest touch to her nipples, leaning into it at first, then pulled his hands low to her hips again.

Before long he let his fingers quest again, this time to where their bodies met, to her clit.

"Okay?"

"Very okay." She bit her lip and pulsed her hips, rubbing against his touch. Deep inside her, his cock flexed and throbbed. It wouldn't take much for him to go off and he wanted to get her there, too.

Love you, he mouthed. She gazed down at him, her eyes hooded, her mouth swollen.

Each slow rise of her body brought a new sway, a hypnotic swing to her breasts, a jiggle at her hips, and it drove him wild. He wanted to bury himself inside her, to claim her and love her and make her his own.

And when she threw her head back, baring the long, sexy expanse of her neck, he felt his orgasm start almost by surprise. She came too, and he said a silent prayer as she clenched around him.

She meant so much to him. He would do anything for her, his beautiful queen who secretly gifted books to people and thought bunnies were magical.

CHAPTER FOURTEEN

NEVER UNDERESTIMATE the sleuthing power of a librarian network.

Chloe wasn't sure who on the CC list was responsible for leaking the emails back and forth, but by the end of the next week, a dam broke and suddenly a deluge of messages from other branches landed in her inbox.

Everyone else on the chopping block was eager to network and discuss options. Librarians from bigger branches offered support and raised new questions. Others had been pushing back as well, it seemed, at the same time Chloe had, and now they all knew about each other. By the end of the day, there was a consensus. It was time to go public.

Oops.

She couldn't say she regretted it, even when an <u>Urgent: Confidential</u> email landed in everyone's inbox from the head office, chastising the loop for running away with rumours.

Rumours.

Uh huh.

They were smarter than that. And now Chloe didn't feel quite so alone—or so small against the invisible dragon.

Five minutes before closing, the door swung open, bringing in a gust of wintery air—and a tall, handsome park ranger.

Like going to the diner for breakfast, having Tom appear in her workplace for the first time since they took their relationship public was an interesting exercise in getting past the surreal thing and re-aligning her comfort levels.

She was the only person in the library, though, so when he stopped in front of where she was sitting at the circulation desk, she stood up and gave him a quick, soft kiss. "Hey."

"You aren't answering text messages," he said with a smile. "So I thought I'd stop in."

She squeaked and reached for her phone. Her lips twitched as she read his three messages, all sent in the last hour.

Tom: What do you want for dinner? I'll hit the store on my way home.
Tom: Busy day?
Tom: I'm going to swing by and kiss you in public.

"You kissed me first, before I had a chance," he said, his eyes dancing.

"I did. Sorry, yes, it was a busy day. So much to tell you about."

"I can't wait to hear all about it."

"Do you want to go out for dinner? We could go to Mac's, or drive over to Lion's Head to the pub." Another place where she'd pretended not to want him, pretended he was simply an acquaintance and not the man who made her pulse race when he pulled her into bed and kissed her senseless.

"Yeah?" He genuinely looked surprised. That might be because she'd been miserably under the weather with nausea for a solid three weeks. But it was probably because she'd spent the last year only having a slice of a relationship with him, in secret, and it was long past time for that to change.

"It's been quite the day." She filled him in. "And since I'm taking Monday off for our next midwife's appointment, I'll probably come back to quite the shit storm on Tuesday. C'est la vie, but still…yikes."

"This is good, though, right? Olivia can take this and run with it. There will be petitions and public pressure now."

Normally Chloe would be all for that. Take on the world, speak truth to power…but right now, she was tired. And hungry. And sometimes, when she was too tired and too hungry, she threw up. Because she was growing a baby, and frankly, the thought of orchestrating a county-wide protest made her feel green around the gills.

"I'm glad others are involved, that's for sure." The clock on the wall ticked to the top of the hour. "And now it's closing time. Can I take you on a date?"

———

IT WAS WING night at the pub. Tom got a double order of medium BBQ, extra sauce. Chloe ordered hers dry rubbed with lemon pepper, extra veggies and dip on the side.

"And to drink?" the bartender asked.

"Sparkling water for me," Chloe said.

Tom asked for the same.

"You could have a beer if you want," she offered.

"I could. I'm good, though." He leaned in and brushed his lips against her cheek, just in front of her ear, so he could murmur the next bit just for her. "I'm just happy to be here with you."

"We missed out on this," she said softly. "Flirting over wings. You getting your ass kicked at pool."

"I got to watch you play across the room," he countered. "That was fun in its own way."

"I'm trying to say that I…" She trailed off and flicked her gaze up to look at him. Her eyes were big and bright, and a little unsure. "I'm sorry we didn't date?"

He shook his head carefully. "I'm not. We're going to have the rest of our lives to catch up on dates we've missed. This is one. We'll go on others. Maybe I can kick *your* ass at bowling."

She giggled. "I think I'd topple sideways right now if I tried it."

"We can wait until the baby arrives. I bet bowling alleys are super conducive to quiet naps, right?"

She was shaking with laughter. Good. That was the goal. He slid his arm around her shoulders and let his fingers dance against the bare skin at the back of her neck as they waited for their drinks.

"Maybe we did things a bit backwards," he said later, after their wings were devoured and she did in fact kick his ass at the first game of pool. "But we're not done doing them, you know? So rack 'em up, Dawson. Because this game is going to be mine, and then I'm going to take you home and show you just how much I like the taste of victory."

"The taste of *my* victory, you mean," she said, giving him a fierce and adoring look.

He circled around the pool table. "Oh yes," he growled. "I want to show you *exactly* how much I like the taste of your victory."

Her laugh this time was low, sexy, and bordering on indecent.

She won the second game in three turns, and when they got back to his cabin in the woods, they took turns tasting everything.

————

BY THE TIME they drove south to Walkerton for her next midwife appointment, Chloe was no longer in denial about the little belly Tom had first spotted. Olivia's maternity pants made the roundness even more pronounced, and she thought it was quite the miracle nobody had asked her if she was expecting yet.

"I think we should tell people after today's appointment," she said to Tom.

He glanced across the truck cab at her, grinning. "I can't wait."

She believed him, too. He'd been holding her belly as they slept each night and he was reading three different pregnancy books at once. If ever there was a man excited for a baby's arrival, it was Tom.

Kerry was ready for them when they arrived, so she ushered them right into the exam room. "Good news. Our next appointment should be in Pine Harbour. No more driving back and forth for you, except if we want you to have an ultrasound at the hospital."

"That's exciting!"

"Do you know Jake Foster?"

Tom laughed. "Yeah. He's married to my sister."

And they were in the army together, had been in Afghanistan on the same tour. The Fosters and the Minellis had been blood brothers long before Dani and Jake got married.

Kerry blushed. "Right. Small town. Well, he's doing the renovations on the new clinic space, and making amazing progress. Apparently some of his crew have extra time right now."

"The winter's slow." Tom grinned. "And in the summer, when it's mayhem, sometimes I'm called on to help out."

"Small town," the three of them all said together.

Then Kerry got down to business. "How has the last month gone? How's the nausea?"

"Still there. I'm throwing up every morning, but the rest of the day is…okay. Honestly, I thought by now it might be improving."

"That's always the hope. But you're keeping food down, right?"

"Yeah. And I gained three pounds, although I don't know how."

Kerry grinned. "That's a good thing."

"It's not too much?"

"We're not going to worry about that right now. Or ever, to be clear. We like to see steady growth, that's all."

"Tom bought some pregnancy books. I may have read ahead. And then I got scared."

"Don't read them if they don't fill your well in a good way. We'll cover everything you need to know at the pace you need to know it."

"Okay."

The midwife flashed Tom a knowing look. "So you're an information junkie, eh?"

He cleared his throat. "Maybe."

"I think he's blushing," Kerry said.

Chloe laughed. "He's definitely blushing."

"He's also sitting right here," Tom groused good-naturedly.

"Nothing wrong with a supportive partner." Kerry grinned. "Speaking of which, now comes the fun stuff. Ready to hear the heartbeat?"

"Oh yeah."

"All right, hop on up here," she patted the paper-covered exam table. "Can you fold your pants down?"

Chloe lifted her shirt and wiggled the stretchy waistband all the way down to her hips. "I've popped in the last week. Tom saw it first, and now…we're going to have to tell everyone this week I think. It's pretty obvious."

"My fingers are a little cool, okay? Pardon my touch." Kerry traced the firm roundness just above Chloe's pelvic bone. "Yep, that's your uterus all right. We should have no problem hearing the heartbeat. I'm going to use some gel —also cold, apologies for that, too."

After smearing the gel all over her belly, Kerry took a small handheld doppler device and held the wand to Chloe's skin.

At first, she wasn't sure what she was hearing in the *whoosh, whoosh* noises coming from the machine. But then there was something faster. *Whomp, whomp, whomp.*

"That's a heartbeat, right?"

The midwife nodded. "Yep. Let's see if I can grab yours for comparison." She moved the wand and the baby's heartbeat was gone, replaced by other noise.

Then she found it again, and Tom reached out to rub Chloe's arm. "This is fun."

Kerry moved the wand to the other side of the belly and frowned.

Tom leaned in. "What is it?"

The midwife's tongue poked in the side of her cheek. The baby's heartbeat sounded good, Chloe thought. Fast, but Tom had read her a passage all about that just last night. Fast was good.

Wasn't it good?

He squeezed her hand, and she wondered if he was remembering the same passage. The way her heart jumped into her throat, he must be feeling the same worry.

Kerry flashed them a quick smile, but the furrow between her eyes didn't change. "This baby sounds like it has a good and healthy heartbeat, don't worry," she promised. She moved the wand lower, losing the heartbeat again. There was nothing for a moment, then she picked it up again. "And so does this one."

CHAPTER FIFTEEN

CHLOE GASPED. "WHAT?"

Tom swivelled his head back and forth between them. "What?"

Chloe's eyes felt ginormous as she stared at Kerry. "Two?"

"Two?" Tom cleared his throat. "I know I'm just repeating everything she's saying, but *two*?"

Kerry nodded. "I think so. I want you to have an ultrasound. I'll call over to the hospital and see if they can fit you in today so you don't need to make the drive back down again." She grabbed a soft, white towel from under the exam table and set it on Chloe's belly. "You can get cleaned up and dressed again. I'll be right back."

And then they were alone.

Tom rose above her, smiling tentatively. "Hey."

"Yeah."

"So that's exciting."

"Uh huh." She fumbled for the towel, and he covered her hand with his.

"Let me." He wiped the gel off her skin, and just for a

second, she felt his fingers tremble. Then he carefully rolled her waistband up over her belly, lobbed the towel into a linen basket, and helped her sit up. "Chloe," he whispered.

She threw her arms around his neck and pulled him in for a tight, squishy hug.

The next three hours passed in a surreal blur. They sat in a too-quiet hospital waiting room for a while, then were ushered into a dark ultrasound room for a set of pictures. The tech didn't talk much, but did show them baby A, and then baby B.

It was official.

There were definitely two fetuses inside her belly.

The entire drive back to Pine Harbour, Tom clutched her hand tightly on the console between their seats.

"What do you need?" he asked after parking next to her car in front of the cabin.

"Tequila."

"I have ice cream and pickles."

She snorted. She'd seen the ice cream he'd stocked up on, just in case, but she'd missed that he'd also bought pickles.

Sure enough, once they were inside, he led her to the ugly anteroom off the kitchen. On the shelf above the deep freeze was a complete selection of pickles. Sweet, dill, bread and butter, gherkin.

"Did you buy one of each?"

"Sure did."

"Why?"

"Just in case."

She opened the deep freeze and grabbed the first tub of ice cream she saw. "Good idea."

He followed her into the kitchen. "So…twins."

Fucking hell. She nodded as she yanked open the utensil drawer. "Twins."

"Two babies."

She jammed a spoon in the ice cream, then jerked it out again. "Yep."

"That's great."

"Uh huh."

"Freaky, too."

She looked up at him. "Tom?"

"Yeah?"

"I'm going to need you to get a spoon and eat this ice cream with me in terrified silence, please."

Terrified wasn't really the feeling, though. Just over-whelmed.

She needed a few minutes to process it.

She'd had hours now, but still...a few more minutes would be great. They hadn't even told their families she was pregnant.

His gaze carefully locked on her face, he grabbed a spoon and dug in. They stood there in the middle of the kitchen, sharing a pint of Cherry Garcia, until the cold sweetness worked its magic and Chloe's thoughts started to re-order themselves into something approaching rationality.

"Truthfully?" She looked up at Tom.

He nodded. "Always."

"I was already freaking out about one baby. How to care for it, what it might do to my body. Two? Gong show. But...they're going to be best friends. They're going to hold hands when they're three days old, and that's going to melt my freaking heart. This is the most magical thing and the most insane thing, at the same time, and I'm really glad you got ice cream. That's all."

"That's a lot."

"Mmm hmm."

He dug out another scoop. "You want my truth?"

"Always."

"I freaked out when she said two. Mind went blank, hands started shaking. And I was fucking scared I'd say the wrong thing, like I did when you told me you were pregnant."

They were both so human it hurt.

She smiled up at him. "I freaked out, too. Obviously. So thank you for sharing that you did, too. That makes me feel better."

He laughed.

"I know I keep saying this, but we should probably call our families." She puffed her cheeks out, wrinkled her nose, and looked up at him. "You know what?"

"What?"

"I think I want the pickles for that."

————

"DO you want to call your parents first?" They'd danced around this. Tom knew Chloe's history, and although she hadn't dwelled on it, he knew she was nervous about telling them she was in a similar spot to what they'd experienced.

Except Tom wasn't her father. And she wasn't her mother. They were their own people, with their own dynamic, and Tom was committed to being the partner Chloe needed—in parenting, and in life.

She made a face, then nodded and grabbed her phone. Instead of calling directly, she texted them both a quick *hey are you free to talk* kind of message.

Her mother replied immediately, so that's who got the first call.

"Mom," Chloe said. "What's up? No, nothing's wrong. Everything is…great. Really great. I know, it was a weird text message to send. Sorry about that. Listen, I have some exciting news."

Tom grinned at her. It was exciting.

"Do you know that guy I told you about?" His mouth fell open. *You told* her *about me?* She winked at him. "Yes, the park ranger. Things have gotten more serious between us. No, I'm not getting married. *Mom*, stop it. That's not my thing. But… I'm pregnant."

The silence after that was deafening.

Tom's chest tightened and his throat went dry.

"It's a good thing," Chloe said softly. "Yes, I'm happy. So is Tom." Damn straight. "That's not all, Mom. We had an ultrasound today. There are two of them. Two babies. I'm going to have twins."

This time the pause was shorter, and Chloe laughed. "I'm sure it's going to be a lot of work. But we'll figure it out. Yes, of course you can come up when they're born. Okay. Sure. Uh… Yes. Later. Love you."

She ended the call, and Tom swallowed hard. "So…"

Chloe shrugged. "It went better than I expected." She looked down at the phone in her hand. "Still haven't heard back from my father. Do you want to call your parents? Is it okay to tell them over the phone?"

"Yeah." Tom frowned. "Are you okay?"

Chloe looked up again, her eyes glittering. "It's a lot."

"Come here."

She crawled up against him and he wrapped his arms around her.

"I am excited," he whispered against her hair. "And we will sort it out."

"I know." She softened against him.

"So when did you tell your mom about the sexy park ranger friend?"

She giggled. "Uh… a while ago."

"That's an interesting secret."

"I've always told her about my dating life. So when I stopped…she had questions."

"I like it."

Chloe squeezed him back. "She'll like you. And she won't be around a lot, so she won't be overwhelming."

"It would be okay," he promised. "If she were overwhelming. I have some experience in handling that. Speaking of which…it's my turn." Chloe went to get up. He gently held her against him. "Hey, stay right here."

With his free hand, he found his own phone and tapped the second contact in his favourites list. **The Parents**, he'd called them in his address book.

His dad answered the phone in his still-accented-after-forty-five-years Italian-Canadian voice. "Hello?"

"Dad, it's me. Tom."

"Do you want your mother?"

"I kind of want to talk to you both. Can you put me on speaker phone?" There was some back and forth conversing on the other end, so Tom played with Chloe's hair while he waited.

Then the connection changed, and he could hear kitchen sounds, and his mother's voice. "Tom? What is it?"

"I've got some exciting news." Once upon a time, Tom had taken a half-day course in how to teach a class with confidence, designed to help introverted scientists engage better with visitors to the park services. The key takeaway message was that smiling helped deliver a message more positively, and when in doubt, try to make yourself smile as you teach something.

Tom didn't have to make himself smile for this. He was grinning broadly. He had Chloe cuddled up next to him, and two babies—two, still a shock, holy shit—brewing inside her.

"Well, out with it," his father said.

"I'm going to be dad," Tom said, his voice thickening up. Still smiling. "My girlfriend—Chloe, the librarian, Mom. You know here. She's pregnant. With twins, actually. Two kids. I'm going to be a dad to two babies."

Chloe looked up at him, and now he knew what it was like to be on the receiving end of that curious, is-everything-okay look as the silence stretched on.

"Well," his mother finally said, projecting from across the kitchen. "That is quite the announcement to make over the phone."

He rolled his eyes. "Thanks, Ma."

"We are thrilled for you," she added.

"Congratulations," his father said. "Maybe come over and tell us more soon, okay?"

"Okay, Dad. Thanks." Tom ended the call.

"Did you get grief for not doing it in person?"

"Of course I did." He kissed her forehead. "But you had to do it on the phone, so I did it the same way."

She laughed gently. "And you were a little afraid of your mother?"

"Obviously. Okay, more ice cream, yes?"

"Oh, hell yes."

———

THE LOUD, persistent beeping woke Chloe from a deep, disorienting sleep.

"Whatsthat?" she mumbled.

"Sorry," Tom whispered. "That's my search and rescue pager. I gotta go."

"What time is it?"

"Dark o'clock. Love you. Go back to sleep."

She murmured and drifted off again, dragged back into slumber by the bone-deep fatigue that had replaced her nausea. Pregnancy was a ride and a half.

Sometime later, when dawn was breaking, she woke up with a panicky start. Tom was gone, and it took her a moment to remember he was at work.

In all the time they'd been sleeping together, she'd never heard that pager go off. Before Babies—BB—he'd blown off a hook-up once or twice because of a rescue, but that was abstract information.

The shrill, insistent alarm still rocketed around in her mind. So loud, so urgent. She swung her legs out of bed, ignoring the now too-familiar wave of nausea—*not now, puke*—and headed into the living room.

One of her favourite things about Tom's cabin was how warm it was in the winter. He had good quality windows and an even better furnace—so she could wander around in tiny shorts and a tank that let her belly hang out.

Which was great up until the moment that someone unexpected let themselves into the house.

A key turned into the lock and she yelped, dashing back to the bedroom just as the door swung open.

"Chloe?" Tom called out.

She poked her head back into the living room. "Oh. Hey. How did it go?"

"Great. Got a bit dicey there, but all's well that ends

well." He gave her a happy, loopy grin. "I'm going to get in the shower. Want to join me?"

She frowned as she followed him. "What do you mean, it got a bit dicey? How dicey?"

He shrugged. "Don't worry about it. I'm a trained professional. This is my job."

Technically, she was pretty sure search and rescue was his hobby, and job-adjacent. But that was his distinction to worry about, not hers. "I know you're very good."

He had to be.

If he wasn't, he could die.

Her frown didn't go away.

"Hey." He cupped her face in his hands. "It was fine."

Sure. But her pregnancy hormones were blaring all the ways it might not have been through her mind. "This time."

"I'm careful. I don't take stupid risks, and I don't let anyone else, either." He brushed his lips against hers. "Do you want to come to the next training night so you can see how much I annoy everyone with my safety rules?"

She laughed gently. "No."

"Hey, I don't mind if you worry about me," he said softly.

She frowned. "I wasn't—" He grinned as she cut herself off. "Okay, yes. I was worried about you."

It was a weird feeling to admit out loud.

Weirder still to keep feeling it inside, a twisty, needy hungry monster in her belly as they showered together and then crawled back into bed.

The thought of something happening to Tom terrified Chloe to the depth of her soul. She couldn't shake it, and when Tom said Sean was going to come over a few days later, she leapt at the opportunity to see if Jenna wanted to come too.

"We could have a little dinner party?"

Tom nodded. "Sure. What do you want to make?"

"I fell right into that trap, didn't I?"

He kissed her soundly. "You make a salad, I'll roast something to go with it."

"We're a great team," she said brightly.

And they were.

So why was she worried?

It was the first question she asked Jenna when their friends arrived, and Tom and Sean disappeared to the barn out back to talk about weight lifting and training plans.

"Because he's your partner," Jenna said, like that was a simple answer.

Maybe it would be for anyone else. For Chloe, that just amped up the fear. "How did you do it? How did you stick it out with Sean when you showed up and things were such a mess?"

Jenna laughed gently. "I didn't really *do it*. Don't you remember? I clung to you and dove into work, and just barely found the balance between keeping my heart open and maintaining some semblance of boundaries. It was rough."

"Oh." Chloe rubbed her belly. "I guess."

Jenna held her gaze. "Tom loves you so much. He's not going to do anything foolish or risky, because he wants to come home to you every single night."

"I don't like how much I need him to be okay. To be here and healthy. That scares me."

"The thing that I realized, when I felt that *oh shit, what am I getting into* feeling with Sean…is that it was too late.

By the time I had that panicky feeling of it being too much, and maybe I should get out—"

"I don't want to get out," Chloe hastened to add.

Jenna smiled. "No, I see that. I'm just saying, that even if you did have that thought for a split second, for self-preservation...it would be too late. You only have that feeling once you've tumbled head over heels."

Well, Chloe wouldn't go that far. She hadn't *tumbled*. Had she? She hadn't even really moved in yet, not for real. Taking a deep breath, she glanced around the kitchen. Tom's kitchen. "How about some tea?"

———

"HOLY CRAP," Sean said when Tom swung the door to his barn open. It was a tad more stuffed than the last time they'd been out there. "What is all of this stuff?"

"Chloe's stuff from the apartment. She hasn't unpacked yet." Tom turned on a lantern and the space heater to add some light and warmth to the space.

Sean carefully walked around the pile of boxes. "Is the pregnancy still kicking her ass?"

"Nah, she's feeling pretty good these days."

"Does she need help?"

"With unpacking?" Tom shook his head. "It's more about space. I don't have a lot of it."

His friend gave him a furrowed brow look of concern. "It's not just your space anymore, man. Make room."

Tom frowned. Right. "I will. I am."

"Uh huh. That's why your wife's stuff is in our workout barn instead of in your house?"

"She's not my wife." It came out without thinking.

Sean blinked at him. "Defensive, much?"

Tom felt his cheeks heat up, and he swallowed back against the rise of awkward feelings. "She doesn't want that."

"Nothing wrong with not liking labels, I guess."

"Exactly."

Sean nodded. "But it's hard to make a case for commitment—labels or not—if she's with someone who won't make room for her stuff in her own house."

Tom wanted to protest again, but Sean wasn't wrong. So he resorted to an age old argument. "Shut up."

His friend grinned. "Ah, the sage advice man is getting his comeuppance."

"It's not that I don't want to share the space with her."

"Of course not." Sean's eyes were twinkling now.

"You're laughing at me."

"Of course I am, man! If the roles were reversed, what the fuck would you tell me to do?"

God damn it. Tom groaned. "I should have moved my own shit out here and put her stuff in the house."

"It's really obvious, I'm just saying. You dropped the boyfriend ball."

"Shut up again," he muttered.

But the messaged was received.

Had he cleared out space when they first brought her stuff back from Owen Sound, that would have been a good gesture. Now? It would be decent.

He wanted to be more than decent.

And the whole conversation kept spinning through his mind as they planned a rope climbing workout, then on the slow, careful walk back to the house. As they all made dinner together, as Sean held his baby with one arm and ate with the other, in the tiny, cramped kitchen, not big enough for four people.

Soon his family would be four people all on their own.

If they had Sean and Jenna over again a year from now, there would be seven people at the table. Seven people couldn't fit in his kitchen, let alone at the table.

Those thoughts continued to spiral over the next few days.

Should they move?

By Friday night, he thought about bringing up house hunting, but when Chloe came home from work, her feet hurt and she was in a grumpy mood because the HR person for the county library system hadn't gotten back to her about the maternity leave details, and how it would affect her request for a different position, should the closure go through.

"I hate being in a financially precarious position," she grumbled.

In that case, he wasn't going to bring up the idea of buying a bigger—and inevitably more expensive—house. Tom owned the cabin outright. That would help them a lot if she couldn't get a position close enough to Pine Harbour and decided to stay home with the babies after her mat leave ran out.

"That sounds really stressful," he said. "Can I offer pickles, ice cream, or an orgasm?"

She blinked at him.

Jokes wouldn't make her very real problems go away. But they wouldn't hurt in the meantime.

He added a more sensible fourth option. "Or maybe all three?"

CHAPTER SIXTEEN

EVERYTHING HAPPENED at once at the end of February. The library board announced it would hold public town halls over the next month before making any final decisions. Tom's sister announced they needed a big family dinner, given the baby news.

And Chloe's libido came roaring back with a vengeance.

Tom's work schedule went into overdrive, too, because the provincial park was hosting a ten-day Maple Syrup festival.

On her first day off, she decided to play tourist in her own town and went to check it out, catching a shuttle ride from Main Street instead of worrying about parking at the park itself. It was a good call, because cars were lined up and down the highway waiting to get in.

Word had clearly gotten out that the park had the hottest rangers all around. Or maybe that was her libido talking.

After disembarking from the shuttle bus, she took a quick stroll through the visitor's centre, but she was wearing her to-the-knees extra-warm down parka, so she headed back to the maple bush part of the park pretty quickly.

At first she couldn't see him. The park was crowded with families, everyone dressed from head to toe for the blast of wintery cold weather expected later that day—the first storm since they'd been trapped on the island together.

So much had happened since then. Now she wanted to do something special for him. That warm, excited feeling grew after she found Tom crouched next to a plastic line running between trees, discussing with a group of preschoolers why the thin hose was blue.

One by one, they suggested sillier and sillier ideas, and he carefully considered each one as if the kids were trusted colleagues.

At one point, he caught her eye—*hey, lady*—and she waved. When he finished, there was a big crowd between them, so instead of trying to fight his way through the people he pointed to the back of the shelter pavilion.

Nodding, she went the long way around the crowd to meet him there, and he caught her hand. He led her to a side door, which opened to a basic office that looked like it primarily functioned as a first aid station.

She needed first aid right now—from her favourite park ranger.

"That was a lot of fun, watching you in your element," she murmured after he kissed her hello. "You're really good with kids."

"Thanks."

"You're going to be really good with *our* kids."

"I hope so."

She leaned in and kissed his neck, trailing the tip of her tongue along the tendon there. "Tom."

"Mmm?"

"I have a present for you."

He groaned happily.

"Not for here," she said silkily. "Because I know you're a complete professional." He laughed, and she kept going. This was a lot of fun. It had been a while since she'd had this much fun. "But I want to give you a sneak peek at what will be waiting for you at home." It was hard to step back from the big, hard warmth of his body.

But she couldn't show him that she didn't have anything on under her parka unless she put some space between them.

Worthy sacrifice. The look on his face as she unzipped, revealing the lush swell of her breasts, the curve of her belly, and the absolute bareness of her body above her low cut leggings was perfect. Sexy, fun, and more than a little dirty.

"Chloe," he growled, yanking her close.

"Mmm?" She laughed as he kissed her, then sighed. Oh, his hands felt good on her skin. She was loving the new shape of her body, and was finally—finally—feeling good again.

"You need to dress more warmly than this."

"It's the best parka money can buy," she whispered. "Very warm. I feel toasty right now."

"You feel *amazing* right now." He nipped at her lower lip, then slid in for a hot, sexy kiss that was completely unprofessional. "Fuck, you've given me a hard on. Feel that?"

She was feeling the hell out of it. "I'm leaving now. And I'm going to touch myself until you get home."

He grinned as they broke apart. "Good surprise, babe."

She winked. "I think I'm back."

———

THEY HAD sex almost every day that week, which meant by the time they rolled up to his sister's place for the weekly Sunday lunch Tom rarely made it to, they were both in very good, very chill moods.

That didn't last long when he realized that his parents' were in attendance as well. The weekly lunch was almost always siblings and offspring only. Dani and her husband, Jake, their two kids, Rafe and Olivia and their daughter, and some combination of all the other siblings across the Foster and Minelli families.

Today, everyone was there, more than twenty in total.

Which should have made it more complicated for his mother to pin Chloe down, but Anne Minelli's super-powers were not to be underestimated. She may have been waiting in Jake's office right inside the front door of the rambling farmhouse, because no sooner had they taken off their coats than she was right in front of them.

"Chloe," she said warmly.

His mother did not do warm naturally, so this was an act.

And Chloe saw right through it. "Mrs. Minelli," she replied just as artificially sweetly. "Good to see you again."

"How are you feeling?"

Tom could see the real answer glittering in Chloe's eyes. *Great, thanks to the orgasm I rode out on your son's face before we came over here,* but she kept that to herself. "That good ol' second trimester glow, you know how it is."

His mother's response surprised him—and in a TMI way. "Enjoyed that four times myself."

God help him. Tom took a deep breath and slid his arm around Chloe's waist. He wasn't abandoning her.

But she didn't need his help. She pivoted the conversation effortlessly to the library. Common ground, and a topic with lots of meat. "I wanted to speak to you today, actually. About speaking at the town hall next week."

His mother cleared her throat. "Yes, I would be happy to. And I have questions, you know, about how this all unfolded. Why didn't we know about these budgetary shortfalls sooner?"

Too much meat, maybe. Because Tom had knocked up the librarian and she'd been thrown for a loop and wasn't focused on what mattered to the town. It was his fault, really.

"That's a great question for the library director," Chloe said. "Why don't we find Olivia and we can coordinate talking points? We want to stay on message. Pine Harbour uses its library at a rate higher than most other communities on the peninsula, and every resident—up and down the peninsula—needs access to information, resources, and books."

He moved forward with them, into the crowd of friends and family, but as they entered the great room, with the open kitchen at one end and a big family room at the other, they got separated.

Chloe winked at him, waving him on to the kitchen to help Dani in the kitchen.

His sister gave him a pointed look. "Hello, brother I haven't seen in years."

"You came to search and rescue training last week."

His idea—she was a paramedic, and a damn good first responder. She'd be a great addition to their team.

Dani shrugged. "Socially. I haven't seen you socially in ages."

"That's deliberate."

"Ouch."

"I'm enjoying my time with Chloe, cut me some slack. And we're here now." Tom surveyed the food prep for lunch. "What are we making?"

"The guys are are out back. Dean brought Jake a smoker back from Nashville, and they put a brisket in like eight hours ago. So I'm doing a lot of salads and sides to go with that. The theme is spring."

He glanced outside, where snow fell lightly on the group huddled around a shiny black dome. "Optimistic."

"My middle name. I bet they could use another round of drinks if you want to take beer out to them."

"Deal." He grabbed a six pack of bottles, caught Chloe's eye and pointed outside, then looped back to the front door to grab his coat. Then he took the outside path around to the back.

"Hey, I was just about to go inside and grab more drinks," Zander said, clapping him on the shoulder. "Perfect timing."

Tom handed drinks all around, ending with Jake, after he finished checking on the meat.

"Nearly done," his brother-in-law said. He took a long swallow of beer. "Cheers, thanks. Chloe here, too?"

Tom frowned. "Of course."

"I didn't mean it like that. Your mom said that she's been feeling really under the weather with the pregnancy."

"Knock on wood, that may be behind her."

"Good. Good." But Jake was still looking at him.

"What?" The two of them had a special bond. They'd done a tour in Afghanistan together. Had matching ink to remember the brothers in arms who lost their lives on that tour. Jake was trying to talk about something here, but Tom was missing it. "Spit it out, man."

"Sean says you're a bit crunched for space."

"Ah." Tom didn't mind a bit of gossip between brothers. "Yeah. The twins thing adds a whole new layer to it as well. It was already going to be tight in my place with Chloe and a baby. But two kids?"

"Got it. You need to build a new house."

Beer sprayed out of Tom's mouth.

Dean laughed.

Jake laughed.

Tom was not laughing with them.

Jake clapped him on the shoulder. "Don't worry, bud. We've got your back."

Shaking his head, Tom swiped his arm across his face, getting the beer foam off his beard before it froze into beer-sicles. "Shit, you guys are crazy."

"It's what we do. Fall in love, build a house for our women."

Tom was pretty sure that if he called Chloe his woman, she'd kneecap him. Rightfully so. The mother of his children, though…she'd like that.

But he couldn't build her a house, no matter how romantic the notion was. He looked at Zander for moral support.

His brother shrugged. "Your cottage is fucking small, man. Come on. At the very least we could fix up the interior, make it nice for her."

"How much free labour are you willing to put in with me?"

Jake looked hurt. "All of it, asshole."

That was the highest honour Tom could imagine. He took a deep breath. "For real? What if we renovated my verandah to be winterized? That would get us another bedroom."

"Less exciting, but do-able." Jake scratched his jaw. "What's your budget?"

"Half of what you want it to be."

"Very do-able."

"I'm serious, Jake. I'm not going to start parenthood in debt."

"We'll all help. Instead of a baby shower, we'll have a nursery building party. We can get a lot done in a weekend. Talk to Chloe, and then we can put a plan together."

He had the best friends in the world. "If you guys are serious…"

Dean leaned in, his eyes sharp. "Let us help. We've all been there. And you didn't plan this."

Tom hated a little how that was public knowledge. "This *is* what I want. You guys know that, right?" It was so important for Chloe to know that everyone else knew he *chose* her.

Zander crossed his arms and scowled. "Of course."

But maybe that was why he'd been scarce lately. For longer than just lately. Because for too long, he'd had to keep how he felt locked down, and the twin pressures of being seen—and not being seen—had messed with his head.

He let out a rough breath. "It'll be good to work on the house. Thanks, guys. I'm going to find Chloe and talk to her."

Opting to go back the way he came—the long way around so he could hang up his coat and take off his boots in the quiet of the foyer—was smart, because Chloe met him at the front door.

"Hey," she grinned. Then she kissed him right on the mouth, lingering just enough to scatter his thoughts, before wiggling her fingers under his shirt for a second to scratch his side.

Someone was in a good mood.

"You survived?"

She laughed, a low, sexy husky giggle. "I'm not convinced your mother isn't going to use the library town hall to publicly chastise us for not getting married, but all in all, I think the conversation went well. What were you guys talking about out there? I saw a lot of gesturing."

"They have a wild and crazy renovation plan."

"Whose house is being rebuilt?"

"Ours." His pulse hammered at the base of his neck. "If you want."

"I…"

"Nothing crazy. Mostly a lot of hard labour over a few weekends, and we could turn the verandah into a second bedroom. What do you say?"

"It sounds like a big decision, maybe best made after lunch." Her eyes sparkled. "Come on. Apparently your father is going to make a toast. I've got five bucks on it being a walk through memory lane on everyone's wedding."

"He wasn't at Zander's wedding," Tom groused.

None of them were.

And if he could ever convince Chloe to get married, it would be eloping for them as well. As much as he loved his family, right now he just wanted to toss his pregnant lover over his shoulder and tromp back to his little cabin by the lake.

"You're grumpy," she whispered.

He immediately softened. "But not when I'm with you."

———

CHLOE HAD A BETTER time at lunch than she expected—probably *way* better than Tom expected for her—and most of that was due to a new friend, the mother of young Emily Kingsley, the newest member of the Foster family.

Emily liked to introduce herself and all of her family members by their full names. "I'm Emily Kingsley. Matt is one of my two dads, but we don't have the same last name. His name is Matt Foster. I don't have the same last name as my other dad, either. I just share a name with Mommy. Her name is Natasha Kingsley."

All of this was announced across the table, proudly. And unnecessarily, because everyone around the table knew the story—and everyone except for Chloe knew Natasha and Emily, and had been at the wedding on Christmas Eve at their home in Wiarton. Matt had moved out of Pine Harbour to live with Natasha and Emily in the small town at the base of the peninsula. It was also where the guys all went for their weekly army reserve training. Chloe had driven through it many times, but never stopped longer than to grab a coffee at the Tim Horton's.

Chloe liked Emily right away. And she *really* liked that Natasha simply beamed at her daughter, not caring one whit about the double-take Anne was making at the other end of the table. It was the exact opposite of her own experience growing up—and in little Emily she saw herself, the precocious girl who loved her life exactly as it was, messy and real.

One day, Chloe's kids might yell the unconventional details of their family down a holiday table, and she would beam at them while they did it. She needed more friends like Natasha Kingsley in her life—and there was nothing wrong with widening her social circle outside of Pine Harbour, either.

"You guys should come over for dinner," she said quietly to Natasha. "So we can get to know each other better."

CHAPTER SEVENTEEN

ON HER NEXT DAY OFF, Chloe met Olivia at Mac's for burgers and plotting. The community town hall on the library closure was only a week away, and Chloe was getting nervous. Talking to Olivia helped. The burgers, though, did not. The babies didn't love them as much as Chloe had thought, so she ate most of her fries and a second helping of coleslaw the waitress brought her, but bundled up the burger for Tom.

"I'll take your dad a bonus lunch, do you think he'll like that?" she asked her belly, smoothing her hand over the ever-expanding curve. One of the babies responded with a head butt to the ribs. "Fair enough."

She found Tom just outside his office, talking to one of the other rangers about a research project taking place over the summer.

When he caught sight of her, he waved her in, wrapping an arm around her. "Chloe, this is Tia Johnson. Have you met? Tia, this is my partner Chloe."

They exchanged pleasantries, then he told Tia he'd find her again in a bit to finish their conversation.

"This is a nice surprise," he said to Chloe once when they were alone.

"Olivia and I met for lunch. But I couldn't eat my burger." She held up the leftovers bag. "Thought you might appreciate it. It's still warm."

"Awesome. Do you want to tell me about it as I eat?"

"Sure." She glanced around him to his office door. "Should we go sit down?"

He hesitated a bit, his cheeks colouring. "Yeah. We can. Okay."

Turning, he led her to his office and opened the door. Inside, his normally pristine space was jammed with stuff. Stuff she recognized from their place. His old camping gear, all of his biology reference books, power tools.

And stacked on the chairs where she thought they'd sit were piles of garage sale signs.

"What's all this?"

"I'm having a garage sale."

"Right now? In your office?"

"Next weekend. Here at the park."

"Oh. Why?"

"To make room for your stuff, because I'm an asshole."

He was really the furthest thing from an asshole. "I'm confused."

"I realized I was making room for you in my life."

"And I appreciate that."

"No, don't. That wasn't good enough."

"I'm not following."

"This whole time, I was making just enough room for you. But I wasn't making enough room for *us*. It's not enough to make room in *my* life for you. I need to make enough room, a blank space, for *our* life to flourish. So I need to sell some stuff."

A blank space for our life to flourish was quite a romantic image for her park ranger. She liked it. "You're serious here."

"Deadly serious."

Warmth bloomed in her chest. "Tell me more."

"When I get home, I'm bringing your boxes into the house. And I'll find more garage sale things and move them into the barn. My shit can move out to make room for your stuff."

"I could stand to get rid of things, too."

"I'm trying to do a grand gesture here. But if you want to be reasonable and meet me in the middle…"

She laughed and tossed her arms around him. "Sorry, keep going."

He caught her chin between his fingertips and held her gaze, his face entirely serious. "I want to build a new life with you. Every step of the way a choice I'm happy to make. Got it?"

"Got it," she whispered, her voice catching. Oh, she got it indeed. She closed the gap between them and brushed her lips against his.

He pumped his fist in the air. "Excellent."

―――――

THE PUBLIC TOWN hall to discuss the library closure was held on a Thursday night. It started at seven in the evening, which was also the time the library closed, and Chloe was working that night. They'd been telling patrons about it all week, but it was hard to read support levels.

She was a bundle of nerves as she set the last of the day's returns on the conveyor belt for the sorting machine and flipped the switch. It whirred to life and the books slid through the reader. The first one was a children's book, the next two thrillers. Then a romance. All of those would be re-shelved here. Then a couple of cookbooks. In her head, she did the sorting along with the machine. Would those go back into the county main supply? Yep, that's the bin the sorter dumped them into.

She knew her stuff.

Maybe they could sell the sorter to pay for a month of rent. She could do the work instead, although she had other things to do. They all did.

Damn it.

She blew out a frustrated huff, then turned the machine off. It was closing time.

Starting at the back of the building, she turned off all the lights, then put on her coat and grabbed her bag. The light switch at the door plunged the place into darkness, and she stepped outside.

Tom was waiting at the curb, leaning against his truck. "Can I drive you over to the community centre?"

"I was going to walk," she said before locking up. "But this is a nice surprise."

"I thought you might want some company since everyone else is already there."

Her co-workers had come by an hour before, to rally together, and they promised to save her a seat. "Thank you," she whispered as he took her into his arms and kissed her. "I'm nervous."

"I know. But rumour has it, the turnout is good."

When they arrived, the parking lot was full. "This is…"

He squeezed her hand across the console. "People love the library."

"I'm glad."

Inside, the crowd was even bigger than she estimated

from the parking lot. It was better than a good turnout. It was *great*. The library director was speaking, to a relatively quiet packed house, but she could see her colleagues and the empty seat for her up front.

Tom waved her forward, and took a spot along the back wall.

As far as Chloe could tell, they were still in the 1984 doublespeak part of the presentation, and she hadn't missed anything good. Blah blah blah, meeting community needs.

Well, hopefully they saw tonight that *this* community had needs that would not be met in the least if the library closed.

When the floor was opened for questions, Olivia was the first one at a microphone. "What other options beyond closure were considered for our town's library?"

The answer was pure bullshit. A general statement about options being considered across the county, some branches contracting hours, others closing.

Olivia didn't let it go. "But for this town, for *our* library, was closure the only option ever considered?"

Chloe grinned at the precision of the question. Yes or no, tell the truth or lie. What would it be?

Deflection, it seemed. How frustrating. "There are significant expenses involved in many alternate plans."

Olivia stepped aside, and other people had turns asking their questions. Chloe saw Anne in line, and was pleased as punch when Tom's mother stuck like glue to the talking points they'd prepped her on. "As a community leader, I'm very interested in what options would be available if we ran a fundraising drive."

"The library service needs to be mindful of financial commitments across the county."

"My understanding is that there are concerned community leaders everywhere on this issue."

The library director acknowledged that, but then politely moved on to the next question. On and on the line went. Even though everyone had a chance to speak, little progress was made.

Chloe was twitching. She wanted to get up to speak. She'd talked about it with Olivia and decided to wait and see how the public-driven discussion went. It hadn't gone far enough. Beside her, her co-workers were similarly amped up. Collectively their vibe was stressed, to say the least.

And when she stood, they all stood with her.

Instead of going to the microphone, Olivia hustled for the mic stand and brought it to them. They turned to the packed house, and Chloe locked her gaze on Tom at the very back. He gave her a thumbs-up in support, and her chest filled with warmth. "We are blown away by the support tonight. The size of this turnout reinforces what we already know. Pine Harbour is a community that loves its library."

"Help us save it!" someone shouted out.

Her pulse hammered in her neck. There was a line to walk here. She couldn't be insubordinate. But she could lead them in the right direction. "As has been stated, there are expenses that cannot be denied. Expenses related to operating a library, or moving a library…"

It could have been a slip of the tongue.

It wasn't, but it *could* have been, and that's all that mattered. Deniability.

Another voice in the crowd shouted out. "Can we do that? Can we move the library?"

That was Chloe's cue to sit down again.

Olivia collected the microphone, and held on to it. "Could we get a response to that question, please? Could our library be relocated to a more affordable location?"

The library director looked pained.

Chloe wanted to punch her fist in the air, but she limited herself to a polite smile.

"Relocation would also come with some one-time expenses that could make it—"

"Excuse me, ma'am," a deep voice interrupted. Everyone in the room turned to look at Owen Kincaid, the oldest of the Kincaid brothers. And the supervisor of the brand new emergency services building just outside of town. He introduced himself for the few in the room who didn't know him. "We have space in our building, and it's already covered by county tax dollars. Depending on the size of the—"

"Mr. Kincaid, this is highly irregular."

"It's a highly irregular time in the world, ma'am. Communities need to band together and get creative to protect resources we once took for granted. Yep. But what you're seeing here is exactly that, and with all due respect, we're probably going to have a solution for this problem whether you like it or not. Is there any particular reason you're hellbent on not liking any of them? Between the firefighters and the army reservists in this town, I'm sure we can find a brigade of volunteers to move the library contents."

Chloe pictured a line of firefighters passing her books down the street, biceps bulging.

She liked that idea a lot.

Possibly too much, and in an unprofessional way.

"I assure you, Mr. Kincaid, that there is no conspiracy to reject any...feasible idea." The library director nodded.

"Please, everyone, feel free to make suggestions. All will be considered."

Chloe stuck her hand in the air. "One advantage of the emergency services building is that it's on the highway, which would make the library more visible to county residents beyond the Pine Harbour community itself."

That sent up another wave of excited chatter.

Chloe dodged the gaze of the library director. Maybe that had been too far. Except she had an excited feeling that nope, it had been just far enough to get a real ball rolling.

CHAPTER EIGHTEEN

BEFORE THEY LEARNED they were having twins, Chloe thought of her due date as an abstract point, late in the summer. Her midwife appointments were only once a month, even after finding out about the multiples.

It felt like she had lots of time.

But two things happened just before her big ultrasound anatomy scan. One of the babies kicked her for the first time—no longer just random, fluttery feelings, but an Alien-esque movement that repeated again that night, much to Tom's obvious joy.

And Chloe's due date changed.

Well, apparently it had already changed, but she'd missed the memo. In her defence, there was a lot to keep track of.

Tom knew, though. It came up when they were discussing time off from work for her appointments, which were about to increase in frequency.

"We're nearly at the halfway mark," she said, tapping her pen against her planner.

"Past it," Tom said casually.

What?

"No," she said slowly. "I'm not due until the middle of August. And remember what Kerry said? First time moms usually go late."

"That's true for one baby," he said. Then he wiggled two fingers at her. "Twins are different."

She blinked. "They *can* be different," she corrected, even though she wasn't sure she was correct at all. "But if all goes well…"

"I think—and you can call Kerry and double check—that we're hoping to get to the end of July." He held his hands up. "Which is a long time from now."

It was barely four months away.

She joked about her belly getting big, but it really wasn't. How could two whole babies grow in such a short period of time?

So time started to speed up.

And as March came to an end, Tom and Jake were still leisurely discussing renovation options.

Chloe was pretty sure they needed to make a firm plan and soon, because she wasn't living in a construction zone with newborns. She'd move in with Jenna and Sean if need be.

"It won't come to that," Tom assured her.

"The weeks are zooming by."

"And my guys are machines. As soon as the weather warms up, it's going to be a big group effort to turn this place into just what we need to welcome the babies home." He gave her a warm, confident grin. "Like your very own episode of *Queer Eye*."

"Army Guys for the Pregnant Lady?"

"Something like that."

She had to trust his confidence. She had enough to

worry about at work. Despite the community support and Owen Kincaid's continued advocacy for the library to move into the emergency response station, the library board was dragging its feet.

And she still didn't have her maternity leave paperwork sorted out. There was something rotten in the state of Denmark. Maybe ghosts were haunting the library head offices.

So when they headed back to Walkerton for the anatomy scan, she asked Tom if he minded stopping with her at the library board offices, too.

"Not at all," he said. "Can I wear my uniform?"

She laughed. He had the army uniform, and the park ranger uniform, and the search and rescue team had reflective gear that counted, too. "Which one?"

He shrugged. "Whichever will put the fear of God into whoever it is that's causing you all these problems?"

"How about you wear a nice button-down shirt and pretend to be a lawyer?"

That made him laugh. She hoped they were both chuckling at the end of the day.

Their first stop was the hospital ultrasound clinic, where Tom waited while she went back to the dark exam room on her own. The technician took what felt like a bajillion different images, from all different angles around her belly. Then after a lot of clicking and whirring from the giant machine, the tech announced she was done, and asked if Chloe wanted Tom to come back and see the babies too.

Did she? And how. "Yes, please."

It was a redo of the first ultrasound, when the fact they were having twins was confirmed. Tom held her hand as they were shown the babies, bigger now, one of them sucking a thumb, the other kicking their feet. They were big enough now that the tech could point out fingers and toes, the spines, perfect and tiny, and two beautifully beating hearts.

Tears welled behind her eyelids, and Tom silently passed her a tissue.

She slid a glance sideways at him. He had one too, and shrugged happily at her as he dabbed his eyes.

Once they were done, Chloe wanted to put some space between that lovely moment and her crusade against the library management. It was still early in the day, not yet noon, and she was hungry, too.

"Let's find some lunch before we storm the library offices," she suggested. Keep the happy feeling a little longer.

They went to a diner on the main drag. Tom ordered a burger and fries, and Chloe chose the soup of the day. "And extra fries for him," she added. "Which are really for me."

When the waitress brought their food out, she brought Chloe a full plate of fries with a wink and a knowing glance at her belly.

They took their time, discussing reno options in between bites, and as they ate the place filled up with a lunch crowd.

Chloe didn't notice the people who sat behind her, but as the noise swelled—and then died down unexpectedly— she caught a part of their conversation.

"It's a mistake to string librarians on for too long."

Chloe froze. Tom caught her eye and nodded slowly. He'd heard it, too.

Holding her breath, she turned her head just enough to point her ear directly backwards.

"The email from the ministry was clear. The spending freeze is confidential until they announce their new plan for library services across the province."

Spending freeze.

New plan.

Her mouth fell open as blood pounded in her ears.

From the other side of the table, Tom reached over and grabbed her hand. He clearly thought she was about to spin around and give whoever was talking a piece of her mind, because how dare they?

But her boyfriend had another plan. He tugged her arm insistently and she turned her gaze back to him as the volume in the restaurant shifted up again.

What? she mouthed.

He gave her a grim smile and lifted his phone. *Smile.*

She gave him a wide-eyed what-the-crap look instead, and he took her picture.

"Are you done?" He asked casually, gesturing to the last bites of food between them.

Yeah, she was done. Done being played for a fool by an organization that underestimated her. "Let's get out of here."

He let her take the lead until they reached his truck. But before she could wrench the passenger side door open and haul her fed-up, pregnant self up onto the seat, he caught her gently by the arms and spun her around. "Hey," he murmured, holding her tight to his chest. "I'm sorry."

"What the fuck, Tom? What are they thinking will happen? They're just going to run out the clock on everyone and surprise us with closure notices?"

He growled under his breath. "Maybe. And they'd be stupid to do that, but sometimes people are stupid."

"I need to call them on that. I should go back in there and—"

"Show that know you know there's a problem but not what the problem is, exactly? We heard a slice of a conversation. You need more intel, okay? Then you can kick their asses, expose them, quietly get them to change their plans…whatever you end up wanting to do."

She blew out a breath. She didn't need this stress, that was for sure. And after all the goodwill that had been built up around the town halls across the county, she didn't want to spread half-truths that could slow that positive momentum with the public support. They might need every single resident in the county on their side at the end of this.

And then there was the sharp, brutal realization that she didn't want to let anyone down, not after she'd worked so hard to give them hope that she could save the Pine Harbour library. She might not be able to save anything after all. Blinking back frustrated tears, she glared up at Tom. "How do I find out just exactly what is going on here?"

"The same way I found you on Christmas Eve. We ask my brother to use his network to get information that would not otherwise be available."

Zander was a good…whatever he was. Bodyguard, private investigator. But now she wondered just how far his reach went. "Hacking?"

"Don't ask me a question you don't want to hear the answer for," he said gently. "I don't ask either."

"I did not peg you as the radical, criminal type."

"I have my moments." He kissed her quickly, then helped her into the truck.

After he'd jogged around to his side and gotten them

back on the road up north, she felt the need to clarify that she wasn't opposed to his grey-area strategic thinking. "About the radical, criminal enterprise. I like it. It's hot."

He winked at her from across the cab of the truck. "Let me tell you about this time I climbed on top of the visitor centre at the park in the middle of the night."

"Recently?"

"When I was in grade ten and trying hard to impress a girl." His eyes crinkled and his nose twitched as he cleared his throat before continuing. "Spoiler, she was not impressed. But the ranger who found me first thing the next morning thought my climbing skills could be fostered and funnelled in a more productive-to-society kind of way."

It was closer to an origin story than Tom had ever shared before. And it reminded her of her own librarian book-dealer story she'd told him at Christmas. She told him that. "We're not that different, are we?"

"Maybe not."

"You're cooler-headed than I am, though."

"On the outside, anyway." He gave her a quick glance before returning his attention to the road. "I was pretty pissed in that restaurant, too. Secrets like that can mess with people's livelihoods. It's not okay."

"You were right to stop me from engaging, though. I don't know who those people are. Maybe they're not in a position to effect change."

"That reminds me. The photo." He handed her his phone. "Do you recognize them?"

She carefully studied the photo. It was a horrifying picture of her. She chuckled. "I should have smiled. But no, I don't recognize them. Should I ask around?"

"I bet Zander can ID them for us."

"You were serious about hiring him to get the dirt, weren't you?"

"Absolutely."

"I can't afford whatever he charges."

Tom's brow pulled forward. "Chloe."

"What? That's a reasonable—"

He held out his hand, palm up. She slid her fingers across it and he lifted her hand, kissing her knuckles. "He'll do it free. He'll do it because he's a dad whose kid goes to the library, whose mom goes to the library, whose wife writes books that are shelved in the library. But he'll mostly do it because he's your brother-in-law, in spirit if not in a strict legal sense."

She gave him a faint smile. "I'm guessing the strict legal sense isn't really his deal anyway."

Tom's face split into a wide, laughing grin. "Exactly."

————

ZANDER CAME OVER THAT NIGHT. Instead of hacking, he had an old school, analog plan to figure out what the real deal was with the library plans for the next fiscal year.

"People who will talk about something confidential in the middle of a diner will also fall for talking to a stranger who knows a little about their secret. There's a bit of ground work to be done first, but I think I could call them up and pretend to be from the ministry that funds them."

"That's… Would that really work?"

"It's a good first step. If I don't get anything out of them, then we reach out to someone in the media, quietly, and see if they can get the emails through a Freedom of Information request, which will trigger some more uneasy chatter. The email will pop up at that point."

"How are you so sure?"

"Twenty years in the military. No such thing as a budget everyone likes. And when people don't like how things are going, OPSEC is low."

Chloe would normally be amused at the idea that there was operational security concerns around library services. But the analogy seemed appropriate now. "I don't feel right keeping this a secret from the other librarians in the county."

"Give me a day. Loose lips can happen on both sides, and it would be better to be sharing solid information rather than best guesses."

That was true. Heart pounding, Chloe nodded in agreement. "Deal."

After he left, Chloe expected to fall asleep early, as she usually did, but the nerves and perilous excitement of the day overrode the low-grade fatigue of pregnancy.

Tom couldn't sleep, either. They read together for a while, but he was restless. "I'm going to get up for a bit," he said, setting his book aside. He brushed a light kiss to her temple. "I might be keeping you awake."

"You aren't," she said, putting her book away as well. "I'll get up, too."

"A crazy day, huh?"

"The craziest. Do you want ice cream?"

He grinned. "I'm not the pregnant one."

"It can't hurt."

"No, it probably wouldn't hurt." He shrugged. "You know what I need?"

"What?" She would give him anything he asked for.

"A hug."

That sounded amazing. She rolled over, pressing her body against his. Between them, her belly was just big enough to feel like a thing between them, but not *between* them. More like it was now a third part of their dynamic, and they were hugging around it. He sighed and she squeezed tighter.

One of the babies slowly kicked, then the other. Tom made a happy sound and pulled her in tighter.

Yeah, a hug was even better than ice cream.

"What's wrong?" she asked quietly into the warm little space between their faces.

"I want to protect you from the chaos of the world."

"I don't think you can."

"Doesn't change the fact that I want to."

That was sweet. She kissed him softly. "Thanks."

He smoothed his hand over her hair and down her back. "What can I do instead?"

"Be my accomplice in crime, apparently."

"It's hardly a crime. More like a whistleblower investigation."

"True." She leaned her head against his shoulder. "You know what you could do?"

"Name it."

"Can you make some final decisions about the renovation and get that started—and then completed—before the babies arrive?"

He pointed to the other side of the cabin. "Do you want to go stand on the verandah and talk about the nursery options?"

She was already out of bed. "You bet I do."

He grabbed the quilt and wrapped it around her shoulders. "To keep off the chill of the night air," he whispered.

She gently fisted the front of his shirt and pulled him in for a lingering kiss. "Same," she said when they broke apart.

CHAPTER NINETEEN

THE NEXT MORNING they had a brief reprieve from renovation and work drama with their next prenatal appointment, this one at the brand-new Pine Harbour Midwifery Clinic.

"This looks great," Chloe said as Kerry greeted them in the waiting room.

"We're thrilled. Jake's crew did a wonderful job." Kerry showed her to the spa-like washroom just off the waiting room, then left Chloe alone to weigh herself and pee in a cup, her usual first steps for an appointment.

Then she joined Tom in Kerry's office, where she had the results of the anatomy scan already.

"So the whole report is quite detailed," Kerry said, taping her fingertips on the folder on her desk. "But both babies are developing appropriately. They got all the images they needed—hearts, brains, spine length. As we saw at the first ultrasound, each fetus has its own amniotic sac, so they're fraternal. And we know gender, too, if you want to find out what you're having?"

Chloe took a deep breath and reached for Tom's hand. He squeezed her fingers right back.

"We want to know," she said.

Kerry beamed. "You're having a girl, and a boy."

Chloe burst into happy, confused tears. "That's great," she said, furiously wiping at her face. "Oh, wow."

Tom already had a tissue for her. "Each step of the way just makes it that much more real, eh?"

"So real." She took a deep breath. "Great. Okay. Awesome."

Kerry went over the rest of the results from the ultrasound, and reminded them that the appointments would speed up soon. "Everything is progressing exactly as we'd like to see it. I'll see you at the end of April. In the meantime, enjoy the rest of the second trimester."

The relief of finding out that the babies were progressing well, and the joy of discovering they'd be having a boy and a girl, carried Chloe back to work as if she were on a cloud.

―――――

TRUE TO HIS WORD, Zander called that night. Tom was cooking dinner, and Chloe brought her phone into the kitchen so he could listen to the conversation, too.

And he thought, maybe, she wanted moral support. Just in case, Tom wrapped his arm around her and held her tight while she heard what his brother had to say.

"I'm in Toronto," he said. "Long story short, this isn't just a problem in our county. Big story is brewing. I've made contact with a reporter who is on the trail. Can I give her your contact information? You can talk to her on background, off the record, if you want to keep your name out of the press."

Chloe didn't hesitate. "Tell her to call me. I'll talk on the record, no problem." When she hung up, she sighed heavily and leaned her head back against his shoulder. "Wow."

"It's the right thing to do," Tom said. He admired that she didn't need to think about it, either. Her principles were a big part of why he loved her, and he told her as much.

She shrugged off the praise. "Only option, really. Dinner smells good."

Hard pivot away from the emotional conversation.

It had been a while since they'd done this dance. At one point he might have bristled at being shut out, but that wouldn't be fair. He knew she would share more about how she felt when she was ready.

Or when he got the conditions just right.

He kissed the top of her head. "Hey, I made a call to Jake's preferred dumpster guy today. They can have a bin here for Friday. How does next weekend sound for demolition?"

"Terrifying. Let's do it."

Over the next four days, he moved as much as he could out of the house and into the barn, leaving space for the guys to work there, too, if needed.

And he booked a hotel room in Collingwood.

He didn't tell Chloe about the last part of the plan until she got home from work Friday, though. Her little car pulled in between the line of trucks, and he met her there, duffle bags in hand.

"What's going on?" she asked as she opened her car door.

He blocked her in with his body, eager to kiss her and tell her about the surprise—in that order. "I promised you Army Guys for the Pregnant Lady, and that includes whisking you away from the house. We're going to Blue Mountain for the night. Tomorrow, Olivia and Jenna will arrive to take over the Chloe Is a Hostage For the Weekend fun, and I'll come back to work on the house."

"What? I saw Jenna at lunch today. She said nothing." Her eyes twinkled as she tried to look past him at the house. "How's it going?"

"So far, so good. Do you want to go take a look?"

She kept her gaze trained on the house for a long moment, then shook her head. "Nope. I'm good with being surprised once it's done."

Good girl. He wanted her to have the least stressful renovation experience ever. "Then I'm ready to go if you are."

She laughed. "Are we taking my car?"

"Up to you. I need to drive back in the morning, so you'll be coming back with Olivia and Jenna."

She handed him her keys. "Then I'll ride shotgun there, too."

They stopped at Mac's for coffee, then hit the road. It would be an hour and forty-five minutes if they didn't hit any traffic, which they shouldn't at this time of year. Two more months and the highway running up and down the peninsula would be crawling with visitors from the city.

Today, though, their drive south and around the bottom end of Georgian Bay was easy.

When they arrived, he appreciated the impressed whistle Chloe let out when he parked in front of the nicest hotel in the centre of the ski resort town.

He handed her keys to the valet, then went around to

her side to help her out before grabbing their bags from the trunk.

"What did you pack for me?" she murmured as they walked toward the reception desk. "Did you remember my favourite vibrator?"

The last part wasn't murmured so much as projected. Not loud enough for the desk staff to hear, but amplified enough to give him a nervous jolt. Someone was feeling playful.

This trip had definitely been a good idea.

"I packed a roll of duct tape," he whispered back as they stopped in front of the clerk. He pivoted his attention. "Hey. Reservation for Tom Minelli."

"Yes, hello, Mr. Minelli. We have you in one of our suites this weekend. Could I see some ID, please?"

He slid his driver's license and credit card across the counter. Beside him, Chloe shook with silent laughter. It hadn't subsided fully by the time they stepped into the elevator, so he yanked her into his arms for a much-deserved kiss. "You liked that," he growled against her mouth.

"Which part?"

"All of it."

"Guilty." She sighed happily and leaned back against the mirrored wall, rubbing the side of her belly. "What should we do first?"

"I have a plan."

"Is the plan semi-public sex?" She wiggled her eyebrows, then bounced a little in excitement.

"It wasn't," he said quietly, pulling her close. "But I like the enthusiasm." And not just because when she bounced, her tits jiggled. But because they'd almost done that before she told him she was pregnant, and then he ruined it. He owed her sex in the open, which was—as far as debts went —a decent one to hold.

"I'm enthusiastic about a lot of things," she purred, rubbing against him.

Yes, his dick said.

Are you sure? his brain asked, and it was a reasonable question. But now was not the time to overthink the situation. Sure, he'd had a goal today, and it wasn't getting laid as soon as they checked in. But the lady wanted what she wanted, and who was he to deny her?

The elevator deposited them on the top floor, and they followed the signs to their room at the end of the corridor.

He swiped the keycard over the lock, then pushed the door open, holding it with one hand while he used the other arm to usher her forward.

The suite was even nicer than in the photos.

And the sounds Chloe made as she moved into the centre of it were even better than he imagined.

"Oh! A giant bath tub? And—ah, nice view. Oh, yes, I love this." She spun around, beaming. "Wow!"

He leaned against the arch separating the entrance from the living room and the bedroom.

In between the two spaces was that giant clawfoot tub, as promised, in a glass nook with a view of the ski hill.

"They promise that's one-way glass," he murmured. "So it wouldn't really be semi-public sex, but we can pretend…"

She turned around and shimmied out of her clothes.

Pretending it was. Tom's cock strained at his fly as he prowled toward her, trapping her against the glass. He grazed her earlobe with his teeth, then asked her, "Like this?"

"Yes," she breathed.

He stroked his hands over her flesh, paying special attention to her hips and belly and breasts, then slid his fingers between her legs. "I want you to come on my hand," he growled. "Get all flushed before I take you out for dinner."

She whimpered and rocked against his touch. Her sounds drove him wild, but he was going to save himself for later. This was just for her.

There was nothing he liked more than watching her come apart for him.

And when she did, he spun her around and held her as she went boneless against him. "So good," she murmured after he kissed her.

"Beautiful."

She blushed again.

When she reached for her clothes, he stopped her. "I packed a change of clothes for dinner."

"Intriguing…"

And risky. But the dress he'd picked for her fit beautifully, a black swing dress that skimmed her belly and twirled loose around her curvy legs. "That's right, spin for me," he said as he buttoned up his dress shirt.

She obliged with two more turns, then stopped right in front of him and helped him with the second to last button before his collar. "Leave it open," she whispered.

Heat surged through him.

"We do have a little bit of time before dinner," he said, pulling out his phone.

He'd heard "I Don't Dance" by Lee Brice a few weeks earlier, and was reminded that the song said a lot of things that resonated for their relationship. And it was pretty easy to dance to, he figured. The song was ready to go, and he hit play. "Could I have this dance?"

Her lips parted in a silent O as he set the phone down, and she nodded as she rubbed her hand over her chest. "Nice choice of song," she whispered as she right into him, soft and pliable. "This reminds me of us."

"That's why I picked it."

Her breath hitched, and he pulled her in for a quick squeeze first, then he moved them slowly, stepping sideways, then forward, holding her tight. She lifted her face, her eyes sparkling with wonder. *Yes.* Their lips barely grazed as he turned them, then stepped back. Still slow, still careful, his hand firmly in the small of her back.

He wanted to show her that he had her, that she could trust him. With a dance, with a meaningful getaway, with a renovation, with thoughtful and considerate dirty sex.

With everything.

As the song came to a sweeping end, she threw her arms around his neck and pulled him in for a searing embrace.

The restaurant was a short stroll from the hotel, made lovely by the picturesque surroundings and lovelier by the company. When he told Chloe that, she blushed and laughed. "You are full of good lines today."

"I feel full of good lines today, yeah. It's because my heart is full, which is really your doing, so…"

She pushed her shoulder into his arm. "Nice one."

Except he meant it, and he wasn't sure she understood just how much.

The street, and then a surprisingly busy-for-the-off-season restaurant were not the right venues for deep dives into big feelings, however, so he shelved that thought for later.

First, a feast for his woman. She might hate that term,

but it was how he thought of her now. His. His precious, his partner, his person. His woman.

And it was glorious to sit across a table from her, to admire her in public, to know that other people might be looking at him and thinking, *you fucking lucky bastard.* Which he was. She glowed. She always had. He'd been drawn to her from the very first time they'd met. Couldn't get enough of her. Went to the library more than he ever had before, found himself heading to Mac's any time her car was in the parking lot.

But she hadn't wanted him. She'd wanted his body, his private company. She finally let on that much. But the rest of him? The family man, the loyal and square member of society—she wasn't interested in that. And somewhere along the way, he'd forgotten to show her that it didn't matter. He'd give all of that up for a shot at a relationship with her.

That she was having his babies was gravy on top of gravy.

All he'd ever wanted was a chance with the sexiest, most curious, and most challenging woman he'd ever laid eyes on.

"You are looking at me in a very interesting way," she murmured. "What is on your mind?"

"The past," he said, keeping his voice low. "And the present. And, of course, our future."

She reached across the table, giving him her hand. "There's a lot I'd change about the past. You know that, right?"

"Yes, of course."

"Good." She smiled radiantly. "And I wouldn't change anything about our present. This is perfect. This can be our future, exactly like this. Although not *exactly* like this." She slid her gaze to the side, then back to him, her eyes glittering in amusement. "This can be a sometimes treat."

He snorted at the Cookie Monster reference.

There would be a lot more Sesame Street references in their future—and not a lot of fancy dinners, at least not for the next while. But they would make time for each other, too.

He picked up his menu. "What do you feel like?"

"Dessert," she said promptly.

And while their first two courses were delicious, it was in fact the dessert menu that got her most excited—and proved the most difficult for her to make a choice from.

"I don't know," she said helplessly, as the waiter hovered, having returned from clearing their dinner plates. "I really want the creme brûlée. And the pistachio cheesecake. God, maybe I should get both. It's too hard to choose between them. I could take one back to the room. What are you thinking?"

He'd been eyeing up the chocolate mousse. "The cheesecake sounds great to me. I'd trade you a few bites for some of your creme brûlée if you want to share? Unless you want to get both, in which case you should do exactly that."

The look on her face was magical. "Really? You'd share?"

Yes, really. He wanted to lay the world at her feet. And he hoped he was showing her that today. He had one more treat for her, back at the hotel.

Back in their suite, Chloe grabbed him and kissed him just inside the door, which scrambled his brain cells and almost made him forget about the plan.

But then he remembered. "I wanted to run you a bubble bath," he gasped.

"Are you going to wash me all over?"

"Every perfect, pink inch."

"I can't wait," she whispered. "I'll just go wash off my makeup and meet you there."

He ran the water first, then added the bubbles provided by the hotel. The towels were already next to the tub, so all he had to do was roll up his sleeves and—

"Ready for me?"

He turned around and his breath caught in his throat. Chloe was naked, completely, and her face was bare, her hair twisted up into two knots on either side of her head. She was a Greek goddess, leaning against the floor-to-ceiling glass window, one arm stretched high over her head, the other curved low around her belly.

"In you get," he said hoarsely.

"Are you not joining me?" She slinked off the glass wall and drew closer.

"If I did, it wouldn't be relaxing."

"But it would be fun," she murmured as he helped her step in.

"Not too hot?"

"It's perfect." She sighed as she sank into the water, the bubbles now big enough they obscured her body completely. A fact he'd bemoan if he didn't know every inch of her by heart, if he wasn't going to enjoy the hell out of finding her in the fizzy clouds.

He pulled up a low, wooden stool, clearly set there for exactly this purpose, and grabbed a washcloth. "Your leg, please?"

She poked her right toe out of the water, and he washed up the outside of that limb, then grazed across the top of her thigh before sliding the washcloth back down again, all the way to her foot.

He repeated the care on the other side, then did her arms. And her back. And her front, without a washcloth, taking his time there, too.

She was flushed and worked up nicely when she finally stood on shaky legs and climbed into his arms.

A water nymph, irresistible and seductive in every way.

"Your shirt is getting soaked," she giggled as they made out next to the tub.

"Take it off me, then."

Wet fingers slid against more wet fingers as they worked together to strip him down, at least the top off, before stumbling out of the bath nook and into the bedroom.

"Take your pants off," she said as she took the towel he was trying to dry her off with and tossed it on the bed, then tossed herself after it.

For a woman growing two babies, she was incredibly agile.

And horny.

Fuck, he loved the second trimester.

He shoved his pants off, then prowled after her, falling between her legs as she giggled.Then sighed. Yes, yes, that. He kissed and licked harder, wanting more of those sounds.

"You are too good to me," she breathed.

He almost missed it. He almost kept going, licking her to an orgasm that would carry that thought away, that would lead to mind-blowing sex that eradicated the thought from his own head, too.

He wasn't too good for her, though.

That was the piece he hadn't quite figured out earlier. It wasn't that she didn't know how much he loved her. Of course she saw how much he cared. It was more complicated than that.

He crawled up her body, loving every inch of her on the way. He kissed her belly all over, lingered at her breasts, and when his mouth traced up her neck, he made sure to hit all of her favourite spots.

Then he braced his arms on either side of her so she couldn't look away. A dirty trick for which he would never apologize. "You deserve everything I can give you and more. You deserve the world. The moon and the stars and beyond."

"Tom…" Her chest rose and fell, but she didn't say anything after that. Didn't argue, didn't minimize what he was saying. She fixed her glittering gaze on his face and just looked at him. And slowly a smile bloomed, her mouth curving up and out, until her lush lips parted and she exhaled. "I love you."

A lovely sense of peace flooded through his heart. "I love you, too." he said. "I'll never tire of telling you that. Never tire of showing you. You are my everything."

If they were two different people, this would be the perfect time to propose to her.

But maybe this was better. This was their truth, without pomp and circumstance.

"I love you *so much*," he growled, and she tugged him down, their mouths sliding together. Carefully he rolled them both to their sides and lifted her top leg. He'd had grand plans for her to come on his face. It was his usual favourite, especially lately. But now? Now they both needed a more primal, intense connection. "I want you like this."

"Take me." She arched her back, rolling her torso away from him, opening up her hips. She was wet for him, slick and ready. Tight, though. She always was now. Too snug for his eager cock, and there was real danger of him going off before her.

That would never do.

He held still as she worked her hips, taking him inside her. He counted ten good reasons to not come before his pregnant partner, and he said a little prayer for good measure.

God was definitely on the side of Chloe coming first. For sure.

Once he was fully seated inside her, he reached between them and gave her his fingers against her clit.

She shivered and moaned. Yes, oh yes.

It was the thing they said to each other the most during sex: *Yes*. He liked it. It had no pretence, no artifice. Just an honest sound, word, plea, offer.

Yes?

Yes.

Yes, more. Yes, harder.

Yes, faster, yes, your fingers, yes, love me, yes, need me, yes, I'm close, yes, come with me.

"Come with me." Maybe he said it. Maybe it was just a thought, but as soon as it flashed through his mind, and maybe out of his mouth, she was clutching around him, a rippling climax that carried him over the edge, too.

When he slipped out of her, he twisted them both around so he could hold her.

"Love you," she said drowsily, her head heavy and her eyes already shut.

"Shhh." He squeezed her tight, then left long enough to wash up and get a cloth for her.

When he returned, he cleaned her up, then tucked

them in together. "Time for sleep, my beautiful one. Tomorrow is a full-on pampering day."

"For me," she mumbled. "You're heading back to work really hard. I should be telling you...to...go..."

She didn't finish the thought. The next thing he heard from her was a soft, barely-there snore. A smile curved across his face and his own eyelids drifted shut.

Time for sleep for both of them.

CHAPTER TWENTY

IN THE MORNING, Tom ordered room service for breakfast and they stayed in bed until it was delivered.

After they ate, he gave her a long, lingering kiss goodbye and promised her friends were on their way.

As soon as he left, she ran herself another bubble bath and put on an audiobook to listen to. Solitude wasn't a problem for her at all.

But when Olivia and Jenna arrived just before noon, she was happy to see them. Jenna had a sleeping baby on her chest, in a baby carrier, so they headed out for a walk around Blue Mountain village.

They finished their walk at a gastropub next to the man-made lake beside the hotel, where Chloe ordered two kinds of French fries and a pitcher of lemonade for them all to share.

"We know how to party," she told the waiter.

He didn't laugh, but Olivia and Jenna did.

"I swear, these kids are going to demand fries as their first food," she said as she dipped a sweet potato chip in mayo. "They have been my staple. Fries, and soup. That's all that Tom's been making lately, and it's truly perfect. Maybe as we get closer to summer, we'll swap that out for salad." She tipped her face up to the sun, bright in the sky, even though the air wasn't really warm yet. "Dunno."

"These are good pregnancy problems to have," Olivia said teasingly.

"Knock on wood." Chloe ate another fry and sighed happily. "This is nice. Thanks for coming to keep me company."

"Since our husbands were otherwise busy this weekend…"

"Who's watching Sophia?"

Olivia's eyes lit up. "She's gone to my mom's for a *week*. It's freaking magical. I've been so productive. Jenna and I drove separately. She'll take you home tomorrow, and I'll drive down to London to pick up my munchkin."

"That's lovely." Chloe frowned. "Don't Anne and Alessandro ever take her?"

Olivia groaned. "For a few hours, sure. But they don't like overnights. That's okay—it really is. Everyone has different boundaries, and I don't think grandparents should be forced to do primary care if they don't want to."

"No," Chloe said slowly. "Of course not."

But it hadn't occurred to her before that her babies would have *two* sets of emotionally distant grandparents. Her own parents were non-starters. Her mother had only enquired about the pregnancy once. And her father had simply replied to her email, informing him he would be a grandfather, with an update on his second set of children —all still young enough to not be giving him grandchildren for quite some time.

And now she was realizing that Tom's parents would only have a limited role, too.

It was okay.

It was just…not any kind of fairytale.

Which was life.

Her children would have adoring aunts and uncles. "We can swap kids for date night," she said suddenly. "I'll babysit Soph. Of course I will. Why haven't I volunteered before?"

Olivia laughed and looked at Jenna, who waved a sweet potato in the air. "You were busy banging Tom in secret, if you'll recall. And then you were tired and sick, and that brings us up to the present. But a verbal offer is legally binding, blah blah blah, I'm totally taking you up on the kid swap plan."

Jenna and Sean didn't have grandparent support, either. In fact, other than Faith's mom, who was a really active part of young Eric's life, all of their friends did the childcare thing on their own. What fantasy had Chloe built up in her head that she wasn't going to live up to? They were all just struggling to make things work.

And she loved them for it.

It was time to trust that they loved her because of her mess, too, and not despite it.

"Deal." Chloe raised her glass of lemonade in the air. "To our own Date Night Network."

Olivia added her glass to the cheers. "Genius."

"Legally binding," Jenna repeated, joining them with a loud clink.

———

AFTER ANOTHER LEISURELY STROLL AROUND the village, they made their way to the spa in the hotel for pedicures, where all the attendants cooed over Chloe's belly and Olivia's child-free escape and Jenna's perfect little baby, asleep in her arms.

Soon, Chloe would have two of those.

"You'll have to show me how to use the carrier thing," she said.

Jenna smiled. "Will do. And you can use it with both babies at once, you know."

Chloe was pretty sure one at a time would enough of a challenge—at least at first.

"Dinner plans?" Olivia asked from the far side of Jenna.

Chloe swished her feet in the warm water. She could go for another bubble bath, but since the tub was in the middle of the suite, maybe that wouldn't be appropriate. "We could order in?"

"I brought cheese plate fixings," Olivia offered.

Done. "That's all we need."

And it was. Once their nails were painted a riotous rainbow of colours, they toddled back upstairs and flopped on the couches for a rest.

But soon enough, Olivia was back on her feet to make dinner. And when she returned to the living room, she looked quite proud of herself. "I will say, this has really set a high standard for our next girls' night."

Chloe cackled. Her high standards had definitely changed in the last year. It was five o'clock, for one thing. She'd bet they were all in bed and asleep before nine thirty, although there was no telling what sort of fun might happen once they busted into the bottle of sparkling peach juice Olivia had set out next to the most elaborate cheese plate Chloe had ever seen in her life.

On second thought, there was nothing wrong with this new standard.

"Cheese is a perfectly acceptable alternative to wine," she announced once they tucked in.

"Hear, hear," Olivia said, raising her glass in a salute.

As they settled in around the cheese plate, Chloe realized her phone was vibrating. By the time she found her purse, it had stopped. She frowned when she looked at the screen. "I've missed three calls."

"Tom?"

She shook her head. "416 area code. Someone from the city." Her eyes went wide. "Oh! The reporter." She quickly filled Jenna in on what had happened. Zander had warned her it might be days before she heard anything.

But on a Saturday night?

Holding up her finger to quiet her friends, she tapped the phone number to call it back.

"Hello?" A man's voice.

"This is Chloe Dawson. I missed a couple of calls from your number."

"Yes, Ms. Dawson, thanks for calling me back." There was a pause, and in that moment, Chloe remembered that Zander had said the reporter was a woman.

An uncomfortable feeling prickled the back of her neck.

When he spoke again, the discomfort grew, because he didn't introduce himself. "Is this a good time to talk?"

She chewed on the corner of her lower lip. Uh… "Sorry, I think I missed your name?"

"I'm calling in regards to library services in Bruce County. I understand you've spoken to a number of your colleagues because you are concerned about your position…"

He hadn't answered her question. And there was something very not right about how much this stranger knew about her life—and still was getting the details all wrong.

Heart pounding, she snapped her fingers to get Jenna's attention. *Can I use your phone to record this call?* she mouthed.

In her best Nancy Drew impression, her friend slide the phone across the table, already unlocked.

And there was a recording app right there.

Thank God.

"Sorry, I missed that," Chloe said as she held Jenna's phone next to her ear, hoping against hope that he'd say something useful. Her voice had a bit of a shake to it, but she got it under control. If this was a union busting move, she was going to nail this guy's ass to the wall. "Did you say you were from the library board?"

"I'm calling from Toronto. I work with the ministry."

"Okay. And what can I do for you?"

"You've been making a lot of noise, Ms. Dawson. But what you don't seem to understand is that the province is entering a period of austerity. Hard choices are going to need to be made, maybe ones that you don't understand. But the way you're running interference has to stop. I understand you are concerned about your job—"

"That's not it at all," she blurted out. She'd heard enough. She'd recorded enough. This man couldn't be trusted and she wouldn't entertain this nonsense a second longer. "I have only been concerned about the people who use our library. Which is a lot of people. We had a packed town hall meeting, but that was apparently all just for show, wasn't it? The decision has been made."

"You would be wise to focus on retaining your full-time position elsewhere in the county."

Her mouth dropped open, then she snapped it shut.

And ended the call.

"So that wasn't the reporter," she said slowly, her hands shaking. There was a solid chance she was going to throw up. She felt sick.

Jenna gave her a look of alarm. "Who was it?"

"Someone from the ministry. And honestly? I think he threatened me. Not personally. But he hinted ominously at my job situation. Oh my God."

Olivia came around to where she was standing and gently took Jenna's phone out of Chloe's hands. "Here," she said, handing it to their friend.

Jenna tapped on the screen, then again, and the recording played from the beginning.

"Sorry, I missed that. Did you say you were from the library board?"

"I'm calling from Toronto. I work with the ministry."

It was small and tinny, but it was there. The recording had worked.

She was definitely going to throw up. Eventually. First, though, she needed backup. "I have to call Zander."

She could feel her friends staring at her, wide-eyed, as she rang her brother-in-law. He answered on the first ring.

In the background she heard the loud whir of power tools. "Hang on a second," he said to her, then to Tom in the background, "It's Chloe. She loves me more than you."

"Never," she said with a shaky laugh. "Although right now, I need you more than him."

The background noise disappeared. "Okay, I'm outside. Your house looks great, by the way. But what can I do for you right now?"

She quickly ran down the conversation she just had.

"And then he told me that my job was on the line. Basically, if I want a full-time job, I'll need to move. So much for the promises of reduced hours. I would take a part-time job in a heartbeat over moving. It feels like blackmail, Zander."

"That's not okay," he growled. "You were right to call me. I want you to make clear notes of the call. Did anyone witness it?"

"Olivia and Jenna both heard my side of the conversation. And I, uh, recorded it on Jenna's phone."

He laughed out loud. "Genius. Good work."

"It felt scary, to be honest."

"That was the hardest part you'll have to do. Don't answer the phone again, got it? And next week, we'll contact an employment lawyer."

She made a small groan. "This is escalating way beyond anything I ever imagined."

"A lawyer will de-escalate it, and quickly. That was offside, absolutely not okay, and a mistake on the ministry's part. Repeat after me: you haven't done anything wrong."

"You haven't done anything wrong," she said cheekily.

"Chloe."

"You say that just like your brother." She sighed. "Okay. I haven't done anything wrong."

"Good. I'm going to head back inside and reassure Tom that everything is fine."

"Thanks."

"He'll probably call you himself in about ten minutes. He's holding up a piece of drywall right now or I'm sure he'd be tackling me for the phone."

"Tell him I really am fine," she said. She didn't feel it. But intellectually, she knew it was true.

When she ended the call, the suite was completely

quiet. She looked at her friends, and they looked right back.

"Well, that's a twist I didn't see coming," Olivia finally said.

That made two of them.

"Yeah."

"You would take a part-time job over moving for a full-time job?"

Chloe blinked. "What?"

"That's what you said to Zander."

"The whole whistleblowing thing, and *that's* the twist you didn't see coming?"

Olivia shrugged. "I like what I like. And I like you in Pine Harbour, so that's exciting and brand new information."

"It's not brand new," she protested. Was it? "I've always liked Pine Harbour."

Jenna snorted. "I think it's more of a hate-like."

"Sure, sometimes. But sometimes it's just a straight-like." Chloe frowned. "I haven't thought about leaving in months."

The way her friends' eyebrows hit the roof at the exact same time told Chloe she hadn't shared that fact with them.

Or anyone.

———

THEY HAD JUST FINISHED HANGING the last piece of drywall when Zander returned from outside.

Tom glared at him. "Library shit?"

"Do you kiss your woman with that mouth?"

He fought to keep the scowl at bay. "What's wrong?"

"Everything is fine. Chloe specifically told me to tell you that everything is fine, in fact."

"That hardly means anything is *fine*, and almost certainly means there's good reason for me to worry about her safety."

"Nancy Drew can take of herself," his brother said. "But you do need a lawyer because some asshole from Toronto threatened her job a little."

"What?" The hammer he was holding slipped, almost falling out of his grip before he caught it again. He shoved it into his tool belt. "Threatened her job how?"

"In the usual spineless way of making vague suggestions nobody can follow up on. It was a scare tactic, because someone has got it in their head that she's organizing shit up here."

"She's not."

"She should, though." Zander raised his eyebrows. "Yeah. I know she's pregnant, but she cares a lot about this. We could have her back while she made some real noise, if she wanted to."

"When did you turn into such a rebel?"

From the other side of the room, Rafe laughed. "When he left town on a motorcycle at seventeen?"

Good point.

Back then, Tom had thought his oldest brother was impossibly grown-up, and heading out to take on the world's promises.

Now he imagined his own kids joining the army at seventeen and—nope. Not okay. Fuck. "Listen, are you sure she's safe right now?"

"Yes. This is political posturing. Besides, she's in a secure hotel room, with friends, in a reservation made by you, not her. Nobody knows where she is. If some numpty was going to show up to threaten her to her face, they would come here. And you'd get to greet them with that hammer, and your brothers. But when she gets back, we'll find her a good lawyer to put a stop to this. Something has definitely gone wrong in the communications pipeline, and once that's brought to light, this will be resolved."

"I'm going to hold you to that."

"That's fair. Now, do you want to go give her a call before we start mudding and taping your new wall here?"

Tom scrubbed a hand over his face and nodded. Yeah. He needed to hear her voice and get all of that again, straight from the source.

CHAPTER TWENTY-ONE

AFTER SUNDAY BRUNCH, which they tried to make as light and leisurely as possible after the previous night's drama, Chloe and Jenna bid Olivia farewell and loaded James into his carseat.

"Full disclosure, once you're a parent, a lot of driving is scheduled around nap times," Jenna said.

Chloe didn't mind that idea at all. "Good to know."

"He'll sleep for at least an hour. But we can stop and do some shopping on the way home, if you want? I'm not allowed to return you until dinner time, but we can also go to my place and wait in closer proximity for the signal."

"Can we give Natasha a call and see if she wants visitors?"

"That's a great idea." And it would keep Chloe's mind off the week to come. The thought of returning to work filled her with dread.

When they arrived in Wiarton, Emily had a tea party set up for them. James woke up cranky, but Emily stepped in to play Very Grown-Up Teacher to him as soon as Jenna nursed him a bit, leaving the grown-ups to talk amongst themselves over their tea.

"She's really good with him," Natasha said. "That's nice to see."

"Were you worried?" Jenna asked.

"A little? It was just the two of us for so long, although she did have her cousins—but they were both older than her. She was my baby, my entire heart. It'll be weird to go from one to two, but she's excited."

Chloe was going to go from zero to two. Built-in sibling and playmate right from day one. And unlike Chloe's childhood, a ton of cousins. No matter what happened with the library, Chloe and Tom weren't going anywhere. She loved her little community, and would fight like hell for it.

They stayed at Natasha's until Matt called her and told her he was coming home.

"That's our cue to leave," Jenna said, picking up James, who looked at Emily and burst into tears. "I know, bubba. I know you love Emily. We'll come back soon for another visit with her delicious tea cups."

Emily held out one of the plastic mugs from her tea set. "He can take it with him if he wants."

Chloe's heart grew two sizes as Jenna took it and handed it to James, and Emily's eyes practically turned into emoji hearts for real.

"She's going to be a great big sister," she whispered to Natasha. "See you soon. I think I'll have a nice new space to host dinner in shortly!"

That was an understatement, it turned out.

From the outside, the cabin looked the same as when she left, although there were a bajillion tire tracks from trucks, now all departed except for Tom's.

But inside…she didn't even recognize it.

The living room was now open to the kitchen, making one huge great room space. "The wall is gone," she said dumbly. "You took out a wall?"

"Yeah." Tom grinned at her. "So we have room for a giant table here," he gestured to the empty space in the middle of the room. "And then—down the road—we can renovate those cabinets, maybe put in an island. That'll be Reno 2.0. But come look."

He led her through the kitchen to the anteroom—or what had been the anteroom before. Now it was a sweet little pantry, with nice hardwood floors that matched the kitchen, properly painted walls, a real window that over-looked the backyard, and the big ugly sink was gone. In its place was a new kitchen counter, with the dishwasher framed in underneath, and a small sink beside that, leaving tons of room for built-in shelves on the rest of that wall.

And on the counter was a brand-new coffeemaker, and a kettle, and in front of both of those were Tom's Thermos and Chloe's mug that she'd taken to the Vances' cottage.

"Oh, Tom," she breathed, trying hard not to cry. "I love it."

"That's not all," he said. "Ready for the finale?" She shook her head and he laughed, then pulled her in close. "Come here."

She kissed him, hungrily, with so much love it felt like it might burst right out of her.

When she'd restored herself with the taste of him, he led her to the other side of the cabin. To what used to be their bedroom, but was now a nursery for a prince and princess. It was painted butter yellow, with white

"So where is our stuff?" She knew the answer. If the

verandah wasn't the nursery, then it must be their new bedroom.

Tom held out his hand. "That's the finale I was talking about."

Her heart thumped like a marching band was in her chest as they walked past the bathroom, to the door at the end of the hall. Before she went away for the weekend, there had been a bean bag stretched across the bottom of the door to keep out the draft. Now, warm light shone from beneath it.

And when Tom swung it open, he revealed more than she'd ever imagined.

"I know we talked about putting the nursery in here," he said as she turned in a slow circle, taking it all in. "But this shares a wall with the bathroom, so here…" He moved around their bed and opened a door on the far side of the brand-new space. "We have our own bathroom. Well, the rough-in for one. We can finish that later."

Chloe zoomed over to him. Sure enough, there was a basin for a shower, space for a toilet, and the rough plumbing for a sink. "Holy shit," she breathed.

Then she turned around and took in her new bedroom from a whole other angle. White walls, exposed beams on the angled roof, and… She wiggled her toes on the new floor. "Is there heating under there?"

"Yep." Tom looked so freaking proud of himself.

As he should.

"How did you do this in three days?"

"Minimal sleep and Jake's entire crew." She wanted to protest, but Tom didn't even let her get started. "They're family. It's okay."

Oh, man. She couldn't hold the tears back, and Tom guided her to the bed, where they curled up together.

"It's so wonderful," she whispered. "And you know what? I had a similar realization about Olivia and Jenna and Natasha all being my family, and how we all need each other, too."

"Yeah?"

"I think I've always thought that I was alone in my experience of being alone, and that's just not true. I feel a bit silly now, but better late than never in figuring that out."

"You aren't silly."

"I came here a loner, and saw a big, sprawling family dynamic, and didn't realize it was just as much one big found family as it is two borne ones."

"Huh," Tom said. "Yeah. That's a good way to look at it, isn't it? Because it's true. Family is desperately important to all of us, because we only had each other growing up. My parents were working seven days a week. Jake's dad was lost in grief over losing his wife. For years. So we took care of each other. Dean, Jake, Matt and Sean are my brothers just as much as Zander or Rafe."

Chloe's heart ached for those little boys, who turned into the most wonderful of men, because they had each other. She squeezed Tom tighter, and hugged him until the babies wriggled and disturbed the cuddle.

Tom laughed and kissed her, then kissed her belly.

"Hey," she asked. "So...do you have a toolbelt?"

"Of course."

"Wanna show it to me?"

Tom's eyes lit up. "Why, Ms. Dawson, are you feeling frisky?"

"Very frisky. Very thankful. Very, very loving, Mr. Minelli." She cleared her throat. "But we take construction standards very seriously, in fact, so I'm going to need to inspect that tool belt, if you don't mind. Please put it on."

He scrambled off the bed. "Here?"

She crawled after him, settling on her knees. The warm floor was kind of nice. "I'll wait here, I think. Oh, and Tom?"

"Yeah?" He gave her the most eager smile. She loved it. She loved him.

"The tool belt is the only thing you need to wear when you return."

————

THE NEW-HOUSE JOY lasted twelve hours. It was replaced by shit-is-getting-real panic at six o'clock the next morning, when Chloe's phone started ringing.

She didn't recognize the first number, although it was local, not from the city. She was still shaking the sleep out of her head and deciding if it was smart to answer a strange call again when that number disappeared, and a moment later Zander's name popped up in a second call.

"You aren't the only one who was called this weekend," he said. "Your union rep is trying to get ahold of you."

"I just missed a call from someone."

Zander rattled off a number.

"Yeah, that's it."

"Give her a call back. She'll advise you on the next steps. My source says there are three of you, and it's not just this library board, either. Honestly? Someone might go to jail over this. It's time to lawyer up."

"I can't afford that," she whispered, panic gripping her fiercely.

"Your union will handle all of that. And if not, we'll take care of it. We're getting into whistleblower protection territory. You'll be deposed, and then lawyers from the union will take over."

"Holy shit."

"Keep breathing, Nancy Drew."

She hung up the call and threw herself into Tom's arms. Then she called her union rep, who sounded totally calm as she instructed Chloe to stay home. "I'm advising you not to go to work today. Call in sick. Then we'll find out what time a lawyer can meet with you, and we'll take it from there."

Chloe patted her belly. "Sorry, kiddos, but Mom's going to use you guys as an excuse." She got the part-time librarian to cover the shift, then pulled the blankets up over her head.

Tom crawled under the covers with her. "I'll stay home with you today."

"You don't have to."

"And yet I'm going to anyway."

She took a deep breath and nodded. "Thanks."

The next call came at lunch. Could she drive to Port Elgin and meet a lawyer at the union local's office? They went in Tom's truck, his Thermos full of coffee for them to share.

When they arrived, Chloe's union rep introduced her to the lawyer, a woman probably around Chloe's own age, with a strong handshake and a serious look in her eye.

"Come on in." She looked at Tom. "You can wait out here."

Inside the meeting room, the lawyer asked if the conversation could be recorded, and when Chloe agreed, read the date and time into a micro recorder.

"Tell me, in your own words, what happened on Saturday night."

Chloe went over it again, explaining about the call, the moment she realized she should record it, and then phone call to Zander afterward.

"That would be Zander Minelli, a private investigator?"

"Yes. He's my boyfriend's brother. He's ex-military," Chloe added, although that probably didn't matter. She felt like it helped, though. *He's a good guy.*

The lawyer scribbled a note, then looked up again. "You have faced an unacceptable harassment. That's our first concern, and hopefully that will be the focus of our grievance complaint. But I've been brought in to talk to you today because there might be a claim that you are a whistleblower."

"A whistleblower?"

"Someone who reveals government abuse."

"I know what a whistleblower is." Chloe's voice sounded faint to her own ears. "I don't think that applies to me."

"It may not, especially because there is a due process for that protection and so far, you haven't followed it."

"I didn't know I should." Chloe's head was spinning now. "What exactly is that *due process*? I ask because there's a reporter who wants to talk to me."

"That's not a good idea. If we're going to claim whistleblower protection, we need to keep this completely quiet for now. There's an internal process to follow, and if you don't comply with that process, you could be terminated for failing to live up to your duty of loyalty and fidelity to the public service."

"That's a mouthful."

"Have you, at any time in the last six months, spoken out against your employer?"

"In public?" She thought about the town hall. "No."

"Have you subverted the mission of your employer at any time?"

She made a face. "I don't think so. What are the limits on what I can tell you?"

"Be honest with me."

"I talked about the library closure with a good friend, who is also a community leader. We planned ways for the community to protest the closure."

"Tell me more about that."

"We organized a message campaign—as in, we all tried to stay focused on the same message—and we found an alternate location for the library to move to at a very low cost."

"All right. I need you to write down for me, to the best of your recollection, the dates of those conversations, and who you spoke to."

"I never criticized the library board."

"But you circulated a photo of two library employees."

"No." She sat up straighter and glanced at the door. "No, that wasn't me."

"Can you be more specific?"

Chloe went over the details of that lunch again. "I heard the conversation, and got alarmed. My boyfriend noticed my alarm, and he took the photo."

"Is he the person waiting outside?"

"Yes." Chloe swallowed hard. "Is he in trouble?"

———

TOM'S right knee was bouncing and he couldn't get it to

stop. He'd done enough investigations at his reserve unit —for chicken-shit stuff, mostly—to know that interviews always happened alone.

But damn it, he wanted to be in there with her.

When the door opened, he jumped up. It was the lawyer. "Tom?"

"Yes."

"Can we talk in that room over there, please?" She pointed across the hall.

"Sure."

He'd been on the receiving end of a few investigations as well. A bogus complaint about making recruits do too many push-ups in the gravel, a concern about improper storage of ammo. Everyone involved in an investigation had an angle, and anyone—witnesses, the subject of the query, even the investigator—would be best served by only answering the direct questions, honestly but as simply as possible.

That rule went out the window when it came to Chloe.

"Is everything okay?"

The lawyer didn't answer his question. "There is a photograph of being circulated of library staff. Are you familiar with it?"

"The one in the diner in Walkerton? Yes, I'm familiar with it. I took it."

"What caused you to take the photo?"

"The conversation. Chloe heard them talking, and I knew she wanted to confront them about it, but that wouldn't do her any good."

"What did you advise her to do?"

Tom wasn't sure where this line of questioning was going. "I told her to keep her head down and let someone else do the investigation."

"Someone else being your brother."

"Yes." He pulled out his phone and found the text message to Zander. "You can check my phone. Chloe was there, but she's *in* the photo. She couldn't have taken it. And then I sent it to my brother and asked him to find out more information."

The lawyer looked at his phone, made a note, then turned off her recorder.

She stood up, gave Tom a slow, careful look, then nodded. "That's a fine line," she said. Then she shrugged. "I like fine lines. They give me something to work with."

"Is that all?"

"For now." She led him back to the hall, then disappeared into the first room again. Five minutes later, Chloe appeared and gave him a wide-eyed look.

They didn't talk until they were safely back in the truck.

"So that was more intense than I expected," Chloe whispered.

Tom leaned over the console and hugged her. "It's going to be okay."

"She said I can go back to work tomorrow. Keep my head down, wait and see what happens." She let out a nervous laugh. "This is wild, Tom."

"It's been quite the rollercoaster since Christmas, hasn't it?"

"I'm ready to just…be…for a little bit. Enjoy the last part of my pregnancy before the babies demand eviction."

"We'll find a way to make that happen."

She shook her head. "No more Zander interventions." Her eyes went wide. "And nothing behind my back, either. I don't need plausible deniability, I need actual peace and quiet, okay?"

It was his turn to laugh. "I wouldn't do anything behind your back, but I like the way spy lingo slides off your tongue like that. Plausible deniability. That's hot."

"Reading all those thrillers has finally paid off." She looked out the window. "This is a tempest in a teapot, though. Right?"

He squeezed her knee. "Whatever it is, we'll handle it."

"I need this to be done soon. Summer will be here before we know it and then...chaos."

"The babies? That's going to be amazing. The good kind of chaos."

Chloe burst out laughing. "Sorry, that's mostly nerves responding."

He gave her a good-natured grin. "I may not have liked chaos in the past, but don't you worry. I'm going to learn to thrive right in the middle of it."

"Feel free to teach me some of that as you figure it out." She took a deep breath. "Can we go and find some ice cream now? Or maybe a cute baby animal to look at?"

He put the truck in gear. "I can deliver both of those, in fact."

———

IT TURNED out there were baby bears at Tom's provincial park.

"You're shitting me," Chloe said, her eyes feeling as wide as teacup saucers. She nibbled the ice cream sandwich he'd pilfered for her from the cafeteria. "Where?"

"A den on the north edge of the park."

"Can we go and play with them?" She was teasing. Obviously not, but a girl could dream.

Tom's lips twitched in amusement. "No. But we can

watch them on the super fun Bear Cam in the visitor centre."

"I guess I don't want to piss off a Mama Bear," she admitted as she followed him across the lobby and into the interactive exhibits part of the park's main building. They had the place to themselves, though, and there was a padded bench in front of the Bear Cam.

Tom sat down first, and she snuggled up against him.

"We need to be patient," he whispered.

"Okay," she whispered back. "And why are we whispering?"

"It adds to the ambience of bear watching."

"Love it." She slowly ate her ice cream sandwich and watched the screen with rapt attention. And her patience was rewarded at the exact same moment she finished her sweet treat. A dark brown bundle rolled onto the screen, then jumped up, testing a tree trunk. When stretched like that, it wasn't as rolly polly as she expected. "He's skinny."

"Food scarcity is a problem. We're monitoring them, don't worry. And they're growing."

"Good." As they watched, the other baby bear appeared, this one more tentative than their sibling. But apparently a better climber. It didn't take long to scamper up the tree, and for the first one to follow.

Chloe let out a happy sigh. "That was adorable."

"Come back tomorrow and watch them some more."

"I will. The bears are going to be my calming self-care strategy until this problem at work gets sorted out once and for all."

CHAPTER TWENTY-TWO

THE NEXT WEEK crawled by in a painful state of radio silence and tested patience. Chloe declined the interview with the reporter, and went to work, and kept her head down.

She also went and checked on the bears every single day. They looked skinny, and maybe it was her own impending Mama Bear status, but Chloe was concerned. She found out that Tom's co-worker Tia was in charge of tracking the bears' progress, and she pinned the other woman down in her office to voice her worry. "How do you know how much they're eating?"

Tia smiled, but kept typing. "We monitor them."

"They're not stepping on scales. How are you sure they're okay?"

"Do you really want to know?" Tia asked, pressing her lips together in amusement as she waited for the answer.

"Yes." Chloe gave her a fierce look. "Consider it a community connection thing. As one of the town librarians, I'm asking for more information—"

"We check their poop."

Chloe cocked her head to the side and gave a slow blink.

Tia shrugged, and grinned, and held her hands out to the side. "You asked."

"I did."

"And that's the answer."

"Tell me more." Yes, it was a touch TMI, but this was fascinating. And it was an excellent distraction from her troubles. "Their *poop*?"

"You can learn a lot from scat."

Actually, she knew that. Pregnancy and stress were doing a double-whammy on Chloe's memory. "That makes sense."

As Tia launched into a detailed explanation, Chloe started making a list of books she wanted to pull for a display for the children's section. Even though it was a distraction, she was going to make this work related after all.

When they finished talking about baby bear poop, Tia leaned forward and propped her elbows on the desk. "We should collaborate on something about this. Take advantage of the park being so close to town. Cross promote the Bear Cam with a library display, maybe get a scavenger hunt going or something like that."

They should.

They really, really should. Chloe straightened up. "Let's do that. Tomorrow. I have to run back to work right now." She stood up, then turned and pointed at Tia. "You are a freaking genius, you know that?"

"What did I say?"

"We need to take advantage of the park being so close to town," Chloe yelled back over her shoulder.

There was a problem with the way the library's patron

count was being measured—and a way to lift those numbers even more in the future. It had been in front of Chloe all this time.

————

TOM WAS HAVING a drink with Sean and Owen at the Legion when Chloe and Olivia arrived, both of them out of breath and pink-cheeked. Olivia had Sophia with her, and his niece immediately climbed into his lap and started babbling at him about the car ride they just went on.

"You're just the man I wanted to see," Chloe declared as she skidded to a stop in front of them. Tom was half way out of his chair before she waved him off. "Not you, my beloved park ranger, although yes you, in a minute. But first—Owen."

"Me?" The firefighter pointed to his own chest.

She pointed her perfect sharpest-sunshine-beam ever smile at him. "You."

"We're chopped liver," Sean said under his breath.

Tom was fine with that for the moment. He liked the gleam in her eye. Chloe had a plan, he could tell, and after the rough week she'd had, a plan was just what she needed.

"The space you indicated the library could possibly move into in the emergency services building—is that the same set of rooms that the open house was in when it opened? With the food drive?"

"Yep." Owen shrugged. "We don't use them nearly enough, and what we did use them for, we could move into the ambulance bay the few times a year we have those events."

"Which is very smart thinking on your part. But also,

did you consider the fact that you got major community engagement for that open house? How many people did you get through there?"

"More than a thousand over the two days."

"That's more than the population of Pine Harbour," she exclaimed. "Right?"

"Right."

She pivoted to Tom, who was already hooked on the plan and he didn't even know where she was going with this. "And you. Do you know what percentage of visitors to the park are county residents versus day trippers from the city versus people on vacation from further afield?"

"We don't track that all the time, but we did take postal codes last year for a test pilot on that data."

She pumped her fists in the air. "I knew it! By the way, you should give Tia a raise, she's very good at her job."

"I'm not really in charge of raises and we're paid on a grid, but—" *Not the point, Minelli.* "What did Tia do?"

Chloe leaned in, her belly swaying as she planted her hands on the table and set her jaw firmly. "She suggested we do a cross-promoted educational partnership around the Bear Cam, and a library display about local animals. For the kids."

"That's a good idea."

"It's a *great* idea. And more to the point, we don't do enough of that. You know what I think? I think our public services are way too silo-ed, and that's made us all vulnerable. First it's the library, but next it'll be the parks, and then it'll be emergency services. But it's harder to take funding away from one if the projects are tightly interwoven. Or at least, that's my new plan."

Tom got up on the other side of the table, planted his own fists right in front of hers, and leaned in to kiss her.

"That's a great fucking plan," he whispered against her mouth. "I love you."

"It may not work in time." This close, he could tell she was shaking. She was scared. But after a week of holding stock still because a lawyer told her too, she was fighting again. So she was scared but she was excited, too.

And Tom loved her with all of his heart.

He wanted it to work for her—and for their town.

Another week went by before she heard back from the union. She wouldn't need to file for whistleblower protection—she wasn't a great candidate for that anyway, being a mouthy hothead—because someone else at the ministry had done it. And there were tapes that made the one Chloe had made look tame.

"I'm glad I've ended up on the periphery of all of this. Is that a cop out?" Chloe asked him as they sat together, curled up on the couch late one night.

His hand was curled around her belly, waiting for the babies to kick. "It's asking a lot for you to anticipate that a personal work kerfuffle will turn into a provincial political drama, and act accordingly from the outset."

"I would have made a really shitty whistleblower."

"But you make a fierce and mighty local librarian, which is what this town needs." He kissed her temple, then her cheek, and then her mouth, slow and sweet. "And don't discount your role in all of this. It doesn't matter that you weren't the big Kahuna. You were a part of the process."

One of a hundred little pieces of protest and better ideas coming from all around the province, turning into a groundswell of relentless messaging to the government: re-think this budget freeze. Re-think these cuts.

And they had.

"I'm proud of you," Tom whispered as Chloe crawled on top of him.

She caught his lower lip between her teeth, nipping him before she gave him a look of pure bliss. "That's all that matters, then."

CHAPTER TWENTY-THREE

SPRING TOOK its time on the peninsula, which Tom appreciated. Every week, Chloe's belly grew a little more. With the library upheaval finally resolved, she was able to focus on planning for the transition to the new space in the emergency services building—and take some of the vacation time she had banked to make a few extra long weekends.

Most of those were spent at home, cocooning together in their new and improved digs. It was a glorious honeymoon of sorts.

But by the last week of June, the temperature started to soar, summer finally arriving with a vengeance. Tom installed a ceiling fan in their bedroom, but Chloe still struggled to be comfortable. It didn't help that her belly now had its own centre of gravity, and rolling over in bed required an Olympic effort—her words, not his, although he would give her a gold medal in baby making if he had the power.

He'd also make the summer heat go away if he had that ability.

"There is a real and present danger that I may strip down to nothing at the picnic," Chloe announced as she stood in front of the closet. "It's too hot for clothes."

Tom was not complaining about her refusal to get dressed. If his pregnant partner wanted to run around in a pair of panties and a crop tank top, he and his dick both agreed that was a spectacular plan.

Their friends and family might not agree when they arrived at the annual Pine Harbour Canada Day celebration, but what the fuck did they know?

"We could stay home." But it was hot here, too.

She made a noncommittal noise. "We should go."

They really didn't need to. "Do you *want* to go?"

"Sort of. It might be the last big party before the babies arrive."

That was true. "You can put your feet up and have some lemonade."

"That makes me sound like a little old lady," she protested. "But yes, and I will." She finally settled on a lightweight red wrap dress and sprawled out on the bed beside him, still in her underwear.

The dress lay beside her, scrunched in her fist.

"What's wrong?" he murmured as he stroked her cheek.

She sighed. "I miss my body. I miss sex. We had some amazing sex, once upon a time."

The last time was two weeks earlier, but Tom wasn't about to argue with her. That was clearly a lifetime ago, and a travesty. There had been a good run there where they'd been intimate almost every day, but she hadn't been up for it, or anything else, in the last little while. "We can have sex right now."

"Not the kind of sex I want to have."

"Come on, you gorgeous prickly pear. Try me. I'm strong."

"What does that mean?"

"It means, despite your big, sexy belly, if you want me to hold you over my head, Dirty Dancing style, I can do that."

"You wouldn't let me soar over your head," she pouted. "You'd think it was dangerous."

It would be dangerous.

But he tamped that down. "Whatever you want. I want to make the next month all about you, because when these babies arrive, it's going to be hard work."

"You're really selling this whole experience. How about I stay pregnant forever?"

His fingers trailed over her breasts. "Okay."

She burst into tears.

Fuck. "No, Chloe, I'm sorry."

She laughed. Through tears. "Me too. I don't know why I'm so weepy today."

"Maybe it's a full moon."

"Maybe."

But it wasn't, and Tom couldn't help but worry that this was the start of a whole new level of pregnancy hormones.

"Lemonade?" She whispered it, a tiny little plea, and he nodded.

"Unlimited lemonade, just for you. I'll kill anyone who tries to get in your way."

"Seems excessive."

"I'm in an excessive mood, apparently."

"That makes two of us." She giggled and wiped her eyes. "Damn it. Okay. Help me up, and then I'll put on this dress and fix my face."

———

THE PICNIC PLANNERS had outdone themselves. The lemonade stand was one of the first tables on the way in from the parking lot, and there were misting stations set up to cool everyone down.

Once she had her travel mug filled and she'd taken a slow stroll through two of the misting stations, Chloe had to admit she was in heaven. "I take back all my crankiness from earlier, with the qualifier that it may return at any moment."

"That is absolutely your right," Tom said. "Are you interested in any food?"

She made a face. "Nope."

"Face painting?"

She shook her head and did a search for her friends. "I want shade and a good gossip session, probably."

"We can arrange that."

They found Matt, Natasha, and Emily first. Like Chloe, Natasha was ready to pop. "Any day now," she said. "How about you?"

"Another few weeks." Chloe rocked back and forth on her feet. The short walk around the park had tightened up her legs, and her back, and she was desperate to sit now. "I'm napping a lot."

"Same. Where did you get the lemonade?"

"Towards the parking lot." Chloe pointed.

Tom gestured to Matt. "I can show you where it is?"

While the guys went back for lemonade, Chloe joined Natasha on some folding camp chairs they'd set up under a tree. They caught up on non-pregnancy chatter for a while, but after the guys returned with lemonade, Emily wanted her mom to go and get matching face painting together.

"Up we go," Natasha groaned as Matt helped her stand.

Chloe couldn't imagine chasing a preschooler around right now. "Have fun," she called out.

As soon as Natasha departed, Jenna arrived, pushing James in a stroller. She held her fingers to her lips. *He's napping*, she mouthed.

Chloe gave her a thumbs up.

Tom leaned in and whispered to Chloe that he wanted to catch up with Ryan Howard, who was manning a booth about the kids' ice hockey program. She nodded, and after he left, enjoyed the silence while Jenna rocked the stroller back and forth, until James was finally out enough that his mother felt confident sitting down.

"How's it going?" Jenna asked.

Chloe blew a silent raspberry. "Crazy rollercoaster of emotions, that's how it going. One minute I'm over-the-moon excited about lemonade, the next I'm grumpy about… literally anything. I couldn't decide what to wear this morning, and then I burst into tears about sex. Sorry if that's TMI."

Jenna laughed. "It's fine."

"And before we came here, I seriously thought about doing the whole Marie Kondo thing on my wardrobe."

"Don't throw out clothes now. You might want them again in a few months."

"Nothing will ever fit me again. I'm Muumuu Girl for life now."

"Don't diss the muumuu." Jenna gestured at her own flowing tunic. "Comfort rules."

"You look cute. I look like—"

"A gorgeous pregnant woman, stop it."

"Sorry." She shifted in place as her butt tightened up again. "And apparently I can't even go for a walk without my body protesting."

"Hip pain?"

"No, more like a sore back."

"What kind of soreness?"

"Nothing major. Just a dull ache. It comes and goes."

Jenna nodded. "Tell me when it stops, okay?" She pulled out her phone.

"Why?"

"No reason." Jenna tapped on her phone with quick fingers.

"What are you doing?"

"Just texting your husband to get his butt over here in case we need to go to the hospital. Keep drinking your lemonade."

Chloe squeaked. "Jenna!"

"Mmm?" Her friend kept typing.

"That's a long message."

"Now I'm texting Sean and telling him to come fetch his child in case I need to go with you to the hospital. Kerry's off this weekend and I'm covering for her."

"I don't think I'm in labour." Chloe shifted. "I'm telling you, it's just a dull ache. It's nothing like labour."

"What is it like?"

"Cramps." She rolled her eyes. "Okay, that makes it sound like labour. But it's really..." Taking a deep breath, which was hard with the distracting ache across her lower back, she waved her hands.

"Still going?"

She rolled her neck. "Mmm."

"Let's go for a walk. See if that stops them."

She carefully pushed herself to a standing position and grabbed her lemonade. This would be a civilized stroll.

They were around the ice cream stand when Tom appeared from the aging community centre building. Now he was jogging toward her, looking casual until he was up close. Then she saw his face was drained of colour.

"Hey," he said, his eyes wide, as he stopped in front of her. "What's going on?"

She made a face. "Jenna thinks I'm in labour."

"What do you think?"

"I think Jenna's a bitch."

Her friend chuckled.

"It's not funny," Chloe protested. "You're very mean for ruining my Canada Day lemonade celebration like this."

"I'm super sorry," Jenna said. "And it may be nothing."

It had been almost five minutes since the last contraction. Correction, back ache. But just as that rebellious thought snapped through her head, her womb tightened up again. She winced. "It's back."

Jenna nodded and tapped her phone screen again. "Keep walking. Tom, do you guys have a hospital bag packed?"

"Sort of. We started."

"Can Olivia maybe finish that for you? Bring it later? Is there anything you definitely wanted to have with you during labour?"

Chloe shook her head. "I have a playlist of songs I want to listen to on my phone. That's it. We're pretty flexible."

"Good. Flexible is great. How's that contraction doing?"

"It's not a—" Chloe's hand tightened hard around

Tom's fingers as the worst of it peaked, then faded away. Oh God. There was no avoiding this. "Fine," she muttered. "But I want some lemonade for the road."

"Deal. I'm going to follow you in my car. You can't speed. This is not that kind of emergency. But we are going to go straight to the hospital in Owen Sound."

"Owen Sound? Not Walkerton?" Chloe looked back and forth between Jenna and Tom in confusion, but then it dawned on her. Walkerton had a birth centre, with lovely labour rooms. But Owen Sound—the bigger city—had the intensive care nursery. There would be no nice, small community hospital delivery for her if the babies came today.

Tom nodded tightly.

As long as the babies were okay, that's all that mattered.

Another contraction started as they headed for the truck. She could walk through it. Maybe Jenna was wrong —and Chloe knew her friend would be happy to be wrong here—but this time the contraction slowed her down, and kept going.

When it ended, after she was buckled into the passenger seat, she was sure her friend *wasn't* wrong.

The babies were on their way whether she was ready or not.

CHAPTER TWENTY-FOUR

THIS WASN'T how any of this was supposed to go. Chloe
needed a bit more time to prepare—but that wasn't going
to happen. She'd run out of time. She had a playlist of
songs to listen to, and that was it.

She hadn't even had a baby shower yet. Sean and Jenna
were having a barbecue for them the following weekend.
Her mom was even going to drive up for it.

Oh, shit. She fumbled for her phone. Tom glanced at
her from the driver's seat as she dialled her mother's
number.

"Hey, Mom," she said when it went to voice mail. "I'm
going to text you, too, but I'm in labour. Don't freak out.
We're on the way to the hospital. Tom will update you in a
bit. Love you."

Then she typed out a text message that said basically
the same thing.

She thought about texting her father, but he could wait
to get a birth announcement. It wasn't like he'd been
excited when she'd told him she was pregnant, either.

"Do you want me to call my parents?" Tom asked.

She made a face.

"I'll update them later," he said wryly. "That's the last thing you need right now."

He always knew.

How had she ever thought she could run away from this man? Not that she'd run far.

Something had happened when she found out she was pregnant. She'd realized that her life had changed the moment she met him. She'd even thought about it like that, how her decision making was neatly cleaved into Before Tom and After Tom priorities.

Deep down, even when she'd been terrified of commitment and gripped in the worst of her fear of rejection, she'd known he was the one.

There had been a time when she'd fooled herself into thinking that The Age of Tom was a fleeting joy, that she couldn't enjoy it too much, couldn't get too attached. Not anymore. She loved him so much, and she wanted The Age of Tom to last forever.

"We have to go home," she said suddenly. "I need the hospital bag."

"Olivia will bring it." Tom reached over and squeezed her hand. "It's okay."

"It's not." Panic swelled inside her. "Tom, I need—" A contraction cut her off, and this one was different. This one felt sharper, longer, harder to breathe through.

She made a high-pitched whining sound—oh *God*, she couldn't sound like that for the next however long this would take, could she?—and then doubled over as much as one could when one was stuffed with two watermelons trying to escape one's body.

"Deep breaths," Tom said.

She wanted to shove his lungs into his throat and see

how well he breathed deeply then. *Fuck*. As soon as that contraction ended, she had the terrifying thought that another was right around the corner. "Tom, I think something's happening."

"We're almost there."

"I'm not having these babies in your truck." She groaned, and that felt better than the whine. She did it again, a growly low noise that didn't spin her head as much, and shoved her hands as hard as she could against the dashboard of the truck. "Feel free to speed," she spit out between clenched teeth.

"Jenna said—"

"Jenna's not in my fucking uterus right now."

He floored it.

When they arrived, Tom let Chloe out at the front door of the hospital. She found a bench to lean back against, to push her hips into as the contractions racked her body.

"Chloe?"

She blinked as Kerry appeared in front of her. "I thought it was your weekend off."

"It is, but I've gotten enough sleep, and I didn't have anything else to do."

"No hot dates?"

A cloud crossed Kerry's normally sunny face. "Nope."

"Sorry."

"It's okay. Let's get you inside. I wouldn't miss this for the world."

They took the elevator, which had a railing at the right height to push her hips against. She groaned through the contraction, which lasted longer than the elevator ride. Kerry held the door and waited for Chloe to catch her breath before they moved into the waiting room for Labour and Delivery.

"Why do my hips hurt so much?"

"The babies are rearranging everything a bit."

"That's terrifying."

Kerry chuckled, then gave their names to the clerk at the desk, who told her a room number. Tom sprinted out of the stairwell just as Kerry pointed down the hall. Jenna was right behind him.

"Perfect timing," Kerry said. She told Jenna the room number, then disappeared.

When she found them in the room, Chloe had changed into a hospital gown and was leaning over the hospital bed, trying to find a comfortable position.

"This is Betsy, your RN extraordinaire," Kerry said, introducing an older woman in scrubs as they both scrubbed in. "The OB team is going to pop in to say hi, and you'll meet the paediatrician who is going to check the twins as soon as they come out. It's a baby party."

Tom chuckled, but Chloe was too overwhelmed with what was rapidly—and disturbingly—happening to her body. Maybe she nodded. Maybe Kerry just picked up on the fact that now was not going to be a talking time.

Either way, the midwife came around the hospital bed and gently touched her elbow to Chloe's shoulder. "I'm going to quickly check your progress, okay?"

She grunted in reply. Sure. What the heck. She climbed up onto the bed, settling on her side, and closed her eyes.

Another contraction seized her body, and Kerry waited until it ended, then guided Chloe's top leg up. "You're progressing quickly," she announced after what was indeed a quick internal exam. "You're already at six centimetres and one of the babies is doing their job nicely. Do you want to wait for the amniotic sac to rupture on its own, or do you want me to help it along? The contractions are going to—" Kerry paused, and Chloe felt it.

A wet, messy pop.

"Well, that answers that question," Jenna said brightly. "Your water just broke."

The next contraction roared down upon her, and suddenly everything was too much. The lights, the talking, Chloe squeezed her eyes shut and buried her face in her hands. She heard Jenna and Kerry in the distance talking about the lights, turning those off. A couple of doctors came in and were introduced to her, then they took a quick bedside ultrasound to make sure the twins were in a good position.

Chloe kept her eyes shut the entire time, her entire world narrowing to the overwhelming waves of movement inside her body. She vaguely registered it as pain, as something she didn't want to experience again, *oh my God*, but there was another sensation, too. One of intense power and adrenaline, like she was spiked full of the good stuff.

Tom would know what it was called, but she couldn't find the words to ask him.

He was behind her, rubbing her back. She should roll over, or tell him to come around. They had so much to talk about still.

But it was too late for that. It was too late for so much. She hadn't prepared nearly enough. She wasn't ready for any of this, and it was happening to her whether she liked it or not.

She was checked twice more by Kerry, and the last time, her midwife told her it was time to start pushing.

Jenna rolled up a stool to sit next to the bed. The paediatrician was summoned by Betsy, the RN extraordinaire.

Tom helped Chloe up, then crawled up onto the bed to sit behind her.

She leaned back against him, grateful for his warm, solid support.

He kissed her sweat-slicked temple. "You can do this, my beautiful prickly pear."

"That nickname is not allowed to stick," she panted.

"Of course not. Push back against me."

"I don't want to. If I do that, one of them is going to come out, and I'm not ready to become a mom."

"But they're ready to meet you, babe."

A sob ripped from her, and she pushed back into Tom's chest as she bent her head low, focusing all of her energy on the babies deep in her pelvis. Or maybe only one of them was. She couldn't picture their descent, and it didn't matter. She wasn't in control of this anymore, if she'd ever been.

They were coming.

Her babies.

She was going to meet them in the very near future, and they needed her to get her shit together.

"No…" she whispered as another contraction took over. *Yes.*

Kerry and Jenna gave her encouragement and guidance as she bore down, again and again. It didn't feel like she was making any progress; the contractions were still the same, still intense and overwhelming and wild and otherworldly.

But then Kerry beamed at her. "One more for the shoulders," she said.

The shoulders? "Wait, what?"

Tom squeezed her. "The head is out."

Good Lord. Chloe trembled.

"Wait for the next contraction," Jenna said.

Chloe laughed. Like any of this was in her control. Wait? Stop? Her body was just doing its thing on its own. She'd birthed part of a baby and hadn't even noticed.

The next contraction roared in, tearing down her spine and spiralling toward the ring of fire between her legs. And then there was a baby in Kerry's hands, a wriggly, tiny mess of a thing. Blue and slimy.

"It's a girl," Kerry said, delivering the wee thing to Chloe's chest with Jenna's help. On the other side, a doctor appeared with a flannel blanket and covered the baby, rubbing her back vigorously.

Chloe was transfixed. Her daughter. "Come on," she whispered, tears sliding down her face. "Let me hear you."

It took forever, but then her baby girl squeaked, and stretched, and Chloe's heart exploded with love. She didn't even notice the next two contractions. Kerry was still between her legs, Betsy helping her, but all Chloe could see was her little girl being worked on right on top of the belly where she'd just slid out of.

Behind her, Tom cleared his throat. Twice. "She's beautiful," he whispered.

Jenna handed him a tissue. "We're going to take her to the warming table for a minute and do her APGAR tests while her brother arrives."

Chloe nodded.

Tom was pinned behind her, and now she regretted that. She wanted him to follow their baby girl and hover over her, but they could still see her. She was just across the room. *Too far*. Chloe's first irrational moment of mom fear, she realized with a jolt. Laughing, she took a deep breath as the next contraction started.

Kerry grinned at her. "You ready for another one?"

Chloe nodded and exhaled, channeling all of her newfound superhuman strength into delivering her baby boy in a single push.

"Whoa whoa," Kerry said, but it was done. He was out, Chloe could feel it, and she reached for him, taking him from Kerry's hands. This time it was Jenna who appeared with the warm flannel blanket. Their daughter was still with the paediatrician.

"Everything okay?" Chloe asked nervously.

Jenna nodded. "She's perfect."

The brand-new brother let out a loud, protesting yell and Tom laughed. "He already objects to his sister's marks."

"This one is perfect too," Chloe said, cuddling her son close to her skin.

They gave her a few minutes with him, then he too was whisked to the warm lights on the far side of the room. At all times, someone was with each of the babies. As their little boy had a full check over with the doc, Jenna bundled up their daughter and brought her back. Tom carefully extricated himself from behind Chloe as Kerry explained the last stage of delivery, and what would happen next.

Because the babies were early, they'd go to advanced care nursery for a few hours. Tom could go with them, see them get settled with specialized nurses to watch them for the night, and then Chloe could go over and visit them as soon as she was sorted out.

"How long will they have to stay in the NICU?" Tom asked.

Fear gripped Chloe's chest as the doc and Jenna traded glances.

"That depends on how they do overnight," the paediatrician said. "But they're both breathing well on their own, and that's a great sign."

Chloe got another cuddle with Baby Girl Minelli, the official name on the ID anklet Jenna attached to her before she was handed to Tom. Then she repeated the cuddle with Baby Boy Minelli before Jenna carried him, leading the way out the doors.

"They're going to be in very good hands," Kerry said reassuringly. "Let's get you cleaned up now. And how does a bath sound?"

"Glorious," Chloe said, her head and heart both swirling with too many feelings to properly count.

Over the next hour, Betsy and Kerry helped her bathe, then get dressed with the fabled mesh underpants and a maxi pad the size of the Bruce Peninsula securely stuffed between her legs.

"Here's your bag," Kerry said.

"When did that arrive?"

"Olivia dropped it off a few hours ago."

"I didn't see her." Chloe marvelled at how intense and inwardly focused her labour had been.

"She's still here," Kerry said. "If you want a visitor? She's in the waiting room with a few other people."

Chloe pulled on a pair of yoga pants and a t-shirt, then tested her legs. "Can I go for a walk?"

"You sure can."

They went to the nursery first, where Tom was sitting next to a clear plastic box. Their babies were curled up together inside it, fast asleep, wearing nothing but diapers. Kerry went to talk to the nurse, giving Chloe a bit of privacy with Tom.

"Hey," she whispered.

He pulled her in close, his arms shaking. "You did so good, babe. So, so good."

She sank into his embrace. "They're going to be okay." A statement. A prayer. A promise.

"The wires freak me out, but Jenna promises they're just monitors." He pointed at the world's tiniest sticky pads on the babies' chests, attached to leads that ran out of the box. "And it's really warm in there. I asked if we should get their sleepers, but the nurse says they probably won't fit yet."

Chloe realized with a start she hadn't even thought about clothes for them. "Yeah," she said, dazed. Her eyes focused in on the cards on the side of the incubator. Baby Girl Minelli. 4 lbs 1 oz. Baby Boy Minelli. 4 lbs 6 oz. "They're too small for the stuff we bought. I think the newborn clothes are for seven pounds and up."

"Diapers and blankets work," he murmured. "At least it's not winter."

She laughed weakly. "Good point."

"You should sleep while they're sleeping." He stood up. "Let's go have a nap."

"Kerry said Olivia is in the waiting room." Chloe left off the rest of it. She wanted Tom to be surprised.

He gave her a slow smile. "Okay. Let's go say hi. But then back to bed for you."

"Deal." She stopped and looked at the babies. "We should name them."

They hadn't talked about names since their time at the Vances' cabin. There had been too much going on. But Tom remembered that conversation. "We'd talked about Mabel."

She smiled, remembering the rest of it. "Mabel and Hank."

"Hank? Or maybe Mabel and Henry?" Tom's brow lifted in a genuine question. Did she want to pick a different name?

No. "Hank," she whispered. "That's it."

The grin that sliced across his tired but happy face was totally worth it. For the rest of Hank's life, she'd been telling him this story.

I love how happy he looks, she thought to herself. *How completely happy he is.*

"Those are the names," Chloe breathed. "We should tell the nurse."

Tom nodded. "Those are our babies' names."

"Wow." As she watched, Mabel stirred. A tiny mouth, opened all the way wide. A yawn that cracked open Chloe's chest and dragged the love right out of her.

Then her daughter settled again, curled right up against her brother. Above them both, the machines beeped reassuringly. Steady heartbeats. Good respiratory levels. It was okay to leave them with Kerry and the nurse.

It would have to be okay, at least for the night.

"We'll come back after a nap," Tom said, wrapping his fingers around hers.

She nodded quietly and let him lead her out of the nursery.

The noise from the waiting room gave the surprise away. There was enough of a din that Tom knew half the population of Pine Harbour had followed them to Owen Sound before he stepped through the door. And yet his face still lit up again. Not quite as big a smile as when she told him his son's name was Hank, but close.

His brothers—blood and friendship borne alike—surrounded him and clapped him on the back, dragging him in for hugs. And then, one by one, they swept her gently into their arms for reassuring squeezes, too.

Their little family of four was loved by many.

Chloe herself felt loved, too—by many.

"This is incredible," she whispered through tears to Olivia.

"You're incredible," her friend and sister-in-law said back. "You carried two Minellis inside you at once, *and* you saved the library while incubating those babies. You're a freaking rockstar."

Normally Chloe would protest. Except she had, and she was. "Two very wonderful reasons to fight the good fight," she murmured, watching Tom across the room. She would do anything for him. Have his babies, fight for his town. Her town, too.

Next to hug her was Faith, then Tom's mother. Anne's embrace wasn't as tight as the younger women, but it was nice. And sometimes, nice was a lot.

It didn't take long for Tom to circle back to her and wrap her in a protective arm. "We'll keep you all posted on the babies' progress," he said. "Now go home. Please."

Everyone laughed, but Chloe knew Tom was serious. They needed some space here to deal with what would come next.

They'd been tossed into the deep end on the whole parenting front. Time to start swimming.

CHAPTER TWENTY-FIVE

THE NEXT TWELVE hours were a crash course in parenting. The hospital loaned Chloe a breast pump so she could start expressing milk for the twins. Tom figured out quickly that she could be away from them for about two hours before panic would set in—and trying to delay her didn't work. So they slept in ninety-minute bursts, and took the pump with them to the nursery so she could do that at the same time as she visited with their kids—all eight pounds of them combined.

They hadn't seemed that small when they were born, but now he would swear they would fit in the palms of his hands. "Are they shrinking?" he asked the the nurse, joking.

"Yep," she said.

Chloe squeaked in nervous panic. "Excuse me?"

"They come out a little extra plump. It's normal for babies to lose a few ounces before they start eating. The IV helps a bit, don't worry. And after the docs do the rounds, we can decide how we're going to introduce nutrition for them."

Nutrition. It all sounded so clinical.

He'd read about premature birth in the books. But it hadn't sunk in that that would be their parenting experience. Maybe he couldn't let his mind go there, but now it was their reality. If they went home without the babies, he'd read everything again.

He wasn't sure how he'd get Chloe to leave them behind, though. It was hard enough for her to be in a different part of the hospital. So he held his breath when the medical team came around and reviewed the charts hanging at the end of the babies' plastic bed.

"They're both breathing well. Let's see if they can eat without tiring and see how that goes."

Chloe's eyes lit up, and the nurse held up a hand in caution. "This is often a one step forward, two steps back type of thing. It's normal to be frustrated. We'll give them each twenty minutes, and weigh them pre and post feed to see how they do. Got it?"

"Got it," Chloe promised.

"We'll wait for them to cue that they're hungry." It took half an hour, but then Hank woke up, his little mouth opening wide before his eyes even fluttered, his head twisting this way and that. "That's what we're looking for," the nurse added, opening the side of the incubator. "Out you come, big guy."

Tom watched in alarm as goosebumps raced over his son's skin. "Should I get a blanket for him?"

"Nope, the cool air will help wake him up more, and feeding will warm him from the inside. It's okay." The nurse settled Hank on the pillow and showed Chloe how to hold him, switching her hands around to try different positions.

Tom would never forget the look of surprise on Chloe's face, wide eyes softening to wonder, as Hank latched on.

"Oh, wow," she said, stroking his bald little head. "Hey, buddy. You're good at that."

Tom jerked his head to the hallway. "I'm going to duck out and call your mom, give her the happy update, okay?"

As Tom paced in the hall, waiting for Chloe's mother to pick up the phone, he saw a familiar face get off the elevator. Owen Kincaid, and with him was his heavily pregnant daughter, Becca. Owen looked tired, but Becca looked relaxed, happy.

Tom raised his hand and waved at them both.

Owen nodded, but before Tom could say anything to him, Chloe's mom answered the call. "Hello?"

"It's Tom. Hi. Just calling with the morning baby update. They made it through the night like champs…"

She had questions about Chloe, and the doctors, and by the time Tom answered all of them a few times over, Owen was gone from the waiting room.

Back in the nursery, Chloe was burping a sleepy Hank. "He didn't nurse for a full twenty minutes, but he did okay. I think. We'll see if he gained anything."

The nurse held out her hands. "Your milk won't come in for another day or two, so it's not a concern if he hasn't."

But Tom's kid *had* gained some weight. A few millilitres, a minuscule amount, but the number went up. It was a win.

Mabel wasn't as cooperative, which frustrated Chloe. "We'll try again in three hours," the nurse said. "And keep pumping. We can always try a bottle, sometimes that's easier for preemies."

Chloe nodded, but as soon as they back in her hospital room and alone, she burst into frustrated tears.

That set the routine for the next two days. Brave faces in the nursery, nodding along as the docs and nurses promised the babies were making great progress. Private tears and whispered fears.

And then, on the third morning of being parents, after Tom's third night sleeping on the world's smallest couch next to Chloe's hospital bed, they woke up to Kerry delivering Chloe's discharge papers. "I can't keep you here any longer," she said apologetically. "And you'll sleep better in your own bed, I promise."

Chloe's mouth pulled tight, but she nodded. "Okay."

They packed up, then went over to the nursery. "I've been discharged," Chloe said to the nurse. "How long can we stay here before you'll kick us out?"

The nurse held up a large brown envelope. "You don't need to stay here at all. You can take the babies home with you, if you have their car seats ready."

Tom wanted to jump in the air and pump his fist, but it seemed inappropriate for the setting. "I'll get the car seats from my truck."

Rafe and Olivia had brought them in the day before and helped him install them in the back seat. Now he unclipped the buckets from their bases, nerves rioting inside him as he thought about maybe bringing the twins back down in an hour or two and taking them home.

But first there were hurdles to cross. Both babies needed to be monitored in the car seats to make sure they didn't have any problems with breathing in the new-to-them position. Chloe and Tom had to be taught how to use receiving blankets and washcloths to pad around their babies, holding them in place in the still-too-big-for-them buckets.

And Mabel needed to drink a full ounce of milk from a bottle.

"Your midwives will follow you closely at home to make sure she's eating and gaining," the nurse said as Chloe focused on feeding their daughter, who was determined to go to sleep instead of eating. "And you'll bring them in to see the paediatrician in the clinic once a week as well."

Tom would do anything it took to have the babies home with Chloe. He nodded eagerly.

Chloe, though, was quiet. Focused. When the bottle was empty, she carefully lifted Mabel to her shoulder. "I don't want her to throw up," she whispered.

Tom held his breath.

Their daughter squirmed and squawked, but she didn't throw up. And when she was placed on the scale, she'd gained a little bit of weight.

"Good girl," the nurse said. "Now let's see how you do in your car seat, and then you can go home."

Ninety minutes later, they stepped out into the sunshine. Chloe carried her hospital bag and Tom carried the bucket seats. The babies were dressed in onesies bought from the hospital gift shop, and covered in light blankets.

It was time to go home.

———

AS SOON AS the first plaintive cry broke the still of the night, Tom was out of bed. It was Hank, with a wet diaper and a snarly attitude. "That's going to take you far, kid," Tom whispered as he set a clean diaper on the change pad. They'd been home for two weeks. He'd taken some vacation time to help with the babies, but Chloe was doing the heavy lifting with feeding two ravenous and adorable growth machines. "But don't try it with your mom tonight, okay? She needs a break."

"She's doing okay," Chloe said softly behind him. "She's got a good partner in crime."

He turned and gave her a tired smile. "I wanted you to get a bit more sleep."

"I'll sleep when they're in college. Or maybe preschool."

He grabbed the nursing pillow for her, and she lifted Hank in her arms, making room for the support.

From the crib, right on cue, Mabel let out a frustrated squawk.

"I'll get her," he said. Which was obvious, because now Chloe was firmly entrenched in her nursing prison. "And then I'll get you water, and ice cream if you need it."

She laughed as she closed her eyes and thunked her head back against the padded headrest of the recliner. "I love you, you know that?"

He did.

And in that moment—with one kid latched on, and the other rudely telling him off for not getting her to her mama fast enough—he wanted to propose marriage so much it hurt.

In the middle of the night, in the nursery, by the dim lamplight.

It was almost perfect. But she would say no. She didn't love the institution of marriage or the strings it came attached to. Besides, he didn't need more than this. This was everything.

He quickly changed Mabel's diaper, then delivered her to her mom. "I'll be right back with ice cream," he promised.

When he returned, he had the fanciest sundae possible at four in the morning in hand, and they shared it together, which was better than getting down on one knee.

She smiled softly. "Thank you for always being so understanding. You always know what I need."

Thank you for dragging me out of my comfort zone and giving me so much to live for. And he would have told her that, except Hank took that moment to have a complete disaster in his diaper, which then exploded out of his diaper, and filled the legs of his sleeper—as Tom was holding him.

"Oh God," he said, gingerly holding the baby tight to his chest. "Okay, I'm going to strip this guy down…"

Chloe and Mabel followed, both babies screaming at the unexpected transition from their cozy nursery to the bright bathroom.

Tom filled the baby tub, then stripped Hank out of his messy sleeper and plunked him onto the sling seat the kid already hated.

"I know, bud. This is the cruelest torture."

Mabel jacked up her protest volume to eleven. Chloe tried to latch her on to nurse again, but she was having none of it.

Tom grinned at his beautiful partner as she bounced and shushed one of their kids as he scrubbed down another.

"Why are you smiling?"

He shrugged. "This is awesome!"

"It's four in the morning. This is madness."

"I know. I love it."

She shook her head. "I'm going to go make some hot chocolate. Or coffee? Are we up for the day? What do you want?"

"Coffee sounds great. We'll have a nap later."

She disappeared, then returned a few minutes later, Mabel in a stretchy wrap on her chest. "She's asleep," Chloe whispered.

Tom had Hank wrapped in a towel. "I bet he'll go back to sleep, too."

She led the way back to the nursery, where she got Mabel into the crib first, then swaddled Hank and rocked him back to sleep next.

"We make a good team," Tom said. "Don't we?"

Chloe gave him a funny expression. "I think so."

"What was that look?" He stepped back into the hall and she followed.

"I was just thinking about how people—not our friends, but on the internet, and sometimes in the library— I see people complaining about their husbands not pulling their weight. And you're just...you're so present. I'm really grateful for that. And you don't even see it. Or you do, but you're doubtful. So yes, we make a *great* team." She pushed up on her toes and kissed him. "Go pour yourself a coffee, I'll meet you in the kitchen in a minute."

Tom laughed when he saw the lid of his Thermos sitting next to the coffeemaker, and beside it, her mug that she'd taken to the Vances' cottage.

Chloe returned a moment later.

"Feeling nostalgic?" he asked as he filled both mugs.

"A little." She smiled at him. "It's been a real roller-coaster."

He gathered her in his arms and kissed her softly, feeling the gentleness of her in his arms. "I love you so much," he whispered. "I wouldn't want to ride this train with anyone else."

"I love you, too." She searched his face. "About that comparison to husbands…"

He shook his head. "I don't care what you call me. But deep down, I'm your husband. That's how I feel. I'm your mate, your partner, your spouse. And if you never want to get married, that's truly, absolutely fine. But if you ever change your mind, know that I will marry you in a heart-beat. I would marry you every year, over and over again, until we're old and grey and so God damned happy it's embarrassing our children and grandchildren."

"Tom—"

But he was on a roll, so he wasn't stopping now. "I love you, Chloe Dawson. I love you with my whole damn heart. I love you when you're cranky, and when you're scared, and when you're brave. I love you when you're pushing back at all the things we're supposed to want, and when you're joyously embracing what you truly *do* want in life. I love everything about you."

"I love everything about you, too." She took a deep breath.

But.

He could feel it coming.

Still, after all this time.

There would always be a but.

And he would just deal, because that's what it was to love someone unconditionally, with everything he had.

He nodded, and she ducked her head. She kept it hanging low for so long his chest started to hurt.

And then she lowered herself to the floor.

To one knee, and when she looked up, her face was wet with tears. "I love how you hold our children," she whispered. "I love how you hold me. I love your patience, and your gentleness. I love it when you lose both of those things and it's so hard for you to get them back, because you just want me to see how much you love me. I see it. I see you, Tom. And when I say I love everything about you, I mean it. I love how fierce you are and how much you want to be my husband, even though I'm scared shitless."

Get up, he wanted to tell her. He wanted to drag her up, into his arms, and hold her the tightest he'd ever held her.

But maybe he couldn't do that, maybe there was no embrace tight enough to get her over this fear.

Maybe he needed to let her do what she was doing, even though it was scary and bold and the most beautiful thing he'd ever seen.

Her fingers shook as she lifted her hands, both of them, and opened them palm up, one on top of the other. There would never in the world be a sweeter or more beautiful proposal. A white gold band shone from its perch on her outstretched hands.

"Tom Minelli, will you marry me? Will you make me your wife, and let me make you my husband, officially and for all to see?"

He sank to his knees, nodding, and yanked her against him. "Yes," he said roughly into her hair. "A million times yes."

She kissed him hungrily. It would be weeks until they could do more than this to celebrate, but God, he loved this woman, and he showed her that with everything he had.

When they finally broke apart, she put the ring in his hand. "It's more of a wedding band than an engagement ring, but you can wear it if you want. Or save it for a wedding."

"It's lovely. Can I get you one, too?"

She laughed. "Sure."

"When did you get this?" He turned it over between his fingers. It's not like she'd had any time to herself in quite a while.

"I bought it before the babies arrived, and stashed it in the hospital bag, in a box of maxi pads. I thought I would do it before they arrived, and then that happened all of a sudden, and there was no time. And I didn't want to link the proposal to anything else. I didn't want you to think I was doing it because of the babies. It had to be its own thing, in its own time. I'm so sorry."

"No." His voice was hoarse, and his throat was tight, but he had to say it. "You were right. I shouldn't have pushed."

She kissed him hard on the mouth. "We're both a bit foolish, but a lot in love. And that's okay. I'll take foolish but in love."

"We'll be that forever."

Chloe beamed. "Good. That sounds perfect to me."

EPILOGUE

December, again

IT WAS A WONDERFUL, magical night—for everyone, but especially Chloe Dawson.

Dani was hosting a Gals Giftmas party, and it was magical. For one thing, she was a little bit tipsy for the first time in more than a year. For another, she didn't have a baby in her arms, and that was a freaking *gift*. And in a short while, she'd go home, and have two babies on her at once, and that would be a gift, too.

Being a mom was the most complicated thing. Feelings that yanked her in different directions at the same time, overwhelmed her and filled her to the brim with joy.

But right now, she was soaking up the friendship. Dani had managed to get everyone out—even Hope Creswell and Liana Hansen, Pine Harbour's resident celebrities.

"Top up, Chloe?"

She beamed at Natasha, who was holding out a bottle of bubbly. "Oh, *yes*."

Just as her glass was filled, another knock came at the door. Dani hustled to answer it, returning with Faith.

"Faith!" everyone called out in unison.

"Just like on Cheers," she cracked. "Sorry I'm so late, but that was worth it."

"Just in time for champagne," Chloe said, dancing over with a flute.

Faith turned pink and shook her head. "None for me tonight."

This time, the collection response was shocked—and happy—silence.

She nodded. "Third IVF was a charm. I'm pregnant."

A celebratory whoop sounded around the room, and Faith leaned in to whisper to Chloe, "Zander doesn't want anyone else to know until we pass the first trimester, but it's twins for us, too. So you know, any advice you might have…"

Chloe wrapped her arms around her sister-in-law, careful not to spill either glass of bubbly. "It's going to be just fine. Congratulations."

"And now you can drink my wine."

"I know. The congratulations were for me," Chloe teased. "Come on, let's find you some sparkling water or ginger ale."

Dani pulled more hot appetizers from the oven and everyone settled in around the island to eat and drink and be merry. Once they were pleasantly stuffed, they moved to the great room and settled in front of the roaring fireplace for a game of Secret Santa.

"Here's how this will work. We each have a random number we've pulled out of the Santa hat. Starting at one, we'll take turns picking a present from under the tree, or choosing to steal from someone who has already picked a present. The only rule is that you may not steal something back in the same turn. Understand?" Dani looked around. "Excellent. Who has number one?"

Jenna waved her hand, then jumped up to peruse the options. She picked a mysterious black box, wrapped in luxurious red velvet ribbon. "Can I leave it a mystery? Or do I need to open it so people know if they might want to steal?"

"Your choice," Dani said over a chorus of *open it!* cheers.

Jenna chewed on her lip, then pulled the ribbon off. Inside was a giant mug filled with hot chocolate packets, two pairs of cozy socks, and a gift card for the liquor store.

"Don't get attached to that," Olivia called out.

Hope was next, picking a not-obscured-at-all bottle of wine, then it was Olivia's turn, who stole Jenna's box of goodies.

Jenna went back to the tree and grabbed a gift bag. Inside it was a Naughty Elf costume, making everyone howl.

"It's not too dirty, is it?" Dani blushed as she looked around the room, outing herself as the person who brought it.

"Hell no," Liana said, waving her number in the air. "I've got the next pick, and I'm stealing it."

Everyone howled. Jenna pouted as she handed it over, but then happily pointed to the stack of books Chloe had brought and carefully wrapped to look like a Christmas tree. "I'll take those, then."

Which made it Dani's turn, who picked something from under the tree—a wooden advent calendar that would go perfectly on her mantle—and then Chloe's number was up.

She waved it in the air and gave Liana a sorry-not-sorry look. "I'm stealing the sexy elf costume."

More howls.

Liana handed it over, then prowled around the room. She snagged the books, Jenna took Hope's wine, and Hope grabbed another bottle-shaped object from under the tree.

And then they were down to just one person. Faith. She side-eyed the elf costume, but then laughed. "I won't fit in it in another week anyway. It's all yours." She took the last present under the tree, a beautiful afghan, and curled up with it. "This is my Christmas speed this year."

Everyone raised their glasses in a toast to that. "Merry Christmas!"

———

WHICH WAS the first thing Chloe said to Tom when she got home, too. He was asleep with the twins in their bed. They'd given up on the nursery after a few weeks and moved the crib into their room, attaching it to their bed like a side-car at the circus.

That's what the last six months had felt like a bit. A non-stop wild circus of love.

Exhausting but wonderful.

Silently, she stripped out of her clothes and pulled on the sexy elf costume. Then she snuck back out to the living room and found a bonus strand of Christmas lights they'd decided to not put on their tree.

Back in the bedroom, she plugged them in and wrapped the lights around her body just in time as Tom sensed her presence and groggily rolled up to a sit.

"Chloe?"

"Merry Christmas," she whispered.

It didn't take him long to shake off the sleep. "Whoa," he said, blinking twice as he took in her outfit. "Hello."

"I'm a little drunk. Jake played taxi, so we'll need to go pick up my car tomorrow."

"A drunk elf visiting me in the middle of the night, I love it." He stood, stretching, then glanced at the twins. "Should I move them?"

She shook her head. "Leave them to sleep here." She twirled, and the Christmas lights fell off her body. "We can go into the living room."

Sex had changed so much after having kids. It was more likely to be interrupted now. It was faster. Less often.

But also better in so many unexpected ways. Tom revered her body in a way that made her feel amazing. He'd always been a good lover, attentive and full of stamina, but now he feasted on her. And her body was so much more responsive. Too responsive some days, too sensitive, but Tom flexed with that.

Tonight, he started behind her, kissing the back of her neck as his hands roamed over her curves beneath the stretchy costume. "Did you escape from the North Pole?"

"Santa sent me on a special mission to reward you because you've been a very good boy this year."

"Santa knows what I like." His mouth drifted to her shoulder, his teeth catching the strap of the costume. He slid it down her arm, then spun her around and tumbled backwards onto the couch so she was straddling him.

His mouth covered her nipple as soon as her bare breast popped out of the outfit.

She'd been looking forward to this since she won the costume in the game. She wanted him inside her, right now. "Tom…"

"Yes, my sexy surprise?"

"Fuck me."

He growled and squeezed her hips, pulling them together. They were wearing too many clothes, but it didn't matter. He tugged her skirt up and covered her sex with his hand, making her clit pulse before he even touched it directly.

"You're ready for me already?"

"So ready," she breathed.

He dragged his fingers between her slick folds, testing that promise. She wasn't lying. She needed him now, hard and fast, on the couch.

Shoving his sweatpants down his hips, Tom fisted his cock. Yes. That. She wanted *that*. Rising on her knees, she gave him space to bring them together, then sank down, taking him all the way inside her.

He shuddered and whispered her name, his mouth on her skin.

She rode him slowly, savouring each thick press deep inside her, each aching retreat. She loved the way he filled her up and made her feel things beyond the physical. Whole, complete, satisfied. Loved.

Her slickness grew with each thrust, and so did how hard he was. He throbbed for her, and after a few minutes of slow fucking on the couch, he gripped her by the hips and surged forward, tumbling them onto the floor.

"Careful," she laughed breathlessly as he cushioned her fall.

"I'd never hurt you," he whispered. "You're my everything."

She wrapped her arms around him as he took over, fucking her hard and fast. Her climax roared to meet his, a rush of need that sounded like a freight train inside her head and felt even stronger than that deep in her belly.

On her last postpartum appointment, she'd had an IUD inserted. No more surprise babies. If they had another down the road, it would be fully planned. Now, sex was just for them.

A gift they gave each other.

"Tom," she cried out as her orgasm crested. "Yes, oh, God. *Yes.*"

He jerked his hips, burying himself as deep as he could inside her for his release. "Chloe," he murmured into her hair. "My beautiful Chloe."

It took them a while to disentangle and stretch out side by side.

Chloe tugged at the costume twisted around her waist. "So this was fun."

Tom laughed. "Very."

She kissed his arm, then flopped back again.

"Hey, so…" Tom pushed himself up onto one arm. "I want to give you your Christmas present early. One of them, anyway."

She watched as he rolled over and grabbed an odd-shaped box wrapped in bright green paper. Taking it, she carefully peeled off the wrapping, only to find inside that box another one, slightly smaller.

"Rip it off," Tom said when she was careful with this paper, too—this one bright red. "There are a few more layers to get through."

Laughing, she tore through a silver box, and a gold one, and then she found a black velvet bag. It was light, and small, but she could feel the ring through it all the same.

Oh. Blinking away tears, she opened it up and smiled as a slim white-gold band fell into her hand.

"We've been busy," he said, curling up around her.

"But I think it's time we start wedding planning, don't you?"

She couldn't agree more. "How does the spring sound?"

He covered her mouth with his.

Perfect. It sounded perfect.

THE END

WANT MORE PINE HARBOUR? Introducing a whole new family of brothers... The Kincaids of Pine Harbour is my next series set in this same world! The series begins with Reckless at Heart, Owen Kincaid and Kerry Humphrey's story. Visit my website at www.zoeyork.com to learn more, and if you want to hear about all my new releases, make sure you're on my VIP reader list at www.smarturl.it/ZoeYorkNewsletter!

ACKNOWLEDGEMENTS

aka The People Who Stuck in There for Five years

My assistant Lori, who doesn't blink when I casually mention that I'm revising three chapters in the week before release. Thank you for being all emotional with me about the end of this journey!

My developmental editor, Kristi Yanta, for helping me piece together jigsaw puzzles of ideas, half-formed but still magical.

My husband, for understanding more than most how much of me is on the pages of this world.

My children, who are the best things that have ever and will ever happen to me. Like Chloe, my first delivery was earlier than expected and not what I'd planned. I did that terrified drive to the hospital knowing I would become a mom weeks early, and see my baby whisked off to the NICU instead of cuddled up in my arms.

And finally, a note of gratitude for my readers:

Everyone who came to Pine Harbour from Wardham.

Everyone who came to Pine Harbour as my first-to-them books.

Everyone who dove right into this Canadian series, set where I grew up, full of strange Canadianisms like toonies and Legions.

Thank you all. It has been a joy to write a series set in Bruce County. There will be more Pine Harbour to come!

Zoe

ABOUT THE AUTHOR

Zoe York lives in London, Ontario with her young family. She's currently chugging Americanos, wiping sticky fingers, and dreaming of heroes in and out of uniform.

www.zoeyork.com

f facebook.com/zoeyorkwrites

🐦 twitter.com/zoeyorkwrites

📷 instagram.com/zoeyorkwrites

▶ youtube.com/zoeyorkwrites

Lightning Source UK Ltd.
Milton Keynes UK
UKHW030628200922
409139UK00001B/194